FALLEN
SPIRE

Other books by Aaron Safronoff

Evening Breezes
Spire
Sunborn Rising: Beneath the Fall

FALLEN
SPIRE

BY AARON SAFRONOFF

NEOGLYPHIC ENTERTAINMENT

CALIFORNIA

To Kylie, my stranger in a strange land.

~ ~ ~ ~ ~

To my amazing friends:

Mark, Jeremy, Jason, Joe, Aaron, Zeke, Nellie, Valerie.

~ ~ ~ ~ ~

To the P2C2E:

V will be fine, Nemrac, D aka His Holy Hand, British.

~ ~ ~ ~ ~

For Brock.

FOREWORD

I'm not a serial writer. It's just not in my DNA. At no point did I intend to create another installment from the Spire universe. This is *Fallen Spire*. It's not book two. It's not really a sequel. It's the end. *Spire* released in the fall of 2011 as the first half of the novel I envisioned. I published it to stop it from squirming around, and metamorphosing on me. I needed stable ground in order to traverse the obstacles presented by the design of the second half: transitioning from science fiction to fantasy, from Joshua to Ezechial, and from describing the evolution of a single character to exploring the life cycle of a universe. And so, the opening portion went to press.

Writing *Fallen Spire* was a rush of emotion unfettered by the slow world-building elements necessary to create its predecessor. So, two years after the first novel's release, I delivered the conclusion without hesitation or an apology for the time between. In fact, I did nothing to help *Fallen Spire* stand on its own. It felt wrong to contrive situations or dialog that would remind readers of what had happened already--like I'd be wasting the time of the fans, albeit few.

Mistakes. Were. Made.

The readers who loved *Spire* didn't want it to end, and the readers initiated with *Fallen Spire* felt lost. So with this latest edition I had to first contemplate the idea of releasing the books as one. Obviously, you know what I decided. The gap between releases had muddied the experiment. I still believe a fundamental context switch happens when you put one book down and pick up the other. Even switching virtual books in an e-reader causes a dramatic pause, and as any musician will tell you, the space between the notes is as important as the notes themselves. Besides, I'm happy with the poetry of the two standing apart in time, space, genre, and binding.

Looking back on it today, I'm confident that I wrote the story as it was meant to be written. Perhaps a time will come when I no longer care about the poetry of the two halves, and all the analogies both cliché and clever the presentation invokes, but for now I'm still enamored of the architecture of the story.

So I'll leave you with this: *Spire* and *Fallen Spire* are intended to sit side-by-side, to be read one after the other, but ultimately how you digest the material is your choice. I cannot direct you. I only hope that you find something memorable, something inimitable in your experience of this one story. Whatever you decide, however you meet me on this journey, thank you.

It is with the utmost pride that I present the second edition of the second half of a lifetime I misremembered. Enjoy.

Sincerely,
-Aaron Safronoff

FALLEN

SPIRE

BY AARON SAFRONOFF

Original cover by Joseph Garhan

Open
One

The room was dark. Not modern-dark, filled with a mix of flashing and steady LEDs, but the dark of a room completely disconnected from the world. There were no indicators of electricity, no furniture, and no decorations of any kind. There was no hint why the space had been carved out of the building... no reason why there was a room at all.

Eerie and isolated, the room felt cavernous although it wasn't really that large. It was a cavity, hollowed out of black, cold stone. The domed ceiling rounded seamlessly down to the matte floor, creating concave walls.

As open and bare as it was, the room was not empty.

There was a man.

He stood at the center of the room and he was not alone. He had voices with him. The voices had led him here, followed him here, tormented him here. He listened to the voices because he believed he had no other choice, because it was excruciating to ignore them.

The man removed his spectacles, which were antiquated, dusty, and scratched. He rubbed at his eyes and then at his whole face. He was very tired. It had been a long walk from Marius' offices, more than a day with little or no rest, but that hadn't worn him out; his leg was fully healed, although it still hurt whenever he thought of Vanya. It was the voices that drained him. The voices were rambling and chaotic thoughts originating outside of him, but they penetrated his consciousness and demanded his attention, stole his will. They spoke in riddles—when they used words at all—and suffocated all other sounds, all other thoughts. The voices were animal and organic, clearly *voices*, but of a language and origin that he could not understand.

When the voices began, he was sure he was going mad; after all, he'd witnessed madness many times before, he'd caused it. The voices seemed random at first, filled with a mixture of anxiety, fear, and confused desire. The voices weren't clear, demanding nothing from him, so he tried to ignore them. Then slowly, it seemed that they were coalescing, echoes spooning echoes, unified by a single purpose. Intentions surfaced. They compelled him to move, and to move in a specific direction. Whenever he moved in a direction opposite to the impulse, there was an outcry to return to the path. He would actively attempt to move against them sometimes, to choose his own way, but then the outcry would turn vicious, becoming an unbearable cerebral cacophony.

The rules changed as the voices gained strength, and it wasn't long before simply *thinking* of going against them became painful. If he pursued a line of reasoning to avoid or to stop the voices, the rebuke was punishing, debilitating. Once, on a crowded sidewalk, recognizing that no one could help him or understand, he panicked and forced himself to simply turn and run. He made it less than a block before he fell to his knees screaming. The pedestrians walked around and avoided eye contact with the screaming, crawling man. He passed out, and when he awoke, he was face down on the sidewalk, pointing in the direction the voices had commanded.

He learned there was only one reprieve from the pain. If he unwaveringly followed the guidance of the voices, he would feel something almost like pleasure. No contrary or tangential thoughts were allowed, no straying from the path. Even considering his destination was seen as a kind of escape from the course.

Eventually, more than voices guided him; at some point—he could not think of when—the Shades had joined them. They first appeared as shadows that were too long. They stretched out from him—from lampposts and street signs—and extended strangely beyond the time of day. Over the course of the journey, the shadow edges turned liquid, like the lip of an over-filled mug of some dark fluid. Eventually, the surface tension broke, and the pools of shadows ran in rivers with him, and within were the Shades. The wake of darkness had followed him ever since.

As he came to accept the voices and the Shades, he thoughtlessly trundled from avenue to street, took a ferry, entered a building, and took one stair-step at a time, to the top. Standing in the hollow room, he understood that he had finally reached his destination.

He shuddered at the memory of the journey; the tormenting voices, yes, but also the physical pain, the complaints of his aged and out-of-shape body. As he stopped fighting the voices, his perspective had changed with each step, so much so that he eventually came to believe that he was leading himself, and that the voices were his own. In fact, now that he had arrived in the room, he began feeling as though the idea had been his all along; this is where he wanted to be. He chose to be here.

Gabriel examined the room and ran his hand along the curvature of the wall. The cold, black stone seemed to respond to him, warming to his touch. As he had climbed the steps of the building, more flights than he could remember, he had not once thought that this was what he would find, an incredible cave at the top of the Spire. Even more peculiar than the room was its door. It was made of wormwood with a manual latch and knob… and no obvious lock.

The voices had quieted when he entered, but were now coming back to him. Soft, comforting, massaging his wounded mind. And even in the darkness he could feel the shadow pools growing around him. They were turbulent and violent, and ever active. Here, in the pitch black cave of a room, he could feel the Shades circling him. *Ring around the rosy…* echoes and ashes. If the voices coerced and argued, the Shades pushed and threatened. Gabriel believed the

Shades wanted nothing more than an excuse to shred him. *Believed.* Absolute.

He struggled to soothe his fears—or heard soothing voices anyway; this was the moment he had been working toward since his first experiment, perhaps for his entire life. He was disappointed that he hadn't begun sooner. All that time looking, trying to explain what he could not explain, was wasted time. All he had to do was try the catalyst himself! Apple was the answer and it was right there all along.

There was quiet.

Without warning, the voices were silenced, and then there was absolute quiet.

Gabriel felt the Shades slithering away to the edges of the room; there was no need for them to pressure him, to threaten him, to push him. He was calm. Gabriel would finish what he had started. There really was no other choice.

He wanted to do it.

And with that thought, slowly and steadily, a resonance began to build in the room. It reminded him of the hum of an ultra-low bass speaker when someone flipped the power switch, thud and hum. He could feel it in his chest, he could smell it in the air, and the hairs on his arms pricked up beneath his dirty shirt. The vibration continued to build. He felt his thoughts coming together around the sound. There were no more conflicting ideas, or anxious and nervous feelings. There was only the one, the simple: Gabriel. He was a single voice, a single persona unencumbered by consequences, compelled only by the present, by this one moment.

The air in the room became thick with the hum. He moved his hands in front of his face and thought he saw ripples. The air was thicker than water, but he breathed easily.

Then he realized he was resonating with more than just the hum, but also with the room itself; the walls, the floor and ceiling, and the cavity between were all powered by the same hum. Then a low throbbing began. Deep. Strong. Demanding. The rhythm seemed distant at first, but it was growing closer.

He didn't recognize the beat from his own life, but his chest knew it well. It was a call to bloody battle: the rhythm of a war drum. It pushed through the thick air with terrifying confidence.

Thud. *Is that my skull?* Thud. *Is that my chest?* Thud. *Is that my heart?* And louder still it came, tribal, relentless, fearless.

Thud.

And the voices returned, following in the wake of each drum beat. They were louder with each strike of the drum, and then faded as they flew into the distance.

The drum would send a crowd of voices flying out, and then, just as silence returned, *Boom*, another beat.

It was a subtle change at first, but he found he was no longer the heart of the harmony; he was a tuning fork. Someone or something was hitting his consciousness against the walls of the room again and again.

Boom.

Boom.

Boom!

The voices flew from him, but they didn't fly away into the distance anymore, they stayed with him. Louder and louder, thicker and thicker.

It was too much. Gabriel fell to his knees and felt his meniscus crush painfully beneath his weight. He clutched at his head, clutched at his chest. His mouth was thrust open wide, so wide he thought his lips would split and peel away from his face. With his chin tucked to his chest, doubled over in excruciating agony, he tried to block out reality. He squeezed his eyes shut, harder and harder, until he felt them filling with sharp tears. Then something sticky seeped out and burned trails down his cheeks.

Mouth still gaping, he rolled his head back toward the ceiling and opened his eyes, pleading for some benevolent force above to release him. He was being pounded into senselessness. There was a primal scream echoing through the cavity of the room.

A convulsion seized him from deep inside his belly and he folded forward, hands to the floor, and wretched. The room shook once, violently, as though the force of the convulsion was coming from the foundation of the building. Gabriel couldn't tell whether he or the room was swaying—were those aftershocks, or was he shaking?

He looked at the floor. The pool beneath his face sent up streams of acrid and decaying smells. The bile was yellow with red runners. Gabe thought maybe he was hallucinating, but what he thought was just bile and blood squirmed and writhed like thousands of larval creatures, like it was some kind of amniotic fluid. Threads of saliva and mucous were strung from his face to the puddle. His eyes bulged painfully as he stared deeper into the puddle.

He laughed madly as he quivered on all fours, struggling desperately to hold himself up. His hysteria gave way to sadness as he accepted this as his fate, and he shook and sobbed openly. A drop of blood fell from his lower lip, a punctuation mark as far as he was concerned, dotting the end of a long journey.

The wriggling wormy bits moved toward the sanguine droplet. There was vomit on his hands and he felt the slimy worms sliding on the backs of his hands. Aware of his body, he was suddenly scared out of his mind, horrified and disgusted. He frantically tried to wipe the fluid off of himself as he stumbled backwards, scrambling away from the center of the room.

Taking a moment to catch his breath, he simply stared at the center of the room and waited. He was sure that some kind of evil was going to rise up out of the vile pool, but nothing happened. It was difficult to see. If anything was happening, he couldn't tell. Maybe he'd even imagined the worms? But the room *wasn't* as dark as it had been when he'd first arrived. Something *had* changed.

There were cracks in the walls and ceiling, and in the floor. The cracks branched out from the center of the floor and spider-webbed their way around the room. They were glowing faintly, but certainly radiant. The color was deep and dark and smoky red. He realized some of the cracks went directly beneath him, and although he was afraid to look away from the center of the room, he stared down at the thickest crack near him, and slid his finger along its sharp edges. The crack responded by turning a brighter red.

He stood and ran to the door. He twisted and pulled at the knob, but the ancient wood refused to budge. Pounding on the door with all his remaining strength sent a booming echo through the room, but that didn't stop him, he just kept pounding and twisting and pulling. Finally, he screamed and pulled with his whole body and the door flew open. Gabriel landed hard and winced at the sharp pain in his tailbone, but he fought against it, stood, and awkwardly ran from the room.

The door closed itself quietly behind him, but Gabriel didn't notice. He just ran.

FALLEN SPIRE

The View

Two

No one noticed.

Why did I think they would?

Ezechial was perched like a gargoyle on a window ledge six stories up. Crouched and leaning forward, he stared at the street below and watched his prey as they slithered and skittered around cars, trash cans, and light posts. Their movements were animal, although their basic shape was more similar to a human's. Some stalked like cats, others hunted like wolves, and one was even hugging the ground like a snake. They all thought they were predators.

A gust of wind blew back Ezechial's hair, but his body was still as a statue. His hands were down beside his feet holding onto the ledge, knees buried into his chest. Many of the street lights had gone out over the last few months, and with no one to replace or repair them, they'd stayed out; it was difficult to see, regardless of the waxing moon and cloudless sky. His eyes saw clearly though, collecting the slight ambient light and enhancing it. If Eve was there she might have noticed his bright eyes glowing softly against the night, but she wasn't there. He wondered if he would hear from her again, hoped he would.

No one noticed.

Those who did notice certainly didn't care. Not then anyway.

Remembering back, it was hard for him to understand what had happened, but the experience was vivid. It was the middle of the day, three months and three days ago. Something went terribly wrong that day. Something in the air—that was the first thing he noticed anyway—it was charged, sharp and static. Then moments later, it became thick, oily, and distorted. Walking around was difficult, each movement heavy and weak. He felt like he was being dunked violently into a tank of water, held down by an unyielding, unimaginable strength. He felt pushed down even harder whenever he struggled against it. More than that though, the presence holding him down also held him open; his lids and lips were pried apart. His heart pounded against his chest, so there was no escape to a quiet place.

There was a sudden stillness in the world; each moment was drawn out for too long. Everyone felt it, like being trapped in the seconds before an accident, in that time-warping sensation of prescience meets absolute fatalism. Like the future is right in front of you, and you're given a vacuum of time to consider it. But on that day, it wasn't just a stretched-out second or two; it was an hour or more. It was torture, pointless and painful. He experienced true fear, and then was faced with the cold realization of his mortality, which deadened his already dampened nerves. Seconds slowly passed, desperate and powerless.

The period of thick-time ended with something that felt like a high-speed planetary collision. There was no recorded quake anywhere though, and there was nothing measurable to explain it. People struggled to describe the event, but almost all of the reports turned into "earthquake"; it was just easier to believe than pursuing the truth. He didn't know what had happened; he only knew that it didn't feel anything like an earthquake.

In that moment, all the people of the world felt the terror together, as individuals and as a community. There was weakness in their selves, and the whole suffered for it. Each person, in that charged and terrified state, felt their society unravel.

10

But that moment of understanding passed.

Trapped and oxygen-starved, vacillating frenetically between panic and acceptance, he finally hit the barrier between desperation and euphoria… and then miraculously passed through to the other side. On the other side of the wall, he floated, his struggling diminished, and he felt that he didn't need to rise to the surface anymore. He began believing that breathing was a myth, that he never needed it. The emotion was a kind of endorphin-enlightenment preparing him for the end. Unfortunately, there wasn't enough soft chemical release to carry him all the way through to the quiet, so the pain— the real pain of oxygen-starved muscles—exploded in his brain. His chest and his heart burned, and his head fired "all alert" across every synapse, sparking echoes of pain throughout his limbs. Like everyone in the world, he was trapped, and like each one of them, he just needed the pain to stop.

That's how he remembered it.

They were all there in the heavy water that day. They shared that fragility, that vulnerability. They shared that last frenzied fit to survive, aimless and incomprehensible.

They were all there in it, but then an explosive went off in the water. It burst bright in their eyes, blinding them. It rang sharp cries in their ears, deafening them. It shattered the glass and the heavy water poured out and to the ground, and they survived.

They *survived*.

And there they were, everyone on Earth, down on their knees or lying on the ground, clutching at their throats and chests, gasping for breath. But even as the echoes of the explosion continued pulsing through their veins, the self-deception began. It was an earthquake.

Sure it was.

There were no reports from the Collective about anything happening at all. The explanations from all other points were varied and numerous. People went back to work. The media blew off the event as mass hysteria. Some speculated that it might have

11

been a kind of attack, maybe even alien, but the magnitude of the attack—the entire planet?—seemed inconceivable even to the most conspiratorial and paranoid minds. Then the denial was ratified publicly across all networks. Nothing had happened. Let's move on. And who could argue? Nothing was perceivably wrong with anyone. The social consciousness, aware for one brief moment—for the first time in human history—of how fragile it is, of how powerfully connected each person is to each other, went back to sleep.

And the Spire cracked.

And no one noticed.

Even several days after the event, no one saw the fractures that had appeared throughout the Spire. The building that stood as the watch tower against war, as a stronghold for order in the world, had broken; the cracks climbed its length and branched at sharp angles across it. Okay, so maybe on that first day it would have been too much to ask for someone to point, and stare, and scream out, but what about later? What about that night, when the deep cracks began glowing dark red, and became visible through the broken walls? Did anyone stop to look? Did anyone call out in alarm or start asking questions? No. It was business as usual. People walked, people ferried and boated, and commerce and productivity went on unfettered.

As the days went by, the cracks grew and the glow deepened, and still the population was blind. They looked past it, around it, and through it. And what of the usual traffic, the comings and goings, in and out of the Spire? There wasn't a single person entering or exiting the building. The usual flow of people in and out of the tower ceased to exist...

The demons began to move in unison below Ezechial. They were communicating, clicks and growls, and rasping tongues. He couldn't understand them, but he could see the convalescence of movement and knew that they were deciding something together, operating on the same question. They took up positions in the darkness, in the blackest corners of the street, beneath cars, through the broken windows of storefronts, or hugged up against the walls of the buildings. One was directly below Ezechial, and a breeze pushed up the rotting sulfurous stench of the beast.

Then, even as Ezechial stared directly at the creature beneath him, it seemed to disappear. He knew the trick, it was his trick. But the creature did it so much better. Ezechial had to fight his own mind, had to fight back the urge to believe the salivating monstrosity was gone. Looking deeper and straining harder wouldn't help; his eyes were telling him the truth, but his mind refused to see.

Why had it taken him so long to figure it out? They were so much better at the trick. They could stand right out in the open, right before his eyes, and convince him they didn't exist. Why was it so hard to believe that they could crack the very foundation of the Spire and hide it from almost everyone?

His heart had sunk when he realized that even the Laterali hadn't seen it coming. They had denied that anything was happening even after the cracks appeared. But that's the nature of the trick really: rationalization. The Laterali wanted to believe the Collective was damaged, that it was a failed experiment in human organization. It only made sense that at some point the damage and the failure would become visible and physical. It was affirming, really.

It was definitely not a shared hallucination that day, but he thought the aftermath was certainly a shared denial. It didn't matter now though, anyway. One week and one day after the first fissures appeared, the Spire cracked wide open, and through the seams poured the fearless and ferocious horde. They ran like blood down the wounds of the black stone obelisk and pooled on the island at its feet. Then when they'd amassed enough to fill every bit of land, and had begun crawling over each other, the horde had moved into the water. Great plumes of steam marked their movement as they swam to the closest shores.

Ezechial heard footsteps, fast and clumsy... human.

Beneath him, Ezechial could distinguish three individuals by the unique sound of each respective gait. He could tell by the sound alone that one was small and quite young. He or she had stumbled twice and caused the others to slow; they dragged and whispered harshly, and ran again. Closer now.

He remembered back to the first wave of nightmares. Not a single person was ready for the attack. The horde fell on them and devoured them. The front line of the flowing horde slowed to eat and tear apart the bodies of their victims, and then they were overrun by the demons at their heels. They rolled up over their gorging kin like a rapidly running river over large rocks. They just kept coming...

Ezechial spotted the runners as they rounded the corner and came into view. They headed toward the building upon which he was perched, a little boy between two young women. Survivors were rare this close to the heart of the City where the horde had taken up primary residence and had their greatest population. These three didn't seem the survivalist types; they carried no visible weapons and they were thin and awkward. No, these were the kind that had survived by holing up somewhere, in a panic room or the like. Why they were out at night was a mystery to Ezechial. Every survivor he'd rescued believed that traveling at night was a deadly mistake. Even if the belief was founded more in fairy tales than understanding, it kept them all from moving in the dark.

He respected that they didn't just wait to die. He'd seen that too often already. He didn't judge the suicides that he found, but this was something different; this was hope.

Then the runners noticed.

The boy did anyway. He stopped and screamed and pointed.

There's a good boy.

The demons slithered from their dark places, lips curled back from rows of salivating teeth. A sound like metal grating on metal, like a transmission grinding, howled through the air, and rose to an ear-piercing pitch before cutting back sharply to a low rumble.

Ezechial picked his hands up from the ledge and slid them inside his jacket. He felt the grips, the handles familiar and warm.

The Devil's Tails responded with anxious anticipation, a kind of vibration and thickening in the grips. They were hungry. He pulled them free from their holsters and allowed them to uncoil slowly toward the ground. The whips wriggled a little as they reached their maximum length, dangling down from Ezechial's relaxed, hanging arms. Each licked at the air sharply, tasting it, like reptilian tongues.

The three survivors huddled close together as the creatures circled tighter and closer, snarling and biting aggressively. They seemed to be having fun. No need to kill quickly. These demons were out for a good time.

The metal-on-metal whine tore through the air again, and Ezechial spilled himself out over the ledge, and fell. He descended head first, Tails like contrails rippling behind him. He seemed to fall forever. An awkward—but not unwelcome—precious calm between. Quiet and confident, he was possessed by only the focus of falling and the certainty of the ground beneath him.

He somersaulted, coiling the Tails once and then unleashing them at the ground toward the beast directly beneath him.

The Devil's Tails became somewhat rigid and distributed the force of his fall along their length. They bent and bowed into long arcs as they sliced through the snarling monster, shattering bone and severing ligaments, while simultaneously easing Ezechial to the ground.

From shoulder to hindquarter, both left and right, blood spilled out onto the ground, and then a pregnant second later, the viscera followed. The blood was magma thick and glowed deep orange. It quickly cooled to black against the night air and gave off the nauseating stench of decay.

The circling stopped, and the demons and three survivors stared at Ezechial, unable to understand how he'd gotten there and who he was. One of the beasts stood up on its back legs, and despite its serpentine movements, it appeared almost human. The rest of the demons began shifting and curling left and right, unholy and eerily human eyes sizing up Ezechial without blinking.

The body of the standing demon was lean and well-muscled, hairless and surprisingly tall. Its limbs were long, ending in agate talons. Its skin was grey with veins of lapis running through it. Standing there, breathing through an open, fanged mouth, its chest rose and fell, shrank and swelled, eager and heavy. Then, any semblance to a human that it had disappeared as it languidly settled back down onto its forelimbs, ducking its head low below its shoulders. The rest of the pack ceased their anxious pacing and matched the leader's posture.

Ezechial didn't wait for the battle cry to sound; he unleashed the full focus of his training. The Tails flew out, sometimes together, sometimes hunting targets independently. The first to be put down was the alpha; Ezechial cut its neck loose from both shoulders just as it was about to scream and leap. Instead of leaping forward, it fell and twitched and jerked forward, the headless corpse grinding into the asphalt. Its scream was nothing more than a gurgling, throaty mess.

Next.

Two more were already in the air, leaping toward Ezechial, but he took one long stride, cut the guts from one and grabbed the neck of the other. He pulled the second from the sky with the full strength of his body, spinning and dropping to the ground, and recoiling his free whip in the same motion. The demon's neck snapped, and it died in the air before its face was smashed into the ground, its body trailing limp, and then wrinkling in behind it.

Ezechial kept moving, each action bringing him closer to the three defenseless survivors. Each step was another kill, but there were more demons than he'd seen earlier. One of the beasts was clever, faster than the others, and snapped one of the Devil's Tails out of the air after it cut loose the flank of another. The razor sharp teeth pushed through the skin of the Tail into the long ligaments and soft insides. Juices flowed into the demon's mouth, and venom poured into the whip. The result was an extraordinary flex and coil, jerking

Ezechial clean from his feet. He held on, regardless of the pain pouring through the grip, as he was pulled into the air then dragged and whipped along the ground.

The burning pain fueled an adrenaline dump, pumping raw focus into his veins; Ezechial pulled himself upright using the rigidness of the bleeding tail for leverage. He unfurled his free whip. The demon saw and tried to dodge without releasing its jaws, but Ezechial just pulled the beast in, ignoring the searing pain of the teeth digging deeper, tearing through the Tail. The free whip went to work and carved the demon up with uncharacteristic brutality. Chunks went flying through the air, and bones were ripped out through the flesh and thrown through windows.

Ezechial howled.

The three kills left steaming, glowing piles of flesh and blood, and after only seconds of furious attacks.

He looked around, coming down from his blind fury, realizing suddenly that he didn't know how many threats remained, or even if the boy and the women were still alive.

Turning around, left arm and Tail hanging off his shoulder like loosely connected rags, he looked around for more. There were more, but where? He was slow to see, and slower to react. Not able to find them with his eyes, he reached back through his memory… there were another three.

Two snapped forward out of the fog of the trick, snatching the adults from behind, claws and teeth rending flesh from bone while returning to the darkness all at once. Blood sprayed the street and the child. There was only the sound of the dragging bodies for several seconds. The boy was catatonic.

Ezechial spotted the third demon hanging from the side of the building closest to the boy, tensed and about to strike. Ezechial braced himself and lashed out. He missed the neck, but managed to lasso the ankle of the demon's rear leg. He pulled, fought momentum, fought gravity, and just barely stopped the outstretched claws from reaching the boy. Then, with his remaining strength, he sent a ripple winding through the whip and yanked the demon back up into the air and past him, then pulled back hard so that the creature flipped and went head first into the brick wall of the building on the other side of the street. Its head was flattened, bursting open and spraying its contents like a starburst on the wall before the body collapsed into it and then fell to the ground.

Ezechial loosened and released the dead body and looked back to the boy. Peering into the darkness, he scanned the surroundings for more of the terrible creatures. The other two were off eating somewhere. It wouldn't take them long to return.

He walked slowly and carefully toward the boy who was stoned silent. Ezechial's Devil's Tails, battle-tired and wounded, trailed behind him on the ground, licking and feeding on the blood, bones, and flesh of the fallen. Finally, standing just less than a meter in front of the boy, Ezechial stared down and wondered if it wouldn't be better to just end the suffering for the boy. What would he do with a child? What would a child do here?

Then, the boy looked up. His skin was white, his hair was black, and his lips were red; each color so saturated that beside one another they created austere, well-defined borders. Ezechial might have mistaken his face for a mask if he hadn't been standing so close to him. The boy's eyes were so dark that it was difficult to distinguish the pupils from the irises in the low light, making him appear dumbstruck with fear.

"Were they your family?"

The boy didn't speak, but Ezechial waited patiently.

Eventually, Ezechial took a knee, "I'm sorry. They won't be back."

The Devil's Tails were still hungrily slurping and slinking through the meat of the dead all around the two.

The boy's eyes welled up with tears, but he didn't seem sad or afraid. There was no accompanying frown or quivering chin. He was tranquil, crying tears of relief, of finally finding something that was long lost.

"You have a choice," he gauged his words carefully and spoke calmly, "You may stay here and… join them, or come with me."

There was a long silence between them, marked by the occasional slitherings and rappings of the Tails against the asphalt. Then, the boy stepped forward and reached out his hand to touch the scruff of Ezechial's face. Ezechial felt the warmth of his cheek in the boy's cold palm, the rough texture of his aged skin against the smoothness of youth.

The quiet of the night was exploded by a high-pitched cry that bounced eerily off the walls of the alley. In seconds, the call was answered by the growling of many more rattling metallic demon engines on the move.

The Tails licked at the air in anticipation, but Ezechial summoned them, looping them back into coils, and holstered them. He scooped up the boy and retreated into the shadow of a building.

They moved quietly and quickly, through buildings and over rooftops, keeping to the shadows whenever possible. They were headed for a safe house far outside the city proper, where Ezechial had quartered his other rescues.

When they finally reached the perimeter of the city, the smell of morning was in the air, and even though it was still very dark, the first evidence of the sun's diffuse light was pushing back the night. It seemed like a safer time to travel, but they needed rest.

Ezechial found an abandoned home with a child's room in it. He put the boy on the bed and watched him fall asleep. He stared at the boy for a long time. The serenity of the boy's resting face brought a sense of peace to Ezechial, which he hadn't felt in a long time.

Absentmindedly at first, he rubbed at his left forearm. It was muscle-sore and slightly swollen, which bothered him, but then he looked at it. A cold sweat broke out along his spine; there were dark lines, like cracks in glass, branching out from inside of his forearm like a tattoo gone wrong. He closed his eyes and tried to massage away the pain.

FALLEN SPIRE

Simon Says
Three

Joshua waited to cross the street. The lights were blurry echoes of the once thriving metropolis. The red light was ringed with a soft halo, and it was reflected in the rooftops of abandoned vehicles and shards of broken glass in the street. The lines of a spider-webbed windshield were highlighted in red, which he thought added something beautiful to the darkening day. He stood staring blindly, long after the lines in the glass turned green, before realizing it was time to cross.

He stepped down from the curb and walked between vehicles with flattened tires, and around those that were crashed and wrinkled up into each other. Doors had been pried open, and in some cases, torn completely off, leaving hooks of metal grasping at the air and frayed ends of colored, wiry veins spraying out. There were stains in the asphalt that could have been oil, but probably weren't.

There was so much that he still couldn't figure out. He never slept anymore, or at least not that he could tell.

Before the suffocating flood, Joshua had spent his days and nights trying to stay corporeal. His emotions would charge up and change him. Stretching out with his awareness, feeling connected to everything, he could become a shadow, or pass through walls and people. Sometimes he did it on purpose, but not always. So, he spent his time trying to master his abilities, and trying to make using them a more conscious choice. But it wasn't just *abilities* that he had; something significant and fundamental had changed about him. It was scary, but powerful.

Joshua was still human, but connected to the world in a way that was entirely new. He still needed food, and had to interact with people, but that didn't always go well. He was confused and distracted most of the time by his new and fascinating changes, so he failed the standard social practices. His greetings would be too long, as he interpreted too many meanings to simple words like "Hello," or, "What can I get for you?" Often, he just stared back blankly, or grinned at a joke that he didn't share. It was difficult for him to distinguish what was said from what was just in his head, resulting in many awkward moments of silence. The end result was that people treated him mostly like a dimly lit child. It didn't help that he was also frequently naked without knowing it. Joshua had only just begun wearing clothes regularly when the flood came.

It was actually during the flood that he'd experienced his last fully conscious moment. The tide came in and kept coming. He remembered feeling the pressure rise with the tide, as though his body was a barometer and his head a bursting bulb. It was like the oceans had swelled up to swallow the land and drown the cities. But the water had been thicker and heavier than the ocean, and impossible to swim against. It sapped his strength and dragged him down with the constant pull of a relentless undertow. Joshua had been conscious of what he thought to be his imminent death, aware of his body begging for breath.

How long he was in the fetal position waiting for the tide or his life to go out, he couldn't guess, but it was long enough for him to see only red. Bloody red turning purple, turning black. But in the black he saw his brother, Bradley, and he made a decision not to join him yet. With his last fully wakeful effort, Joshua imagined himself not as a human body ready to collapse and be crushed under too much pressure, but as a container whose contents were volatile, the pressure forcing them together, resulting in a massive explosion; and with that, Joshua became the focus of an atomic explosion.

Joshua's explosion let all the water out, and he could breathe again. Everyone could breathe again. Since then though, his life had become a lucid and recurring dream. Some days were more vivid, other days less, but the dream was always the same and he never woke up from it.

Wherever Joshua walked, he felt like he was consciously experiencing the transitions most people forget while they are sleeping. Like dreaming that you're giving a presentation to a bunch of people and you realize that you're naked. But how you got there was a detail your dream left out. Joshua seemed to be dreaming all the details, living all the details, but from the perspective of someone who was creating the details as they happen. So, in this waking dream, he had the distinct impression that he knew what was there before he arrived. Despite this feeling of omniscience, he still managed to be completely lost most of the time.

Having made it to the other side of the street, he stopped, turned, and waited for the safe-to-cross symbol to light up. He'd been there all day, crossing and re-crossing that same street. But it seemed new to him each time. He felt strongly that he was really getting somewhere, and he was continually surprised with how familiar the street looked, confirming that he was indeed headed in the right direction.

The night was not especially cold, but he was wearing a black sweatshirt with the hood pulled up over his head. He was oddly proud of himself for continuing to wear clothes even though he couldn't remember the last time that he'd seen a person who might be offended. It was taking him some time to get used to them scratching and pulling at him, blocking out stimulation. He couldn't sense the changing direction of the wind, the change in temperature coming out from the shadows, or the time of day as the warmth of the sun moved across his skin. Still, clothes had their uses, especially when blending into the population of a city.

Of course, there was little need for that now. He knew, or was at least peripherally aware, that most of the people of the city had died or fled, but he was unable to react to it. The emotional draw to the places and people he used to know was distant. Now that the

23

places were deserted and his friends and people he knew were gone or unable to be reached, the feelings just welled up and then out of him. Maybe that was the real reason why he wore the clothing—more emo than camo.

Somewhere, the sun was setting colorfully and magnificently, but here in the heart of the city, the sepia had already gone out of the waning light, and the dark buildings and streets were turning black, with only the odd remaining street lights and the traffic lights offering some illumination.

As though the lighting were a cue, familiar sounds began rippling through the air, bouncing off walls and windows, through the dark alleys and down the streets leading to Joshua.

The recurring dream. The beginning, the middle, or the end, it mattered very little to the cycle, but this section always stood out for him. He liked it.

The music was distant, '*Seems like I've been here before, seems so familiar, seems like I'm slipping into a dream within a dream.*' And the whispering began, gravelly and incomprehensibly low. It was the sound of someone pretending to whisper a secret, though not words, but impressions of words, streaming through the air to his ears. But they were not for his benefit. These were not teasing sounds. These were the voices of the demons hunting.

Joshua wondered if anyone else could hear them—if anyone was around to hear—or if it was just him. He stood in the center of the dark intersection, hands in the pouch of his hoodie, a dark silhouette outlined by the 'stop-red' glowing over his head.

The demons padded slowly out of their hiding places in the shadows, but Joshua knew they were there—he knew each of them intimately, though they'd never met. Some crawled along the walls, and others prowled low to the ground. All of them came with a reverberating, growling whisper that grew louder as they closed the distance.

Joshua waited. He knew this had happened before—just like this, but not quite like this—and the anticipation was something he savored. There was some kind of progression, subtle changes to the nature of the encounter each time. *How many times had it been?*

The changes implied they were learning, but Joshua didn't think they were better, only different. More this time than ever previously; that much was obvious. The subtleties were in the manner of their approaches, more cautious and more controlled each time. This time they were purposefully staggering themselves, leaving some hanging farther back, creating a formation of concentric circles so that there were layers of foul-smelling, slavering beasts surrounding and closing in on the intersection.

He waited with his heart beating heavier in his chest, feeling the strength of his pulse pushing hard through his veins, slowing the world down, thickening the air. The closest demon was only a couple of car lengths away. It was walking on all fours with an aggressive sway, but it switched to a serpentine movement and slid its way onto the roof of the closest car. It held its body only a few centimeters above the roof, knees bent deep, tensing its long claws slowly until they pierced through the metal. As the others continued to close the distance, it began pushing back and forth, rocking the vehicle, before—unable to contain its blood lust any longer—the demon heaved its chest forward and up, arched its head back, and released a high-pitched, metal-on-metal, grating growl.

The beast looked down at Joshua for a reaction and saw that he remained an unmoved, red-rimmed silhouette. It shook in frustration, head swiveling hard left and right, whipping its long dripping tongue around, letting out another grinding cry.

The light turned green.

They were faster this time, but they bled just as easily as they always did.

The light turned red, and Joshua stood alone with his long arms flexed out from his sides. His forearms were covered with the smoking blood of the demons, which dripped down his tensely curled and clawing fingers. The blackened veins visible across his entire body were thick and pulsing. A feverish heat radiated off him, sweat covering his naked body and steam rising from it. He snapped his hands sharply down. Once, twice, drip, slop, spatter, and then he felt they were clean enough to carry on.

Joshua opened his eyes. His pupils were so wide that the irises were hidden, save for the slightest edge of marbled blue. His pupils were flat golden discs when you looked at them directly, reflecting the light they gathered from the few fluorescing sources around.

Steaming, smoking, and eviscerated bodies were strewn all over the intersection, and Joshua wrinkled his nose at the sulfurous smells saturating the air. Demons and cars, skeletal, stripped down to nothing.

The dream. Recurring. He began to float his way back to the clothing store to find another jacket.

Take a Look, It's in a Book

Four

It was an affluent neighborhood in an entirely residential part of the city. On any given day, the streets and sidewalks might have had walkers, joggers, bicyclists, and families, young and old. On a day like today—bright and sunny and warm—one would expect to find many people out and about, fighting off the stresses of modern life with sunshine and physical activity, but now the neighborhood was vacant.

There was refuse in the streets and sidewalks, a small amount of loose debris visible in every direction. It was like the population had suddenly and simultaneously abandoned their homes with no thought of ever returning. There was no evidence of squatters or looters; there was wealth, abandoned and unprotected, and no one was taking advantage.

The stretch of houses along the street was built in the fashion of the late 1900's, a kind of suburban throwback. The houses were single-family *homes* rather than apartments, or at least, that was the tagline used to sell them. The houses were designed as shelters from the fast pace of the modern world by those responsible for demanding that pace, priced so only they could afford them. But it didn't seem to matter who built them or why anymore; there were few signs of anything living, much less a happy family, wealthy or otherwise.

The sun was high in the clear sky, and the street was quiet. The neighborhood was like an archaeological site, the preserved and abandoned exhibit of an extinct society. While a person might feel safe in the exhibit, there was a creepy, lingering sense to the neighborhood that whatever had caused the people to leave was powerfully evil.

But the neighborhood was not entirely deserted. Quickly and quietly, a man rummaged through an antique dresser. He threw clothes onto the floor without care for the mess he was making. Moving from drawer to drawer, he eventually emptied all of the contents and moved to the next dresser in what was apparently the master bedroom of the large home. Portraits on the top of the second dresser depicted a man and a woman posing and smiling in front of an oceanic background. They held each other close in every photo: lovingly arm-in-arm in one, hand-in-hand in another, and classically, humorously false-fighting in the last. There were no rings on any fingers.

The man assessed the frames, sliding his finger along the outer edges. The photos within flickered from one shot to the next, rapidly, but he saw nothing that interested him.

The man was average height and build with reddish hair. It was longer than he liked these days, because he hadn't bothered to care for it. He wore an oversized tee with an electronic poem stalled out from back to front, creating a blurry, but colorful display of a tree or an explosion.

Once he'd finished with the second dresser, he moved without hurry to the bed and ripped the covers off with a single swift pull. Each sheet, as well as the duvet, was tissue thin and soft, but heavy and cool like metal, and they rolled languidly and gracefully to the floor. Beneath the sheets was a body-molding foam mattress. Apparently, the owners had spared no expense with regard to comfort; a king-size bed of that material would have cost them a small fortune.

Mark whispered harshly, "What in the hell am I doing?" He was frustrated with himself, tearing apart the Falken residence, looking for clues in places he knew they couldn't be. Bradley had worked on a quantum communications project for years; it was his baby. His company had lost the backing of the government at one point, but Bradley's intellect and charisma had allowed him to amass funds to continue his project regardless. He'd worked from his home office, and left money in his will to maintain ownership of the home even after his death. So Mark was confident there was something relevant to the project in the house, but he was never able to discover what it was from a distance. Still, it was absurd to think Bradley was going to hide a secret under the covers of his bed, in the mattress, or in a photograph. It was ridiculous to be here searching his home like this, and more than that, it was completely outside of Mark's experience and comfort zone.

He was used to having all of the information of the world at his fingertips. With his vast network of *Marks*, Mark had been intimately connected to every facet of science, medicine, nature, and the Collective. He got whatever he wanted with his hands at his Desk, not by rummaging through someone's clothing drawers. He had been powerful and capable—rumored to be omnipresent and omniscient—but standing there in Bradley's bedroom, looking for something—he didn't even know what—Mark felt powerless and capable of nothing.

Mark wasn't one to be kept in ignorance about any subject for long. If he wanted to know something, he would know it. Somehow though, Bradley had kept his project secret. Mark was only privy to the published documentation and the speculative ramblings of the investors and government liaisons. The latter had come in contact with the project irregularly and only superficially to discuss progress, and of course, Mark's information was only as good as the sources were savvy and trustworthy. All of it was suspect.

Before the Spire cracked, Mark felt like he was an observer on the edge of a colossal step forward for mankind. He'd understood that the world was changing in an extraordinary way, but he hadn't necessarily understood how or to what end. Reality and expectation were married in his mind, holding hands, inseparable. They fought occasionally, but inevitably, with a little work, and a little time for inspection, he would uncover the misunderstanding or the

29

miscommunication that led to the disagreement. Upon resolution, he felt that they were even more strongly intertwined than ever before.

Mark had seen to it that Eve went undetected as she protected Joshua from the Collective. He knew that Joshua would play an integral role, that he would be able to survive exposure to Apple. It was all there in the data he had been compiling for months. He didn't really understand where the catalyst had come from, but he knew its purpose was to unlock human potential in a way previously undiscovered. Despite all of his misgivings about society, he held strong to his belief that this potential would unlock an unprecedented era of understanding and creativity among people, the likes of which would make the golden age nothing more than a shadow staining history.

So, he worked to bring about the change. He kept secrets where they needed to be kept. He moved pieces on the board. He helped Gabriel continue his Apple experiments on his own after he'd fled from Marius in paranoia. Fed the Collective enough information to keep them satisfied, and kept them from launching an all-out search for Gabriel. Possibly the most difficult change for Mark was preparing himself to let go of his beloved and masterful technophilic ways in order to support the changes he predicted: a self-possessed culture, eager to grow and change, enchanted with understanding itself as individuals and as a whole social organism. He saw truth in his vision. Transparency without fear.

But the Spire cracked, and hell fell like phosphorescent tears down the length of its broken body, burning the surface, burning the night. And there was death and darkness. His union of expectation and reality cited irreconcilable differences and went separate ways. And both had left him, orphaned and alone, searching for answers where apparently, there were none. He'd been so confident that Apple was going to cure the world...

He walked from the master bedroom into the hallway, a grandiose expanse overlooking the living room below. Above, several panes of glass allowed the natural light of the sun in, warmth and glow reaching every corner of the spacious home. Looking over the rail, he wasn't sure where to go next.

Maybe there were no answers here, but there was a connection, he was sure of it. The catalyst and Bradley's work, they were linked. Bradley's brother, Joshua, was one of the few to survive exposure to Apple. No way was that a coincidence. It was, in fact, one of the criteria Mark had used to determine that Joshua would be a survivor. Mark was no fool; it was possible that he was just wrong, that his conclusion was coincidentally correct even though he was wrong about his reasoning... but that was pretty difficult for him to believe.

Mark made his way back down to the bottom floor. He'd searched through everything in Bradley's home, and he understood little more than when he first arrived. He wandered into the kitchen and examined the front of the refrigerator. On the display, several items were listed as past their expiration dates, and replacements had been ordered. Mark touched the screen and reviewed the contents list and a notes page containing some dinner ideas for which ingredients had been found, as well as prices calculated, but nothing confirmed. He slid his finger along the front edge of the unit and the door became translucent. Inside were the foods on the list, the bitter greens decomposing in the crisper, the milk and the orange juice—containers swollen—in the middle of the unit, as well as some exotic, though presently unrecognizable, cheeses and meats.

Sliding his finger the opposite direction along the surface, the door became opaque again, and Mark looked around absentmindedly. He wasn't probing for information anymore, so much as trying to *live* in the space and see where he ended up. There was a large sliding glass door opening onto a porch behind the house, and a tiny yard beyond. Walking around the dining table and chairs, Mark walked up to the glass door and stared outside for a bit.

Motionless out there. No birds, no squirrels, no insects. They'd all left with the residents. It was difficult for Mark to not feel responsible for the stillness. He'd been working to create a better world... hadn't he? Not the end of it?

He looked away from the oddly inanimate scene. Walking back out to the living room he saw the door to the den, and figuring since it was the first place he'd looked, why not let it be the last?

The den was dominated by a large wooden desk, opposite the entrance. It was designed in a style to match the era that defined the rest of the house. It was simple and natural and warm.

There was a fairly luxurious and opulent display of books filling several shelves along the walls. Somehow, the number of books managed to be tasteful; they were certainly expensive and unnecessary items to have. Furthermore, though generally recognized as fragile, they were not hermetically sealed behind glass or displayed with extravagant flourishes; rather, they were free to be touched and handled. Indeed, the books even looked worn from frequent use.

There was a large abstract painting acting as a backdrop to the desk. What it depicted or what it had once represented for Bradley was difficult to discern. Organic structures held brightly colored circles filled with smaller circles, ellipses, and other oblong shapes. The painting was hung dead center behind and above the desk, and framed it rather well.

Mark walked around the desk and ran his hand along the back of the chair on the other side. He examined the painting closely. It was a true oil. Mark wasn't an expert, but there were textures, strokes in the paint, that were pretty convincing. He stared at it a while longer. It was easy to get lost in the image, color-echoes of each circle repeated in the others, and the lines and curves connecting and holding them, seeming to convey something from one to the next.

Finally, he pulled the chair out and sat down. He placed his hands on the smooth, cool surface of the desk and pulled himself forward to sit as he imagined Bradley might have sat. Unexpectedly, the chair adjusted to his body, automatically making him more comfortable; he had mistakenly thought the chair was an antique. Mark took a closer look at the desk, sliding his fingers along the surface in typical ways, trying to activate the interface he hoped to find, but there was no response.

There wasn't much to the desk really. It seemed that it was only wood, and the only items on it were more ornamental than functional. There was a feather pen sticking up out of a brass holder, and a closed well of ink beside it. Also, a Newton's Cradle and a compass were displayed, but apparently unused.

He sat back and looked from bookshelf to bookshelf. There was something odd, a pattern in their distribution that was nonsense to him if he looked too closely, but that also somehow made sense to him intuitively. The shelves were not mirrored, but at the same time, there was a strong sense of symmetry. He looked back and forth to figure out how they appeared so symmetrical, trying to identify one book and keep it in his mind as he looked for it on the other shelf; eventually, he would just lose the book. The effect was disorienting and a little alarming.

Mark struggled to grasp what he was seeing, 'There, the book in the middle, left shelf, with the ruddy binding, roughly textured, thick, black lettering and symbols on the spine. Right shelf... book by book, carefully, cover by cover, it's definitely not there, wouldn't expect to see it there, but what about that one? Looks similar enough, not sure if it is exactly... look left... where did it go?'

Again and again, he tried to hold a book long enough in his memory—his memory had never been suspect, and he trusted it implicitly—to confirm whether or not the same or similar book was in the other shelf, but he couldn't. Back and forth he looked, becoming more and more desperate and frustrated each time. It was as though whatever the details were, if he tried to pick them out and pin them specifically down, he couldn't. They changed in his mind, and when he tried to identify them again, he couldn't. Once, he felt certain that a very specific book had swapped shelves, but then it was gone; though, not that it had moved or disappeared, but more that it was not the way he remembered it.

Mark grinned.

He stood up and walked to the shelf on the right. Pulling out a book, he flipped it over to read the cover, but found that he couldn't read it. The words on the cover were written in a completely unintelligible script. The pages were filled with words, but he couldn't hold them together long enough to form a thought. Sentence meanings eluded him, not because they were written in gibberish, but because the words slipped in and out of his consciousness seamlessly.

Mark laughed in a forest with no one to hear him. Reading—or attempting to read—the book in his hand, was the visual equivalent of in one ear and out the other. By the time he had processed one word, he'd forgotten the preceding word, but didn't notice until he'd finished the sentence.

He slid the book back into its position on the shelf and lost track of it immediately. Reaching for another book—thinking it might be the same one—he opened it, closed it, and prepared to return it when he thought better of it. Opening it again, he carefully tore half a page from the middle of the book before returning it to the same spot on the shelf. Then, holding the page firmly in his hand, he walked across to the opposite shelf, to the far corner, retrieved a book, and leafed through the pages quickly and found not one, but two torn pages. He held his torn page up to the missing edges like a puzzle piece, and found that it didn't match at all. 'Of course it doesn't match up, how could it? But, why were there two pages torn from this book?'

Utterly confused, he stood staring at the book with the two torn pages, and his jagged half-page.

Marius wondered about Mark's intentions now that everything had changed. When Mark first ambushed Marius on the Javelin—he was Jasper then, oh so briefly—he had spewed some nonsense about *global transformation* and *social evolution* in an attempt to convince Marius about the importance of their return to the city. Apparently, Mark also needed Marius as a connection to Gabe, because Gabe— pawn though he'd seemed to be—was supposedly critical to the massive changes coming to the world. Gabe had maybe considered him a friend once, but he had doubted he'd have much pull with the old chemist.

Marius had betrayed Gabriel—years of friendship, even if it was mostly an act—to a Stranger, a client he didn't even know—likely dead at this point. Somehow, Gabe had still sought a connection with Marius though, still trusted him, and Marius had turned him away. The chemist had proposed that Marius ingest Apple as he had—the inexplicable compound they'd both seen kill untold numbers of subjects—because he thought it would help. Marius had yelled at him and walked away. He had hoped to leave Gabe in his past forever, but then Mark dug him up.

Marius had smiled and nodded, and waited for the punchline— to hear how Gabe was so valuable to Mark—but the punchline never came. Mark thought Gabriel was integral; therefore, so was Marius. At that point, Marius had few choices. This was Mark, a man who knew more about Marius than anyone else; it didn't seem that running away from him was much of an option. Mark had built Marius' new creds and hid his former identity, making Marius untraceable. Mark had a reputation for never blackmailing a client... until then.

So, Marius' dream of retirement quashed, he tolerated the raving technophile as best he could, hoping to glean valuable knowledge, and eventually an upper hand if one presented itself. He hadn't become a Ghost by being impatient, after all.

Despite the underlying motivation, Mark's words had been compelling and full of confidence. He was full of himself, as well; for all his knowledge, he wasn't particularly socially cultivated. According to Mark, where the world had sewn discord, he'd provided harmony; wherever chance had pulled threads, Mark had sewn them back up. In other words, Mark saw himself as puppet-master, not only trying to ensure that the change would come, but also that it would not be forestalled by any error on nature's part. Confidence and arrogance were easily mistaken for one another, and Marius felt Mark had succumbed to the latter.

Marius was careful not to allow the arrogance to creep in; on a daily basis he changed the lives of many people and sometimes, took them. But he knew there was always someone better, that he wasn't all-powerful, and *that* knowledge kept him from making mistakes.

Unfortunately, he also loved a challenge, which is what got him into this mess. The Stranger had been out of his reach, above him, but he'd dealt with him anyway and landed right in shit.

Marius hadn't made the rules of his old life, but he'd lived by them. Annoyingly, Mark had been working on changing those rules for some time, and succeeded. And he had seemed to feel pretty good about it for a while... until the changes actually came.

As Marius entered Bradley's house, he grinned smugly to himself. Seeing Mark's over-confidence destroyed—as the news of the murdered masses reached him—had been pretty satisfying. Mark's idea of a better world and a time of enlightenment had disappeared, and slowly, too, was his sanity. While watching Mark slowly lose his grip had been a little entertaining, he had become a pretty depressing companion in these last several weeks, and it was getting a little old.

"Find anything?" Marius stepped into the den and unceremoniously toed aside a book on the floor as his grin slid down his face. Mark was sitting on a desk, surrounded by books. Some of the books were organized into piles, while others lay in disarray all over the floor. The bookshelves on both sides of the desk were empty. Since the entire room was littered by either books or pages from books, Marius stayed at the entrance. Mark ripped a page from the book he was apparently reading, and then threw it carelessly away without looking up. Marius watched, "I guess not."

A few moments passed, a few more pages were ripped and cast aside. Marius put his gloved hands into the pockets of his grey trench, and stared reproachfully, although somewhat amused, at the once great Mark as he sat on the desk, unraveling. "I think it's prudent to state for the record that you most certainly did this to yourself."

"I certainly did," Mark looked up, smiling and a little wild-eyed, and he let the book he was holding slide out of his hands. "I didn't find it like this."

"The room?" Marius raised an eyebrow, "That's not what I meant, but I'm sure it's true as well."

"Marius, have you ever played cards?"

"Up for a game? I think I would likely feel bad taking money from you right now, although I am not entirely certain money is worth much anymore," both eyebrows raised now, "What are the stakes?"

"So, you have a shuffled deck," his hands energetically and emphatically creating and shuffling an imaginary deck, "and it is full of possibilities. What happens when you draw that top card?"

Marius, having been talked both over and through by Mark several times these past few months, decided to humor him, "One probability becomes reality, and the odds for each of the remaining cards to appear next, change."

Placing the phantom drawn card back in the deck with a flourish, "And what about now? I've returned the one card we know back into the deck, but definitely not at the top." Mark beams, "Would you bet on the card you just saw appearing next?"

"I wouldn't bet on it at all."

"I'm playing with a full deck, I promise."

"I wouldn't bet on that either, but again, that's not what I meant." Somewhat exasperated, "Could you please arrive at the point? Or at least advise me when you plan on arriving and I'll meet up with you then?"

"These books... Marius! They shuffle themselves!" Gesturing to the books scattered throughout the room, "And! And they are pulling from a deck that is larger than what you can see in this room!"

Skeptically, "There are more books in here," mockingly repeating the all-encompassing gesture, "than the books in here?"

"Well, it's the deck of cards, really," carefully choosing his words, "I kept drawing the top card, and I couldn't tell if it was what I had drawn before or not, and then I marked the cards... and now I just keep pulling new cards." Mark looked around himself, showing some signs of distress in his face, "Just when I thought I knew the contents of the deck, new cards showed up that I'd never seen before..."

Marius stared, posture unchanged, tall and severe in all angles, his salt-and-pepper hair complementing the grey of his trench coat. He stared and waited.

"I thought it was my mind at first," somewhat beseechingly, "playing tricks on me, but I know it's not. I mean, I can't keep track of what I'm seeing; the details are slippery, but…."

The man is completely broken. "I've no doubt that someone is playing a trick on you," narrowing his eyes at the pleading man, "You're describing, if your mind isn't completely broken, a kind of magic trick or something similar."

Mark came down from his perch on the desk, invigorated with an idea. He started quickly placing all of the books back on the shelves in no particular order. Even working as frenetically as he was, it was taking several minutes to put them away. "You could help me, you know," he held out a book to Marius, who made eye contact, but moved in no other discernible way. His hands remained in his pockets, and eventually, Mark returned to his task alone.

All of the books replaced, Mark looked at Marius, "Enough talking," spoken too flatly to be taken seriously, but without enough sarcasm to be funny, "You try."

Marius gave no indication that he understood or cared. He considered just leaving.

"Just try to keep track of one book. Draw one out of a shelf, put it back, and see if you can find it again."

In spite of his best efforts to detect signs of insobriety, Marius admitted to himself that Mark appeared lucid, and maybe a little participation might get them back on track. He strode across the room, drew out one book, leafed through it, and replaced it. Facing Mark, "I hope my performance was satisfactory. Should we get going now? Is there anything else we should be doing here? You never did tell me what you expected to find, or how this helps us…"

Interjecting, "Which book did you select?"

Marius impatiently turned around to the shelf, "This…" he looked confused, "one…?" He pulled down a book.

"Your confidence is overwhelming," mockingly, arms akimbo.

Marius slid the book back into position on the shelf, and after several moments of pulling out books and returning them, "So, what is your explanation?"

"The probabilities are ever in flux! Even while you hold the card in your hand!" he was standing beside the taller Marius now, sliding a hand along the bindings of the books. "It's like playing face up with cards that are all shuffling constantly, and even after you play a card, you still aren't sure what card was played!"

Replacing the book he'd only half-pulled from the shelf, Marius thought to himself for several moments. "That makes no sense whatsoever."

"Of course it does. You're just n…"

"Your explanation doesn't match the context," and perhaps for the first time in their short relationship, Marius flashed his teeth and reflected violent intentions in his eyes, "Why would this *game* be here? In Bradley Falken's home?"

Mark took an almost unconscious step back from the Ghost. His shoulders dropped, and his enthusiasm drained from him as the blood did from his face.

Satisfied that he still had the touch, and that he'd appropriately established who was talking, "Your explanation does not fit the larger picture. This isn't just a game of solitaire here." He stepped around to the oil painting on the back wall, and Mark's eyes followed him. "Communication was Bradley's area of study," mumbled to no one in particular. He reached up to touch the painting, "You are not playing alone."

"Huh? I don't understand," some of Mark's vim returned as he realized that he might have been wrong about what was happening with the books, but that he had found something important, and that Marius was suddenly more than a little interested.

"You wanted to play cards, didn't you?" Marius turned to address Mark directly, "And how many people do you need to play a game? What good is a magic trick or a card game if there is no one else with whom to play it? The cards do not matter," he paused thinking the idea through, "they are just a medium... a vocabulary."

The hairs on Mark's arms prickled, and for the first time, he felt afraid, incapable. Even the Spire cracking, even the Spire opening up, hadn't really frightened him, probably more from arrogance and lack of understanding than courage.

"Someone is playing with you... but who?"

The Pit

Five

Ezechial woke the child after little more than four hours sleep, but the boy seemed well-rested when they started walking.

The boy was reticent and spoke only when spoken to, and then only if a nod or shake of his head wasn't enough. It was past midday before Ezechial learned his name. He didn't push Pallomor for any more personal information though, so they continued together in silence. They were well out of the heart of the city and, he hoped, well away from the host of demons. The dark dwellers seemed to come out mostly at night, mostly.

They walked on a double yellow line, which only seemed to divide cars parked facing northeast from those facing southwest in a long narrow parking lot. The vehicles were mostly intact, and even orderly, as though the drivers had calmly decided that it wasn't necessary to drive any farther, turned them off, and exited. Most of the doors were left open, sometimes causing the pair to walk around awkwardly. Where the drivers and passengers had gone was difficult to discern. Without signs of struggle to follow, there was nothing for Ezechial to track.

His voice carried farther than he expected in the stillness, "I thought that the city would have a chance to die with a great fight, with a struggle that would leave everything destroyed." The boy continued walking without comment, without reaction. "I pictured a city mauled and ravaged when I studied the prophecy, but these people seem to have vanished."

They looked into the buildings as they passed, quietly deeming them empty.

It wasn't like the shore where the demons rolled out of the water, destroying and ravenously devouring everything in sight. The streams of that attack had run red with blood, the feeds difficult to watch, but impossible not to. People had died watching. At least that was how he saw it on his feed before the signal stopped, before every signal stopped.

Each time Ezechial left the city he entered and exited by different routes. Though it was true that he was running out of variations, he still observed the surroundings carefully. He'd seen similar scenes along all his routes: streets filled with vacated vehicles and no explanation or sign of a struggle. No matter how many times he saw the scene, it made him uncomfortable. So he returned again and again, making his treks to the city, hoping for some indication, some hint of what had happened.

On his journeys, Ezechial found signs of life here and there and rescued people when he found them. But *rescue* was a strong word for the small hope he gave them, which only lasted until he got them out of the city and into his restaurant hideout.

Ezechial guided each of the three people he'd found to the basement of a small French-Italian restaurant, which provided little more than the perception of protection. He had no confidence in the security door, which was meant to dissuade burglars, not withstand a demonic attack. Still, he hoped that keeping them inside—off he street and bunkered—would keep the demons off the scent and give them no reason to come knocking.

There was food—dried and canned goods—that would last for another month or so, and *some* remaining salvage from the freezer and refrigerator, which were powerless in their struggle against time and its weapons of decay and rot. They hadn't found salvation and the residents knew it, and it drained them. If surviving the initial slaughter was difficult, surviving after wasn't any easier. They would need to move on soon or lose hope, and life would follow hope as it always does.

Ezechial inspected his forearm, black and blue cracks crawling beneath the skin. The ache had only gotten worse during the night. He made a fist, flexed and released the muscles, and felt the soreness of a muscle burnt from overuse. It was tight, and as he imagined holding the whip again, he felt a twinge of nausea-inducing pain. Going through the motions in his imagination—a practice in his lifelong training—he found himself avoiding the left arm, and instead always choosing a position to favor his weakened left side. He wasn't sure that the demons would notice or understand, but if there was any sentience among them… he would have to be wary and quicker to retreat.

Looking up from his wound, Ezechial noticed that Pallomor was staring at him with an odd expression twitching across his face, as though the muscles of his face couldn't decide whether to smile or frown.

Stopping, Ezechial frowned at the boy for a moment, trying to get a sense of what he was thinking. Sliding his sleeve down as far as he could over the wound, "It's okay. Sore, but nothing to worry about." He waited to see if his words had any effect, but the only noticeable change was that the boy seemed to make up his mind to frown exclusively.

"It's okay." He started walking again.

Pallomor continued in silence, looking into a building or car occasionally, but mostly looking forward, staring blankly into the middle distance. As they walked on, Ezechial decided the boy was in shock, probably stuck in the images of his friends, whoever they were, being bled and dragged away in a flash. He decided to keep the child ahead of him as they walked, always in his vision, so that Ezechial would be able to protect him.

They walked together like that for an hour or so, Ezechial a few strides behind Pallomor, the boy apparently unaware of his surroundings. More than once, Ezechial had had to step forward, and gently nudge the boy around an obstacle. He seemed to think he was safe between the yellow lines, and didn't want deviate from them if he could help it. As they came to the center of an intersection, the boy stopped again. There was nothing obvious in his way, and he stood staring to the northwest, perpendicular to their path.

Stepping up beside Pallomor, Ezechial followed his gaze down the crossing street. Only thirty meters or so away, there was a large break in the parked cars. The space was large enough to hold a couple of large tankers side-by-side and end-to-end.

Ezechial looked back down at Pallomor and thought he saw that odd, uncomfortable smile again. It was faint, almost a smirk; nevertheless, he felt sure he saw the corners of the boy's red lips turning up ever so slightly. He found that he was staring at the boy, staring hard at him. Finally, the boy looked back and tilted his head up slightly, directly meeting the gaze of the elder Laterali.

Ezechial took a hesitant step back without breaking eye contact. Then, after a moment, he shook his head, and rubbed his forearm. He closed his eyes hard, and felt a slight cold prick of sweat breaking out from his spine, and beads began standing out on his forehead. Wiping his brow and opening his eyes again, he took a deep breath and looked at the boy. There was only concern on his face, and maybe even a little fear.

"It's going to be okay."

Pallomor continued to stare up with concern.

"I want to see what's over there. You can stay here if you wish, but I'd prefer it if you came with me."

Pallomor took a shuttering breath and reached his hand out to Ezechial. He wove his small fingers in and around the fingers of Ezechial's right hand and held them there for a moment. Then, without prompting, he began walking toward the empty space, tugging gently at Ezechial to follow.

As they approached the open area, Ezechial was able to see the outer edge of a hole broken through the asphalt. They walked steadily on, and it became clear that the absence of cars was from the road being swallowed up from beneath. There was wreckage, plastic and metal debris, and dark oily stains all around the jagged lip of the crevasse.

There was a sound—shuffling and faint footsteps—approaching from the other side of the gaping maw. Ezechial wanted to reach for his Devil's Tails, or run, or both, but his left hand hesitated in pain, and he felt a tug in his right. The boy was looking up at him, pleading eyes begging him to stay.

The shuffling grew ever closer, and Ezechial listened closely. He decided it was two humans walking their way. He got his first glimpse of them, and even without the trick of perception, Ezechial could tell that they would never spot him or the boy. They walked with their shoulders hunched, a woman and a man, who was carrying a small child, probably not younger than the one holding Ezechial's hand. They were looking down at their feet, but somehow they managed to avoid walking into cars.

Less than a meter away from the edge, they stopped and finally looked up. Ezechial recognized the stare, as they seemed to look right through him. It was the stare people held when he tricked them, but he was not hiding from them and still they couldn't identify his presence. The child in the man's arms was asleep against his chest, undisturbed by the darkness at their feet.

The man, still seemingly looking right at Ezechial, held the boy out in front of him, stepped forward, and dropped him unceremoniously into the pit.

One.

Two.

Three.

Thud.

There wasn't a scream. Just the thud. A few seconds passed, and then there was rustling, louder and louder until it became thrashing echoes welling up from below. The man stepped forward until he stepped on nothing, and went toppling into the hole.

One.

Two.

Three.

Thud-crunch.

The rustling from when the child was dropped hadn't stopped, and now it was just louder and more fervent. The tearing and crunching sounds were punctuated by occasional bone-snaps. Then the low rattling engine sounds began, shaking Ezechial from his stupor in a rush.

His senses focused acutely and he felt a rush of blood through his veins, and the throbbing ache as his arm began to burn and tighten. He was peripherally aware of the woman starting her slow lurch forward toward the brink as he gathered up Pallomor in his arms.

Ezechial ran. His heart pounded heavily into his head and ears, but it still couldn't drown out the sound of the demon calls winding up and whining high into the air behind them. Their metallic rattles and winding sounds were mixed with gurgling and choking, predatory sounds that spurred him on even faster.

As he ran, Ezechial desperately tried to identify his surroundings and realized that he hadn't been paying attention for quite a while. He didn't have a working map of his location running in his head, he couldn't remember the turns he'd taken to get to the pit, and he couldn't say exactly what street they were on. These were things that he usually knew inherently as he moved, always with a sense of place, an understanding of distance and direction determining his choices... but now, he was lost.

He looked up to the sky and felt the sun on his face, and smelled the air. Still running, sweating, and carrying the boy in his arms, he searched back through his mind and began rebuilding the pieces. His left arm was nothing more than a large burning cramp, numbing and weakening with each step he took. Despite their distance, the sounds of the demons eating seemed so close.

Finally, he turned the corner and met recognizable surfaces, cars, and store fronts. All the pieces of his broken mental map snapped together at once and he found his bearings.

It was still hours before dusk, and they would make it to the restaurant long before that, even if they walked. The thought was comforting, but it also meant that the demons were much closer to the hideout than he'd realized. The group would have to move on from the restaurant sooner than he'd hoped.

He was glad he'd found Pallomor before that had to happen. He couldn't say why finding the boy gave him that intuitive sense of relief, because he'd been looking for Joshua, not for survivors. Believing that his future was intimately interwoven with Joshua's, Ezechial had been patiently searching for him. The rest of the Laterali had faded into the shadows when they finally realized the prophecy was upon them. As the demons poured down the giant obsidian obelisk, their seers saw clearly that they needed to retreat and wait. The demons were meant to cleanse the world; the Laterali were not meant to interfere.

Ezechial saw something else for himself. Not against the prophecy, but hidden within it. He wasn't a seer, but nevertheless, he'd seen references to one who *would* interfere. Ezechial didn't believe it was him, but he didn't believe it wasn't either. There was still too much in flux to judge or act on. He even saw something different for his brothers and sisters as well, but that was much later, if any of them survived.

Pallomor would be the youngest of their group, but perhaps he would give them all renewed hope. He needed to tell the others that the demons were close, too close, but maybe he'd leave out some of the terrible details of the discovery. Perhaps they needed to move inland, where he knew how to forage for food and water and maybe there was safety. Without any kind of modern communication working, he wasn't sure how the cities farther from the Spire had fared, but he knew enough to get away from the immediate threat.

Slowing down, but still walking with purpose, Ezechial chose a route he'd taken previously. A couple of hours remained of the day's light, and he thought they'd make the safety of the restaurant before sunset.

The air was cool and getting colder already, the days shorter this time of year. He could feel the heat of his run, and saw steam rising like a mist from his body. He stopped and Pallomor finally moved from where his head had been buried in Ezechial's chest. The odd smile appeared again, curling back up at him, red lines carved into an alabaster mask of a cherub.

He knelt down and landed the boy softly on his feet. As he stood, never breaking eye contact, the strange expression remained.

Finally, "We can walk now. We're almost there."

The boy's answer was to turn and begin walking.

Ezechial followed.

The Chosen One

Six

"The world has chosen me." The man was tall and slender, and exuded confidence and strength. His tone was matter-of-fact. He wore a loose-fitting linen shirt and pants, which were both creamy white in contrast to his chocolate skin.

His arms were clasped behind his back as he continued to address the room. If the other man—doubled-over, writhing on the floor, and clutching at his stomach—was listening, the speaker seemed not to care. "By desperately seeking to advance—in every way, save spiritually," he paused almost as a cue to thoughtful contemplation from a well-practiced lecture, as if to ask the audience, *Why do you think that is?* But the pause ended without more than a drooling whimper from the floored man, "the world has chosen me to unmake it."

The day was beginning, and all the Views in the luxury apartment were showing the last of the sunrise, softening and warming the room. The interior lights had dimmed, and were almost off, as the man inspected the couch in the sparsely decorated living area. He moved aside a pillow and brushed a seat cushion with his hand, patting it finally, but not sitting down. He paced the room, admiring the Views, hands once again clasped behind his back.

"Demetrius… may I call you Demy?" he stopped, bent down ever so slightly, and looked to the man for an answer. Demetrius, eyes squeezed shut against the pain, convulsively coughed once and sprayed bloody spittle over the white carpet.

"Demy, it is." Smiling, he returned his attention to the room, and began to walk around again as he spoke, "You know, Demy, we have an awful lot in common."

Silence.

"Your research, all of your efforts, were directly contributing to my, uh," he ran a palm along the length of his smooth, bald pate, front to back, "awakening? You will have to excuse the term; I've not had anyone with whom to discuss it for such a long time. It hadn't occurred to me to name the transition."

He waited for Demetrius to finish groaning through his gritted teeth.

"The Upper Spire was filled with conjecture about the catalyst's purpose and usefulness, so I had to clue them in every step of the way to keep everything in motion." Looking again directly at Demetrius, "Do you know how much work it is to manage management?"

Demy's breathing came in labored gasps, and chokingly restrained expulsions.

Returning to his slow meandering gait around the living room, "This is a pivotal moment for you, Demy. So few are given the opportunity to actually *know* the critical moments of their lives as they happen, but you? You, I've given the gift of presence." Smiling, "Of course, there won't be much opportunity for retrospective, but that hardly diminishes the gift..."

Demetrius managed to roll a little to his side, and reached up for his couch. His slick red hand left tracks as he tried to pull himself up. He barely lifted his chest, his head still hanging low between his shoulders, and through gritted teeth, "Fuck," choking back a cough, "you."

The man frowned down slightly, disappointed, "I would say the same to you, but evidently," gesturing toward the bloody drool stretching down to the carpet, "you're already pretty fucked."

Composed and smiling at the sky in the Viewer once again, "You've been given a gift and you should know your benefactor." He walked around Demy to the opposite side of the couch, "You may call me Deliah." The man smoothly, casually sat down on the couch.

Deliah put his arm up along the back of the couch, legs crossed, "I was a Secretary until recently, but I've dispensed with the title. Well, dispensed with those to whom it would have mattered anyway," spoken as a pleasant anecdote, shared in passing.

"You may not recognize my name, or the role I've played in your life so far, but today, I am the narrator of the end."

Nodding toward the expansive and expensive accommodations, "You've done quite well for yourself. BioGen takes care of its best and brightest. Along with the perquisites though... so much responsibility."

Demy tried again to pull himself up, only managing to drag himself an inch or so closer to the couch.

Deliah sighed, "You're only making this worse," as Demy dragged himself ever so slightly closer to the couch again, "Whatever you need to do, I suppose... I mean, I chose daybreak for you. Peaceful. Serene. Beautiful. This doesn't have to be any more of a struggle than it already is."

Folding his hands onto his lap, he resumed, "The responsibilities, yes? So many. In particular, your responsibility to BioGen, your project, your team, compelled you to make a report that night... about your friend, Joshua Falken?"

Demy froze. That night, seeming so long ago now, had never felt right to him. He'd been trying to reach Joshua ever since he was sure Joshua had tried Apple. Joshua's first story about being kidnapped could have been nothing more than a vivid nightmare, but with everything else? Demy was positive that Joshua had become a subject. He hadn't any idea how or why, but he'd recognized the effects. He was worried about his friend. He wanted to help. He'd only made the report to try to protect Joshua, but Joshua had run from the apartment and hadn't looked back.

Demy had seen what the compound could do to people. So few had survived, and all of them were tormented and ill. Even after filing multiple times for the research to be discontinued, BioGen persisted. Apparently someone else had survived it; not only survived, but become something new and powerful.

In spite of his high-ranked position and several inquiries, he'd never even discovered how Joshua had become a test subject. Demy had been in charge of acquisitions… he should have known.

"I apologize that your friend became a subject. It wasn't my intention either. Honestly, I was as shocked as you were," then leaning slightly forward, "and isn't it interesting that we both made the same arrogant mistake? Thinking we were the only ones in the game?" He let out a deep, dark, reverberant chuckle as he leaned back against the couch.

Serious again, "If I may be blunt though, your mistake was greater than mine. I had all of the resources of the Spire at my disposal and you had what? BioGen? I *own* them." And something flashed in Deliah's amber eyes, firing them up briefly and ferociously.

"Do you know how you've managed to survive up here? With all the prowling demons out there, rounding up and devouring every human body in sight?" he waited courteously, "Because I wanted this meeting. I'm here to tie up the loose ends."

Demy started to laugh a little as he gave up trying to get on the couch. Instead, he turned himself over to face Deliah from the floor, and scooted himself back against it. Propped against the couch, he put his arm up across the seat cushion, mimicking his assailant. If not for the blood all over his hands and stomach, it might have been a playful mockery.

"So… you're afraid of Joshua?" He stopped a moment, weakening and wincing a bit. "I mean, he does okay with the ladies, but once," coughing, "I saw him hit on this uptight guy…"

"Where is Joshua?"

Wagging his hand dismissively toward Deliah, leaning heavily against the couch, "This guy's girlfriend comes up," he wiped away some of the blood and spittle from his lower lip, "she was tiny, and five ways wasted," spreading the fingers of his blood-sticky hand, Demy was distracted by the texture for a moment, "and gave him the most sincere ass-kicking I've ever seen," he slapped his hand on the couch cushion meaning to be emphatic, but the motion was slower and weaker than he'd hoped, more pat than slap. Still, he managed to grin wickedly back at Deliah.

"It always starts the same, you know? This scene. I try, I honestly do try, to create something new, something beautiful and unique with each one. But, it can be difficult because so many of you are the same."

Deliah continued with affected distaste, "Arrogance. So much arrogance. And the banter… really? You believe that someone courageous is going to arrive to save you? There is no one courageous left! People chose comfort over courage, safety over dreams. There are no heroes, just people living their dreamless lives, rationalizing their servile existence as happiness, waiting to die. No one is going to save you… they can't even save themselves." Deliah was leaning in so far at the end that he looked more like a snake than a man.

Relaxing back against the couch again, and amusedly reminiscing, "One at least had the decency to supply the weapon of his unmaking. He loved that tiny knife. I thought it was poetic."

Deliah sat for a bit longer, lost in thought. Demy stared back at him intensely when he could, but spasms kept forcing his head down. Then, silky smooth and without ceremony, Deliah stood.

He began walking toward the door with his hands behind his back. "There are many kinds of poetry in the world, Demy," he slid his finger down the side of the door, which activated a view of the hallway. Outside were demons, filling all the space available from the door to the elevator. They crawled up and over each other, and occasionally snapped or clawed at one another. In the middle of the hall, there were several hunched over an indistinguishable mass of red and brown.

There was no sound, and then Deliah unmuted the feed. Crunching and slobbering noises entered the apartment, muddied with strange slithering sounds of movement. One of the demons huddled in the middle suddenly looked up, blood-red maw agape, and howled. The whining pitch was like a needle stabbing and scratching at Demy's ear drum.

When the metallic howling finally diminished to a low rumble, the demon briefly looked through the door and into Demy's eyes before returning to the muddled mass of flesh.

"You may choose your poetry, Demy." A harrowing scream, human, came through the door, and not just through the Viewer's speaker. "You may be alive while they dine… or not," eyebrows raised patronizingly.

Sweat beaded all over Demy's body, cold and prickly. All the heat and blood fell out of him. He looked down at his hand still covering the compound fracture in his chest. The rib was punched out through the skin—yellow, bright red, and dark purple-red.

"Oh, that?" Deliah's hands were still behind his back, but he nodded at Demy's chest, "That won't kill you. I promise."

"I don't know where he is," he just sagged there on the floor, propped against the couch, eyes low, but looking at nothing.

"I think I like the banter better. This lack of vigor is… well, it's sad really. Do you know anything that would help me find him?"

"Would it make a difference?"

"Absolutely!" Deliah sprang forward. His linen garb trailed behind him and then snapped as it caught up. In the same motion he transitioned to his knees, hands cupping either side of Demy's face gently before he could blink, or react in any way.

"It would make a difference to me, your generous benefactor, and to the future. You won't be present for it, but any information you share may change how all of this ends! Imagine! You could end all of the suffering Joshua caused by delaying the inevitable. All of you chose oblivion; I was only trying to deliver it." Deliah's eyes were glistening, filling with emotion.

Demetrius looked into Deliah's eyes and mistook the passion displayed as compassion, and began crying, simple tears welling and trailing. "But... I don't know where he is. I couldn't find him." Pleading, "I tried, I tried so hard! But, he just dis...." A long, gasping, choking cough interrupted him, but Deliah held his face strongly.

"What did you do when you received the message from him, from the diner?"

Demy was unable to respond as another coughing fit shook him.

"I understand that it's surprising how much I know about you, but that's a simple privilege of the Upper Spire. Just explain what you did next."

"I didn't do anything," he was whimpering now, "I don't want to die."

"You went to investigate. I know. I would have done the same. In fact, I did, but I didn't find him." Deliah was close enough to kiss Demetrius, "What did you find?"

Weakly, "I don't know. I saw that he was showing signs... that he'd definitely taken the compound." His speech became random and pleading. He was reaching for words that would change the inevitable, the promise of what would happen to him. "There were C.O.s involved. Joshua did something to them, broke a face or two or something... he was, he was definitely getting the fever, yes. You probably didn't know that, but the sweat and heat...he left a trail of dripping sweat all the way to an apartment complex, but that took me a long time to find, special equipment, you know? Special equipment. I had to steal stuff from my office, and BioGen interrogated me... not like this though, not like this... I didn't tell them anything. I wanted to make sure he was okay first. And, and... and I wanted..."

"You wanted to protect your friend from *your* experiments? The horrible things you did to all of those other poor people you selected for the tests? As subjects?"

"Yeah, uh, yes…" deliriously.

"Did Joshua even know about your current work?"

"No. I mean, I showed him some of my research, but it was nothing… inconclusive, inconclusive like everything…"

"Demy, I've decided that your soul is irredeemable." Deliah squeezed Demy's face between his hands, and as Demy tried to squirm away, Deliah held tighter, claws growing and penetrating the skin. "You've given me nothing to go on, and you've done nothing with your life, really."

Releasing his grip, leaving fresh blood streaking down Demy's cheeks, Deliah stood and strode to the door.

Once he made it to the door, he stopped and turned, "When there is no heart at the center of your choices, no expression, no desire to expand your soul, you wither… become nothing. I try not to be prejudicial. I like to think of myself as one who will accept all comers. I so rarely turn away a lost soul at my door, no matter how poisoned, no matter how weak. I accept the offers. The deals are cheap. For a pittance in comfort and material accommodations, I claim something endless."

Deliah slid his finger along the door, and the latch released and the door opened, "The only thing that ever mattered to you, Demy, was you. Every decision you made was for your benefit. Joshua was your only real connection and you couldn't even hold on to that."

"Let me show you what becomes of your soul when you don't take care of it."

The creatures stood or shuffled to the side quietly, heads bowed, looking away from the former Secretary. Suddenly, Demy noticed how human the demons appeared—fragile and scared, subservient. But people are more than that…

At the elevator, Deliah turned, bowed toward Demetrius, and stepped in. As the doors came together, Demy could see the soft amber glow of those terrible eyes laughing back at him.

Demy closed his eyes and wished he could close his ears. The shuffling became rustling, and the rumbling became atonal, high-pitched whines, and then… screaming.

FALLEN SPIRE

Sides

Seven

The alleyway was dark, even at midday, living entirely in the shadows of buildings that stretched to the sky and blocked out the sun. With the exception of a few weeks in the summertime, the north-south alley was in shadow during the day and was tar-black at night. Only the temperature told the time. In a shelter made of shipping pallets, with newspaper and cardboard wadded and folded into the spaces between slats, Gabriel sat whimpering.

His spectacles were dirty, smudged and dusty like his face and mussed hair. A thick fog of pungent smells floated around his makeshift home: greasy body oils, urine and fetid feces, and rancid animal fat—there were scraps of flesh, raw meat and integument sticking to the asphalt and walls. Hugging himself, legs crossed beneath, Gabriel rocked forward and back, and waited for the demons.

Every day since he left the room at the top of the Spire, they came for him. They prowled in from the shadows, and approached him with a kind of playful anger. And like an older brother proving dominance, the leader at the front of the pack growled and spit at him, but never scratched him, never left a mark, as though he was protected. Gabriel sat through it each time, staring blankly, catatonic eyes shimmering wet behind his spectacles, his face pale and drawn. The demons would laugh-metallic in his face, rattling and threatening him with grinding whines, but just like their leader, they left him completely unharmed. Not only did they not harm the one-time chemist, they left him food, or at least he was hungry enough to eat whatever they left behind.

It was no kind of courage that kept Gabe from running; it was sheer hopelessness. His un-living days kept stretching out before him, and it didn't matter whether or not it mattered. The Chemist had used people his whole life, then he was used, and now, he was used up.

Gabriel's journey through the city, with the voices and the Shades, had been the crawl of a mad, disinterred cadaver looking for its grave. When he finally arrived at the Spire, Eve was there watching. She'd imagined the man had found his grave, but not only did the mumbling madman make it all the way to the front entrance, he walked right in, without harassment, seemingly invisible to the stationed C.O.s. Eve could only watch as the doors closed behind him, and wait.

She hadn't expected the Chemist to appear again. She'd camped the Spire hoping for something, some direction, some indication of the great changes she'd hoped were coming. Ezechial told her a war was coming—Armageddon, as the Laterali had foretold it—but nothing had happened since she'd freed Joshua. He'd floated out of her reach, out of Ezechial's, disappearing completely. Invisibility was a talent both the Laterali and the Collective possessed, but employed by different means. Ultimately, both the Laterali and the Collective employed nothing more than tricks, technology, or psychology, but Joshua used something else, and she found nothing but smoke where Joshua had once been.

Not being one much for prophetic ramblings, Eve had not taken the Laterali prophecy very seriously when Ezechial told her about it. But that was a long time ago now, and when you have nothing else—and Eve was pretty thoroughly without—superstition has a way of becoming substantial. Besides, the Laterali were almost as capable as she was—a fully outfitted, high-ranking officer of the Collective—without GEaRS.

She *had been* a high-ranking officer of the Collective, capable of a great deal more than she was now. It hurt her to think it. Now that everything had ended so anti-climatically, she wondered if it was worth it. She'd followed her heart, her gut, instead of her training. What had compelled her? It was impossible for her to tell, but she thought that the answers might be within the Spire. Or maybe she was functioning on pure inertia, and with nowhere else to go, she'd simply returned to what she knew? *At this point, what else can I do?*

So when Gabriel appeared, she had watched intently as the tormented scientist did what she could not: enter the Spire.

As Eve waited outside, she pondered how she could possibly find out what Gabe was doing. She didn't have access to listen-in to SENTRy anymore, the Leader had seen to that personally. There were standard protocols and measures that were followed whenever an Officer left the Collective, but that wasn't good enough for the treasonous Eve. Leader 127 executed all the termination measures himself and sniffed out all of Eve's little, seemingly innocuous, security-breaching functions. He'd even had the foresight to scrub the entire system for any listeners attached to Eve's deactivation, and found several of Eve's latent tunnelers: code that wrote code that wrote code that opened portals back into the Collective. He would not have had trouble finding them after they were triggered, but finding them beforehand meant that he could see her work and see her goals, learning everything from her and giving nothing in return. Eve was severed from the Collective completely.

So Eve had waited that day, blind, deaf, and dumb. The Spire wasn't a retaining center for criminals, insane or otherwise, so how long could he possibly be inside? He would be escorted out, and transferred immediately for a plug and scrub. But hours passed uneventfully, and with each came another twist of the wrist, screwing her anxiety. And as she waited there, the supposed *earthquake* hit; she was too tightly wound to notice at first.

She wasn't sure what actually happened, but she had felt Joshua all around her, protecting her and helping her to breathe, and though she was scared, she knew she would live... she evenly vaguely knew that the world would live. When the drowning quake finally stopped, Eve looked up from where she'd fallen to the ground gasping for breath and saw the cracks. Saw the cracks in the Spire and one portly man hobble-running from it.

Eve watched the whimpering old fool in the dark alley and could not imagine how he'd survived; the pathetic man could barely keep the slobber from running out of his mouth. Still, he was the only link to whatever had happened within the Spire. No one else had come out of the dark building since the cracks appeared—nothing human anyway—except Gabriel. No one had gone back in either, which Eve had it in mind to change.

Having observed for many days, she didn't expect the demons to be back for several hours today. Though they appeared to be keeping Gabe alive, they certainly appeared to have no love of him. Still, she did her best to see into the shadows—the damn beasts had an uncanny ability to sneak up undetected—before she descended the utility stairs of the building she was holed-up in.

The bottom of the utility stairs offered no view into the alley, and Eve's access to the Collective's satellites was gone, so she approached the door with all of her senses amped. Listening carefully, she slid her finger along the door, and a soft and satisfying thud was followed by a whir as the door slid open.

The stench was almost unbearable with her heightened sense of smell, but Eve refused to dial down her sampling; it was information and hopefully an edge. Her view of the alley was limited to the aperture of the doorway and didn't offer much, other than a dark-stained brick wall. So she stripped down to naked, folding her clothes neatly and setting them on the dirty stairs, and began bending what little ambient light there was before stepping out.

Peering down to the south, she saw the bright light of the sun blinding her from whatever stood at the mouth of the alleyway and beyond. To the north were thirty meters of filth, capped by another building at that end. On the far side of the alley, beneath a slight overhang, was Gabe's shelter. Even if she was uncloaked, he wouldn't be able to see her from there; though, she thought, if he was listening at all, he would have heard the door open. She doubted he was aware of anything.

She walked slowly over to him, her long graceful legs picking their way through the trash. As she moved, her silhouette came in and out of existence as the light curved around her like she was living liquid. When she was directly across from Gabe, she stopped and became practically invisible. He was seated, rocking and drooling, eyes vacant and unfocused, but opened toward the ground.

Stalking forward, Eve got a better look at the refuse within the small space. She was searching for weapons, or maybe something that he was using to communicate with the demons, or maybe even ward them off? But there was nothing to see, except that now, somehow, Gabe seemed to be staring at her.

Swaying a bit from side to side, she saw that he tracked her movements, and that he was focused. Behind the dirty spectacles, she could see a glint of life, and sparkling insanity.

Eve continued forward until she was bathing in his sweat and stink, less than a meter away, and then knelt down in front of him. They never broke eye contact, though a passerby would have thought Gabe was looking at an imaginary friend. There was eagerness in his face, a kind of childish happiness for the arrival of a playmate. Eve found it unsettling.

"An angel has come to see me." His voice was coarse and cracked, though he beamed through the statement. The look he gave her was a perversion of happy surprise, as though he was unsure what trick might come of her. At the same time, there was lunatic lust in his tone, but for sex or violence, she couldn't be sure.

Tilting her head a little to the side, Eve evaluated the little man. Her quick survey was an unintelligible mix of results. His body temperature was fluctuating, his pupils were pulsing arhythmically, as was his heart, and the various muscles of his body were vacillating between twitching spasmodically and falling flaccid. She stared into his eyes and thought that even his consciousness was wavering, like she could see him cycling from sleep to consciousness, though his gaze never faltered. He saw her as a concrete thing kneeling before him, and then suddenly, as something fantastic, ethereal and floating. His behavior reminded her a little of some of the test subjects who had survived the fever only to die soon after, unable to cope with whatever their bodies had learned.

Coughing, then speaking through phlegm, "The Shades, they follow me everywhere," coughing clear, "Have you seen them?"

"The demons?"

"Ahhhhhhhh!" beaming broad, a little drool forming in the corning of his mouth, "Silky sounds, silky sounds, your voices... say more, say more," he trailed off to a whisper and then to silence.

"What happened in the Spire?" *Why not ask the wise old trash heap?*

"Oh. Uh. Nothing. The Shades brought me, or... I wanted to go, of course, but I didn't know how," watering eyes, "They showed me."

"Who are *they*?" He must be talking about the people in the Collective, running the Apple testing.

"They're not there. There's nothing there," a clear flash across his eyes, "The building is empty. They're empty."

"Well, it's not empty. Hundreds of people live in the building," her factual tone was met with a grunt, "How far up did you go? Did you speak to anyone?"

"Mmmmm, your voices are warm and honey."

Exasperated, "Did you see anything inside?"

"I saw them bubbling up out of the shadows. I heard them," fearful and quivering, "banshees shrieking, and the choir singing painfully to me. Not like your voices... not like your voices."

"Well, it's been great to see you again, Gabriel, really," Eve had no sympathy for the craven scientist. The choices he'd made had brought him to this point, she was certain of it. She looked down toward the entrance to the alleyway, and adjusted her vision. Half to herself, half to Gabriel, "I'm going in."

"They gave their souls to the devil, and the devil gave them purpose. I opened the door to them. I opened it... I wanted to believe it wasn't a choice… but it was. I wanted an excuse. I need excuses for…" he stopped short.

Eve looked at Gabe, and saw him looking with intense fear at the ground beneath her feet. She examined the river of grime she was standing in and saw nothing interesting.

"No, no…" it was a harsh whisper. His eyes remained fixated on the ground.

"What…"

"No!" his scream was a begging cry against nothing that Eve could see. She took a step away from the pallet-house, curious but also wary.

His rocking began again, this time accompanied by shaking his head back and forth slowly, full of denial. "It was quiet… it was quiet… I deserve the quiet!"

Eve experienced a mixture of contempt, disquiet, and fear. Something in the scientist's voice was compelling. She believed he was seeing or hearing terror incarnate. It was the voice of someone who had sucked Satan's cock and feared the return visit. Maybe, right? After all, what was reality anymore when demons ravaged the city and devoured people, and those same demons left this poor excuse to live?

It was clear to her that it was time to leave, but she tried again regardless, "What is it? Gabe… Gabe!" she snapped her fingers in front of his face, "What do you see?"

"The shadows are growing up your legs," he paused to listen, "and the whispers are calling your name."

That was enough. Eve moved quickly and purposefully, but without fear. Whatever happened to Gabriel, she had no doubt it had broken his mind. If he had taken Apple, it probably wouldn't be long now before his body was broken as well. His temperature shifts and muscular spasms couldn't be good for him, although she had seen worse. Nevertheless, she grabbed her clothes from the building and got dressed, ignoring his loud whispering gibberish.

As she walked out of the building, she looked once more in his direction, then turned and walked out of the alley. She pulled up a map on her IOL; although she knew her way to the Spire, she wanted the bird's-eye view while she moved.

Eve had just entered the light of midday when she turned the corner out of the alley and heard a spine-shaking scream, "Eve!"

The angel came to him like a light trapped in a shard of glass. She floated toward him, wings flowing and bending around her, pushing back the darkness. In her wake, the shadows melted away, purged like some kind of disease, from his tiny bitumen river. She was naked, beautiful.

He had never seen an angel before, but he'd heard of them. The voices told him about the angels, and how they would come for him, and want him. Gabe could not figure out for what they would possibly want him. There was no will left to find answers, or to explore, there was only his aging body and his continued departure from sanity.

Gabe had heard you can't diagnose your own sanity, but his consciousness had bifurcated so strongly that he felt part of him could rationally evaluate the other part. Each personality was different, almost like different people, but with all of the same shared experiences. The perspectives, though—the feelings and conclusions from those experiences—were universes apart at times. So, Gabe, or one of Gabe, looked at the others and said, "Hey, this isn't a coherent whole. You have fallen apart," and another spoke up jovially, "Fallen to pieces!" and most of him smiled.

As the parts deviated and moved farther from each other, Gabe felt his connection to the world diminishing. What would an angel want with a shattered man? But the question hardly mattered to most of him...

The shard of glass melting toward him with soft rays bending and piercing the darkness of his home was real, and whatever her reasons, she was here for him. "She has come for some part of me, anyway," some of him thought.

Around the beautiful, amorphous glassy she-creature, he saw the shadows begin to ripple. The Shades, only a few so far, had come to swim around and examine this new entity. "You guys are always here," another, "In my mind," another, "In your mind," another, "Always following me," another, "Does she know them?" "Do you know them?" His own voice was echoes of the different ways he might have said something to her.

She shimmered and a golden glowing river, thick and warm, poured out of her from a newly formed sliver. An overwhelming sense of elation began in each of him, and he resonated harmoniously, albeit briefly. One of him, "She wants to know about the people," another, "What happened to the people," another, "Their souls," another, "They're souls," another, "They're sold," another, "They chose."

More shimmering, and the sliver flowed again, and he resonated less harmoniously, "She wants to know what you did," echoes, "I did,", "Why I did?", "What I did?", "What I did." And much of him was quiet, and he thought he was sorry. Sorry for so many things.

Sorry for the darkness swelling up around her. It pooled at the ground beneath her feet and reached up to her, over her naked feet, lapping against her ankles. For a moment, he thought the she might be sinking, but he thought he was powerless against the Shades; if they wanted her, they would have her, and he would be left only to weep for his loss. Besides, the voices—he could no longer tell if they belonged to him or not—were shouting too loudly for him to finish a coherent thought.

Finally though, he managed to at least tell the pretty light that she was being attacked. She didn't seem to know. Still, he felt relief as she left. Something in her movement, floating away from him, reminded him of someone else, of a person he once knew, but the memories were wiped away as the Shades turned to him.

They were displeased now. Angry now. Hungry now.

He cried as they covered him in tarry saliva. He felt his heart shrink and quiver as though it was backing away from the surface, trying to bury itself deeper in his chest. It whimpered there, covering itself the best it could, closed its eyes, and hoped the demons wouldn't find it.

Gabriel cried out one more time, with a timbre that pulled at Eve's nerves, begging for help. Eve wouldn't be stopped by the dead-behind-the-eyes chemist. She had to admit, she felt an overwhelming compulsion to do something for him, but it was followed immediately by a sense of *knowing* that there was nothing she could do for him. Whatever the nature of his madness, it was nothing that she knew how to cure; and if she was right about him, about his exposure to the compound, well… there was nothing that could be done.

The day was cool, but the sun was out, and the abandoned city looked welcoming, though almost unrecognizable. The city without its people was composed of eerily familiar shapes and spaces, but stood only as a mockery or poor imitation. As disorienting as it was to see the city without its patina of people, she could still find her way; Eve set off for the Spire.

Scrubbed

Eight

The Spire was empty. She made her way down corridor after corridor on the lower floors, but there was no one to be found. There weren't signs of struggle or any kind of conflict. There was a disturbing nonchalance corresponding to the departure of all of the inhabitants; coffee mugs—half full and growing mold—were distributed normally among work areas. Some of the Desks were tilted upright to accommodate those who preferred standing to sitting, and most—when prompted to wake—revealed current tasks, in-progress projects, as though whoever was working was certain to return. Some offices were locked up, but none of the security at the lower levels was enough to fetter Eve, so she looked on with impunity.

One floor after another, Eve stopped off to see if she could find anyone, and the results were all the same; everyone who had occupied the building had essentially gone on break and never returned. That was the first hundred floors anyway. She didn't check them all thoroughly except to confirm that all shared a similar story. It didn't take her all of those floors to realize that the necessity for stealth was gone, so she moved pretty quickly, taking in everything she could. After only a short while, she thought that triggering an alarm might actually be a good idea. If she could get someone, anyone, to show up, even if it meant her capture, at least then the universe would resemble the reality she had known for so long. She *would* have felt better. But despite her every effort, or lack of effort to conceal herself, no one came.

At the hundredth floor, she balked. Even though she'd seen no response from SENTRy for her activities below, it was difficult for her to conceive that SENTRy had been taken offline completely. No closer to having the answers she needed, she pressed on regardless. If SENTRy decided to employ lethal counter-incursion measures? Well, chances were that she wouldn't know she'd been caught, she'd just cease to be. Her deception of Adam had required her to have extensive and illicit knowledge of SENTRy, so she knew what it could do, and the heart-stopping electrical charge it could create across almost any surface in the building was just one tool within its broad and deep arsenal.

Everything upwards of the hundredth floor was increasingly more difficult for her to access. Leaders generally worked and lived on the middle-upper floors, and the security protocols employed for each of them was unique. Leaders typically didn't have direct access to each other, and the concept of a master key didn't apply; Leaders were cells, independent and self-sustaining. All of their information was rolled to the UpperS, where the big picture could be kept safely away from the contributing artists and actors.

Eve had seen into only a handful of offices this high up the Spire. Really, she was only intimately familiar with 127, Adam, her Leader. The man she'd betrayed for nothing more than a sense of overwhelming and inexplicable destiny.

Overwhelming. Inexplicable. Destiny. The words did not come easily to Eve, but she had no others to describe the emotion, the emotion that caused her to break free of the Collective and the Leader who had taught her so much. She wished she could have shared more with him, but equal to the strength of her need to find Joshua was her need to keep her activities hidden from the Leader. How well had she known the man? Well, she knew more than he thought she ever did. She knew that as much as he might sometimes disagree with the tactics and politics of the Collective, they gave him a home and a purpose, which he would not leave by choice. Eve knew that he would not undermine the Spire without sufficient, irrefutable cause. As she looked through another vacated set of cubicles, *This would be enough to convince you, but... where are you?*

Leader 127 had assigned Eve to the Apple project because he trusted her most among the members of his cell. When she accepted the assignment, she sunk her teeth in fully, as he must have known she would, and she was consumed by it. The project was simple, and in some ways she thought it was a joke when she was first briefed.

They called the compound they were testing "Apple," but the project reminded her of every other attempt to create a super soldier she'd ever known. Some lab tech made a rat more vicious and stronger than ever before, and the studies and experiments began. The results, when they were favorable, were the groundwork for new tools, which Eve and other high-ranking C.O.s like her put to good use. Unfavorable results? Well, she was confident that there were confidential files on all of the prototypes, and some storage rooms filled with the frightening remains as well. But apparently Apple was different. The reaction was uncategorized when she was assigned, and the results ranged from death to catatonia to insanity... so why continue?

Working on the project though, had altered Eve. It opened her eyes to see all that she was not being shown. The effect it had on her was potent and irreversible. Doubts—she'd never cared about the reasons for her assignments, only executing them with extraordinary precision—about her assignments had crept into her every day. The doubts drove her to delve deeper, and to inspect with greater scrutiny, everything she thought she knew. She began questioning authority, and through those questions, she began to develop the big picture for herself. Eve didn't like what she saw.

The UpperS were bent on discovering the nature of the compound, and no expense was too great toward that end. There must have been a positive result in order to keep them pushing, despite all of the failures, and it must have been nothing short of miraculous. But if it was true that Apple had worked in a test case, it had been left out of the briefing and materials to which Eve had access. She couldn't stop thinking about it. She didn't want to let it go.

It was not in her nature to press on Leader 127 for information, and certainly not in her nature to lodge formal inquiries regarding the impetus for her assignments, but she'd done both, regardless, and she'd been shut out. Eve was savvy enough to keep from being reassigned—which probably wouldn't have stopped her, anyway— but she stopped questioning her directives to avoid inspection. Eve's betrayal had begun.

If SENTRy was working, it wasn't reacting at all to Eve's attempts at bypassing the elevator security system. She could have used any number of DNA samples she'd acquired surreptitiously from the members of her cell. Combined with her chameleon Credentials, it would have been a quiet entry to the 127th floor. Instead though, she placed her Glass against the Wall of the elevator and accessed the security system directly, a trespass that should have elicited an immediate response. There was none. She continued, and eventually she was riding up to the 127th floor. She remembered that SENTRy could synthesize any number of colorless and odorless gases because she'd used them frequently. She wondered briefly if the ventilation system would allow SENTRy to pump one of those gases directly into the elevator to incapacitate her or kill her, but then thought better of it. If this was a trap, it was overly and unnecessarily elaborate.

The elevator took only a couple of seconds to traverse the distance to the Leader's floor. As the doors slid open, Eve felt a slow push of adrenaline, and an uncomfortable increase in blood pressure. It was anxiety: the anticipation of something awful. It's the open connection in the middle of the night. It's the friend not showing for lunch, not answering your calls. It's coming home to a dark and quiet apartment where your husband or wife is usually already making dinner. You know what's happened, but you haven't understood it all consciously. You know something is terribly wrong, and you know you're about to find out what it is.

She stood there surveying the black entry room through the open lift doors; only guide lights illuminated the corners of the ceiling and floor. Eve realized the feeling of the slow push, that preparatory rush, as what she felt whenever she targeted a new subject for Apple. Usually, they were selected for her, but she'd begun selecting them for herself, and whenever she actually slipped them the compound, she felt this way; inexplicable knowledge of events that had already happened. Choices already made. Destiny unfolding in terrible ways.

Well, not always terrible.

The lunatic rants that flew from the mouths of the subjects who survived, albeit briefly, were powerful, raw, and without contrivance. She found solace in them, convinced of their importance. No matter how hysterical or unintelligible, there was belief in each word, and a sense that their words were accurate, describing something real.

Eve could never get away from the dreams those voices created in her. The test subjects tapped into her, and made her feel close to something better, to something greater than she was. Eventually though, the subjects lost coherence. The connection with Eve, the words they chose to express their new-found understanding, would crumble and become garbage.

Eve was frustrated by the deaths that followed the brief moments of clarity. She wanted to see the pattern. She wanted a subject who could live through it all and explain it to her.

In retrospect, she thought her exposure to the test subjects corrupted her. It broke her to feel so close to the answers, only to have them turn into incoherent madness. And then she'd ended up in that room, with her own dose...

That room hadn't looked very different from the Leader's hallway in the dark. The Leader decorated his floor sparingly, so there wasn't much to differentiate it from any other regular room, but the rooms of the Spire were somewhat hive-like in there construction, with repeated dimensions and shapes on every floor. Nevertheless, it was the same dark—she knew that lights sometimes irritated the subjects—and the same feeling of impending knowing.

The one thing she knew about the feeling was that there was no turning back from it. Sometimes it was wrong, but inevitably, fatalistically she would continue forward to find out. Without any further hesitation, her eyes already brightening with gathered light, she stepped off the lift.

Instead of allowing her adrenaline levels to be dictated purely by emotion, she started all of her usual augments and regulators. She instinctively cloaked and pulled her clothes from her body, not caring where they fell.

Utilizing a full spectrum of scans, she observed the reception room. The Leader's hand-picked assistant, Jacob, had left his usual position behind the only Desk in the room vacant. The door to the rest of the floor was open, revealing nothing but a dark hallway beyond. With her enhanced vision, Eve magnified into the hallway and found that all the doors were open. Compounding the strangeness was the presence of what she thought were burn marks on the ceiling, floor, and walls.

Walking quietly over to the Desk, Eve fought back an urge to pull up the display. Maybe she was being observed. Maybe there was nothing she could do about it. Her elevated awareness and somewhat controlled paranoia were conflicted, but her training helped her quickly conclude that she could check the streams later, and that if she looked at them now, she couldn't trust them anyway.

Crossing the threshold of the security door into the hallway, Eve sampled the air and ran it through several scent analyzers. The entire floor should have been too atmospherically controlled to allow anything foreign or strange to exist in the air, but she searched anyway. There was sulfur and carbon, and burnt human flesh.

What the...

If there had been a fire, which was almost entirely inconceivable—not to mention inconsistent with the spherical and localized melt and scorch marks—SENTRy would have cleaned it up, casualties would have been removed, and repairs would have been made, but apparently nothing had been done since... well, since whatever happened here. Eve carefully crept over to a melted portion of the hallway and looked at it more closely. The charring and the distorted material radiated out in a more or less elliptical pattern. Roughly the same shape and size, the pattern repeated in a few places along the hall, discontinuously, as though each had a separate source.

Inconsistent with any explosive in Eve's knowledge base, she began breaking down what it would take to create the melting pattern. Supposing a single source of consistent incendiary heat, how close would the source have to be, and how hot for how long to create the pattern? Starting with several assumptions, she created several plausible amorphous heat sources. She ran through the possibilities quickly, but none fit very well. Really, none made any sense. The best she could determine in her hasty analysis was that a vertical source probably more than two meters tall and near a meter wide had generated the enormous amount of heat necessary to account for the pattern. But neither the source nor the environment had ever ostensibly caught fire, and somehow the source had gone away without causing any other residual damage, nor leaving any other evidence of its existence. It never occurred to her that the heat source might have been moving.

Stalking to the first open doorway, Eve looked in and began capturing images before realizing that the burned area in the room contained human remains. The heat had been so intense that even the bones were carbonized. The mound was too small to have been Adam. She stopped looking. She ran to Adam's office.

Stopping just outside his office, Eve felt her heartbeat, uncontrolled, unreserved. The office was unmolested. The View was beautiful; the entire Wall was used to display the sky and the ocean to the east of the Spire. The last time she was here, she'd seen that view and thought she would never see it again. Seeing it now though, was only an eerie reflection of that day.

She'd battled the Leader and his personal guard that day. Shots were fired, and she had torn into the ceiling with her nails, but there were no scratches in the ceiling, no indication that a fight had ever taken place.

The smell of decaying flesh was stronger in the office than in the hallway. Eve gazed at the doorway to Adam's personal chambers. Caution seemed suddenly unnatural and unnecessary. Eve walked across the office and into the inner chamber of Leader 127's residence.

The entire room was scorched and melted, and different than the other burns she'd seen; there were signs of concussive force, not just heat. She scanned carefully, remembering a day long ago when the Leader had shown her his pride, the symbol that embodied his attitude toward life and excellence. He'd brought her into his personal chambers to invite her to be on his team, a member of the legendary cell of 127. She'd taken the invitation as the highest compliment and responded unreservedly in the affirmative. At the time, it was her greatest achievement. Where was his symbol now?

Her scan finally reached the wall on the left. It took her mind several seconds to catch up to what she was already seeing. The fatalistic feeling she had earlier was right this time. Everything she'd seen upon entering floor 127 had prepared her for this, yet she wasn't prepared for this. To accept this.

She stared for what felt like a long time. Finally, she walked over to him and kneeled down in front of the great man. Wrapping her hand around his, which was wrapped and melted to the handle of his Wakizashi, she bowed her head and closed her eyes.

Several seconds passed in silence. She didn't think. She just felt his passing from present into memory. He passed from possibility into the quiet. He slipped from the possible into silence. He was already gone, but she took the time to let him leave.

And then Eve stood. Her hand still on his. She stared into him where his eyes should have been. Spiking her strength, spiking her adrenaline, and embracing her resolve, Eve wove her fingers through and beneath his so that they held the hilt of the Wakizashi together. She pulled steadily. As the blade began to slide free from the wall, she had to work her fingers against his to help him release, but even with her delicate effort he held long enough that he fell forward as she stepped back. Languidly, he fell forward onto his thighs as his hand stretched toward Eve and finally let go.

Her chest heaved slowly, her heart thudded deep and strong. His hand rested open toward her on the floor beside his feet, head bowed between his knees. She looked at his hand; the palm and fingers were melted, prints replaced with alien swirls, charred black and cracked.

She examined his inner chambers one more time, found the sheath and some leather ties that had been well taken care of, though never used. Opening his closet she found a white, one-piece linen robe with a hood. Slipping it on over her head, her lithe body was lost in the billowing garment; her fingertips didn't even peek out of the sleeves.

Eve reached inside through the neck and pinched a small flap and the robe shrank to fit her frame. There was warmth in two long lines running down either side of her body for a second, and then two long, thick linen braids slid down to the floor. The excess was bundled up neatly, ready to feed back into the system. Eve bent down to retrieve the bundles, slit the binding thread with one of her nails, and held it out long.

She tested the strength of the braids. Satisfied, she pulled the robe up over her head and set it to the side. Looping one length of braid around her waist and the other over her shoulder, she tied them both quickly. They were silky smooth against her bare skin. With the help of the leather ties, she secured the Wakizashi sheath to her makeshift harness, and slid it around to her back. She made adjustments until she was happy with the fit. Slipping the robe back on, she walked out of Adam's room and closed the door.

In his office, Eve walked over to Adam's Desk, "Let's see what secrets you have."

FALLEN SPIRE

Red Light

Nine

He saw the world in echoes, visual and aural, temporal and tactile. The ripples flowed out from him in all directions. The ripples bounced back from the world, altered by whatever they touched. He absorbed the returning waves, and from the shifts in frequency and the changes in amplitude, Joshua found himself.

The image he held of himself, though, was fuzzy. The edges softened as he faded forward and back, but he was learning to see through the distortion, to pick out the pieces that persisted. Usually, he was only able to identify a consistency the moment after it changed… perhaps because it had changed.

His jacket was army green in this version of his recurring dream and he remembered that the wintering man wore a similar one when Joshua had seen him last. Joshua thought he didn't wear it as well as the aging assassin, but he liked it just the same. He put his hands casually into the rough denim pockets as he fondly remembered the man who had helped him and Sara. It was probably true that Joshua understood Ezechial and his motivations better now than he had then, but he felt too detached to seek him out. But the time for reminiscing was over.

He followed the echoes.

He followed the dream.

Green.

The contrast of the color was diminished by the daylight and by his fluid, fuzzy nature, but Joshua eventually processed what it meant: time to move. He knew he had a long way to go if he wanted to arrive on time. Crossing the intersection of broken-down cars, he stepped lightly around the various obstructions and looked forward to the other side. He expected to see twisted and monstrous corpses littering the intersection, but there were no bodies, only stains and rotten air.

Arriving safely on the other side, Joshua began spinning around to get his bearings. Turning around, he wasn't sure which way to go. Across the intersection he saw familiar canopies and store fronts. He felt himself stretching out in both directions, imagining himself at one corner or the other, feeling his way through the decision. The answer was there on the periphery of his awareness, standing up on the tip of his tongue. But he couldn't see it clearly, so instead, he continued to look for some hint, any indication of right or wrong.

A light turned green.

The walk symbol came on.

Joshua grinned widely, knowing exactly where he needed to go.

He became introspective for a moment. He wondered if he could remember the answer, and if he could drop breadcrumbs in his mind to help him find his way back to it if he lost it again: patience and signs. The light was *green*.

Green.

And though he missed the concept the first few times he reached for it, he did eventually grasp it and so he began crossing the intersection.

There was a long way to go to arrive by nightfall. Joshua always made it, though, in this dream. No matter how far the distance, he always arrived by dusk, as though twilight itself was his destination.

Joshua remembered her eyes, the opaque green humors staring back at him; Eve staring him down with a playful grin. He knew nothing about her really, but knew that she'd saved him, helped him when she didn't have to help him. Having chosen and achieved a prosperous life, she'd taken a huge risk for him and left that life behind. Why she turned traitor to the Collective, why she chose him, he didn't know, but he liked to imagine her as courageous for doing it.

As he continued across the intersection, he stepped onto a layer of safety glass from the broken-out window of a car door, which was resting there, apparently ripped from its body. The crunching sound had a way of scratching at his ears, which was familiar and welcome. Joshua looked up at the crispy blue sky, and wondered about the time of the year. But the air was wrong. There were no people flowing along the street creating a current for him to follow. He thought—if the two could actually be separated sensibly—that it was neither the right time nor the right place.

But it didn't matter as a shift of echoes, red and blue, stretched and compressed him and forced him to engage the present; right time, wrong time, there were demons coming to find him. Already found him.

The winding and grinding began. High-pitched whines mixed with heavy metal rattles bounced off the buildings, creating echoes of their own, deconstructing Joshua's.

They came on without the usual taunts, or staging. The order and plan of the attack—if there was one—was indecipherable, as one demon after another emerged from the shadows. They climbed along the buildings, hurried through the vehicle wreckage, and picked up speed as they closed the distance. And there were colored lights in all directions, but the daylight had washed away the contrasts, along with their meaning.

Joshua's eyes were wide, blue, swirling marbles. He drew his hands slowly out of the pockets of his jacket, held them out in front of himself and opened them, palms to the sky. As his fingers parted, large butterfly wings spread open between them, as though he was drawing them into existence with the motions of his hands. The butterflies tested their wings twice, and then flew into the air, leaving purple-ashen dust trails through the air, which billowed and spread out quickly but softly. Silhouettes of commuters who'd once travelled through the intersection appeared, some faint and some strong. There were blurs moving in cars, in pairs and groups, and there were pedestrians walking, some wandering, a clear pair intertwined who must have stayed there embraced for a long time.

The entire intersection was filled and covered with dust as the first demon came at Joshua in a loping run. It pushed through the suspension of ashen fog, igniting the dust wherever it touched, leaving an ephemeral burnt-orange trail through it. Joshua couldn't understand the demon. It was too fast and too hot. It was like he stuck his hands into a fire by trying to read the demon, and he recoiled painfully. More demons entered the intersection, a few bounding in like gorillas, others slinking in like snakes, and some running like dogs. They were all grey, hairless, slavering beasts, and they all burned, and Joshua's butterflies were snuffed out in an upward draft of heat and fire.

Joshua braced himself for the first demon as it leapt at him. Its claws were stretched out in front, tongue lolling out the side of its mouth, as it growled viciously through the air. Joshua's veins were black, thick, and pulsing through his face, hands, and forearms. He slipped between the clawed hands by stepping quickly forward instead of retreating. The demon wasn't surprised for long though, as Joshua caved in its face by driving its nose back to the base of its neck. Viscous blood exploded out into the air and plastered Joshua. It steamed in the cold air, and splattered over his face. The demon body crumpled to the ground at Joshua's feet. Ready to move forward, he stepped up onto the mound of its lifeless back, but it slid around beneath him, so he crouched down to steady himself.

He took in the intersection with his opaque, marbled-blue eyes. There were many, and they came from every direction. One lunged at him from the side, but Joshua knew it was coming from reflections in glass, in the movements of the other demons, and had already shifted himself to face the attack. His hands felt stronger than steel with edges as sharp as broken glass as he swiped at the creature's legs, blood gushing out in two thick waves. Its legs went limp, but the demon's momentum carried it forward and it viciously clawed and bit at the air, falling toward Joshua.

Joshua screamed and spit in its face, and was surprised at how easily his hands impaled and lifted the demon. An arch of blood formed over his head as he stood and spread his arms apart, tearing the beast in half.

His veins were onyx black and bulging out over his whole body, a branching map of the life flowing through him. The next demon came from behind him, but he spun around, his hands tearing through the air haphazardly, and caught the beast on the shoulder and side. His hands penetrated up to his elbows and he grabbed the demon's spine and threw it to the ground. The force of throwing the beast down was too much for Joshua's perch though, and he slid off of the first corpse.

He scrambled for a foothold as he fell, but ended up lying flat on his belly, face buried in the flesh of one of the demons. A demon pounced onto his back, but before it could sink its fangs in, Joshua shifted himself through the creature. It burned badly as he shared space with the demon, but suddenly he was riding the back of his attacker. It snapped at nothing where Joshua used to be. Squeezing his legs around the beast, Joshua arched himself up and began mercilessly tearing through its body, arms swinging wildly, cutting through the back and neck and eventually driving it down to the ground.

Joshua didn't stop. He kept at the body, bits of flesh flying away from him. Two other demons attacked, but he wouldn't be distracted. Pausing only long enough to eviscerate each in turn, he kept at the body beneath him. Finally, he found himself cutting up his own jacket, which he'd left with all of his clothes, beneath the demon.

Naked and covered in steaming blood, down on all fours, hands and feet buried in demon flesh, Joshua felt himself grow. His perception and his senses poured out from his body until they filled a new space, a body larger and different than the one he was born in. His body remained, growling and screaming at the sky, but a smoky black shape shrouded him. Insofar as his new body had a definite shape, it was three times as large as Joshua's usual body, with furry black edges. The excessively long rakes of claws at the end of each limb were the only aspects that remained starkly outlined no matter how he moved. When he moved, his body and his projection moved in unison. Joshua's human body was a blood-red heart at the center of the beast. And they moved with terrifying speed and purpose.

No more waiting. Joshua turned from hunted to hunter. He punched holes in the surrounding buildings full of demons that continued to leap at him. He picked up a car door and squashed a demon through the hood of the car it was standing on. Still holding the car door, he caught a charging demon in the window frame, turned it over and crushed it into the ground, cutting the demon in half.

Down on all fours, he jumped corpse to car, then to run along a building, heading away from the intersection, corpses of demons thudding to the ground in his wake.

Those in the intersection poured down the road after him. They came with more ferocity than before, whipped into a frenzy by all the dead bodies and blood. Biting and clawing at Joshua, they rarely hit him, but there were so many, they sometimes caught flesh.

The pain started only as a tickle, but then became a scratch, and eventually an open wound. Joshua felt each talon and each fang now, as they came at him with greater numbers, sensing him weakening. Two demons had managed to gain purchase on his back, their talons sunk deep, and they were biting, chewing and spitting out the black smoke of his flesh, which wisped out from him in brief, orange, fiery bursts.

Joshua couldn't shake them, and the searing pain was weakening his attacks. He charged forward and bit the head off of a demon and spit it out at another, which he impaled while it was stunned stupid by the head toppling through the air.

Finally, Joshua roared. From his chest came a growl that was louder and higher-pitched than the whines of the demons. Cycling the growl down and then up again abruptly, he shocked the demons into a brief, silent hesitation. He turned and dove down an alley out of the sun.

Standing up, he ripped the riders from his back. Arcs of ash were drawn through the air as the demons took his flesh with them as they flew. The arcs, sparked by the mouths of the demons, burned the trails of ash like a flame following a path of gun powder.

Joshua let go another roar as he pounded one rider, and then the other, into a wall of concrete. Shards of concrete and bone flew into his face. Hot blood burst onto the wall and covered Joshua, and the spatter glowed softly in the shadows of the buildings.

His body, the heart of his beast, ached and shivered with weakness. Joshua looked out to the street and saw more coming, but they'd slowed down. Winding up and down, but not attacking. Hands still pressed against the wall, holding up the limp and lifeless bodies of their brethren, he imagined they weren't as eager to die as he'd thought before.

One, though, emerged from the shadows beside Joshua. He'd seen it, but not understood that it was there… the trick. It shouldn't have worked on him, and suddenly he was scared. The demon pounced, and he wasn't able to get away from it. His shadowy beast went up in a brief curl of ember smoke, as the demon went through, all the way to the body of Joshua.

Joshua felt a little resurgence, and he was able to catch the demon's claws; they toppled to the ground grappling with each other. Finally landing on his back, it was all he could do to keep the demon from biting his face. Its long neck reached farther than he would have thought it could, its rank furnace of a mouth pushing stinging heat into his nose and eyes. Its forked, prehensile tongue slipped around its fangs and then rolled out, scrub-licking his cheek. He would have turned his face away, but he noticed the demon's eyes for the first time, and in them he saw something he didn't expect to see: they were human. As the tongue reached into Joshua's ear, he peered deeply into those windows and saw a tortured human soul behind them.

It seemed to grin. Reeling in its tongue, it pulled back slightly, revved up, then hurled a rattle-cry into Joshua's face, snapping and biting at him in frustrated fury. But before the saliva dripping from its teeth could fall, Joshua slid into the shadows beneath them and the demon was left grappling with emptiness.

The other demons fell in, and found nothing there to eat. They couldn't contain their frustrated need to feed though, so they attacked one another. They spit and ripped at each other, and even mounted each other in an orgiastic frenzy. Eventually, there was enough blood-mist, enough slick on the ground, to satisfy those that survived.

Joshua held himself, shivering and sweating though the day was cold, and watched them devour their fallen. He was hurt.

The recurring dream was finally over.

Mistaken Identity

Ten

Keln had just finished cleaning the dishes from dinner, and was making his way down into the storage room beneath the restaurant.

"You guys don't have to use every dish in the place every time you make dinner. You know that, right?"

"You don't have to make so much damn noise." The young man was lean-bodied and average height if you didn't count the five centimeters of spiky, royal blue hair. He was fidgeting with the supplies on one of the shelves.

Shifting his weight, a little annoyed, Keln tried to make his next step down the old plank stairs silent, challenging Oishi's point. But Keln was large, thick-muscled from years of working wood the old-fashioned way, and the stair squealed beneath his weight.

Oishi raised a rueful look and pointed it at the man, who frowned and continued down the steps without further regard to the noise.

"If you used fewer dishes, I wouldn't have to clank so many of them around." Keln spoke matter-of-factly, not wanting to bicker with the youthful and rash Oishi. They hadn't lived together long, but it was clear enough that Oishi hated being there. When Ezechial brought him in—saved him even, from the story he told of it—he'd introduced himself by complaining about the decision to stay in the restaurant. He was convinced of the need to move farther inland. He rarely stopped talking about it. And it had been a struggle each day since, antsy and headstrong, pushing for them to pack up and leave. The only thing that calmed him down was Naddalia.

She'd overheard their conversation from within the walk-in cooler and peeked around the door. "Sorry about the dishes, Keln. I'm not as good as you are with the cooking." She poked her head out around the door. Her hair was braided in tight tiny bunches that stood up from her head, ending in bright tufts of variegated colors where the hair sprayed free of each braid.

"Don't apologize to him… klaxon over there is going to alert every demon in the city to our location." He stopped fidgeting and faced Naddalia, "We take turns doing the dishes, and you and I don't ever make as much noise as he does."

Kicking away the box she used to prop the cooler door open—she didn't trust the mechanical, heavy door and she was scared that she would somehow get locked in—she exited the cooler, her cheeks a little flushed from the cold. The heavy door wasn't the only antiquated aspect of the cooler; the cold was provided by the *almost* obsolete use of solar panels. It was why Ezechial had chosen the restaurant. "Ezechial said that we were fine cleaning up… it's not even night yet," she glanced at her Glass. It hadn't synced since the first wave of attacks, but she was sure it was still accurate.

Oishi frowned, "It still bothers me… we gotta go, get as far as fuck away as we can." Quieter, "I can't believe we're still here, still here with dead weight."

Hearing the last comment, Keln felt embarrassed, but wasn't sure what to say about it. He was a talented woodworker—commissioned to build an immense sculpture for a city park—which didn't seem very useful these days. On the other hand, he was at least a better cook than the rest of them.

Naddalia looked reproachfully at Oishi, "Instead of slamming him all the time, you could try to get to know him." She beamed a glowing smile at Keln, "Have you seen any of his works?"

He shrugged off her question. He stared at his feet, and then at the wall, and attempted a furtive glance in her direction. Her porcelain skin was tattooed and pierced, decorated lavishly with color. The many layers of her tattoos could be turned on and off with a sub-dermal interface in her inner wrist. Today, she was wearing a blue sky with flying dolphins. Well, it was ocean and sky, flying and swimming at once. He couldn't see the tattoo through her shirt, but he remembered it vividly from when she'd shown him one night, not that long ago. He knew which tattoo she was wearing because he could see the head of the dolphin that came up her neck toward the lobe of her left ear. There were wing-like ripples that slipstreamed from the fins of that dolphin, he knew, that wrapped around her shoulders and folded down over her breasts. "…shit, Naddalia." He stalked past Keln, and then hopped the stairs two at a time and left.

"You shouldn't go outside," Keln advised the empty staircase, "He shouldn't go out right now. It's getting dark."

Naddalia walked up to the dark-skinned craftsman, "Don't worry, he just needs some fresh air. You know how pent up he gets staying down here."

"Yeah." His grey-blue irises were sad, but only for a moment, "Thank you. I mean, for helping with him," motioning loosely in the direction of Oishi's departure, "I don't really know how to handle him. Confrontation isn't really my strong suit."

As she walked over to him, he almost seemed to grow in size, comparatively so much bigger than the slight woman, "It's not a thing," easy, lilting.

"Well, it means a lot to me," wringing his immense, strong hands, "Everything is so confusing right now." He focused on something distant, "I used to just put my hands to work when I felt like this, but now I'm not sure what to do."

She wrapped her hands around his, and the warmth and smoothness of her skin calmed him down immediately, *I guess she has that effect on me too*. He offered her a wan, but grateful look, lines of age wrinkling around his face, highlighting the decade-plus between the two of them. It was nice of her to stand with him like that, to make him feel special, but it would have been better if things were like they used to be; bending and scorching, cutting and scarring his life into sculpture.

More than twice the size of hers, he opened his immense hands and gently wound them around hers, holding them and moving them down and away gracefully, before letting them go. He cleared his throat, "I don't know if we ever talked about what you did before… well, before."

Disappointed at the change of subject, but not dismissive, "Why do you ask?"

"You suggested we get to know each other," he sat down on the third stair up, his feet all the way down to the cement floor. They were about the same height then.

Squinting back at him, playfully accusing, "Fine, fine. You backed me into that one." Continuing with a shrug, "I ran the company that manufactured and distributed these braid-stands." Shaking her head vigorously, the tufts of her multicolored hair shifted and swayed as though the braids were springs instead of hair. Keln couldn't help his cheeks lifting up, the feeling of joy he felt in response to the pretty young woman dazzling him with her beauty and apparently, her ingenuity.

Naddalia reached up with both hands and deftly pulled and pinched at one of her braids, and then slipped what looked like a rubber O-ring off of it. The braid fell limp down her forehead and the tuft of powdery pink fell over her eye. She held it out for Keln to inspect.

He stared for a minute, curious, and then she excitedly grabbed his hand and put the ring in his palm, "Here."

Keln rubbed it at first, and then held it between his fingers. Eventually, he pinched it and it split open length-wise, springing and twisting and growing into a cylinder about five centimeters long, a ring at the top and bottom separated by three rigid hair-thin spiraling wires, "Ahh."

"You like it?"

He looked very satisfied, "Yes, yes." Thoughtfully, he continued, "I could use a much bigger version of something like this to help me create my next sculpture. I'm always looking for new ways to hold and position the wood as it dries, or while I bake it." Continuing to examine the device, he made affirmative sounds with his lips pressed together.

"Really?" Naddalia hadn't felt so flattered in a very long time. The man made gigantic and beautiful sculptures, organic and priceless... she invented a device that held up hair.

"Yes." He handed the spring back to her.

She snatched it up quickly, pinched it and squeezed it down easily, "There's a little electrical impulse that goes off when you pinch it," as she slid the ring back over her loose braid, "and it lines up all of the molecules, and makes it rigid. And it prefers to stay like that until you knock them loose with another pulse." Her tuft of powder-pink sprang back up, "Voila!"

"You'll have to explain it to me in detail sometime. I'm not sure I'll understand it all," shrugging, "but I've needed lots of tools made for me over the years, and been lucky enough to have friends to help me create them."

There was a moment where neither knew what to say. The world as they knew it was had turned upside down, demons practically knocking on their doors... but they didn't want to admit it. Maybe. Maybe.

"You said you actually ran the business?"

Rekindled by question, "Yes. I designed the braid-stand for my..."

"Why 'braid-stand' instead of something more catchy?"

"Well, sometimes simpler is better, you know? I was trying to sell it to stylists, not to the general public. You know, like hair-ties or whatever. I just thought..."

Running across the floor upstairs, "What the?"

91

Keln stood, alert, and looked to the door at the top of the stairs.

"Come on! Come on! Open up you piece of…" then the door slid open, and Oishi came barreling down the stairs. "They're out there!"

Keln was quicker than Oishi expected, stepping aside, but at the same time, reaching out to grab Oishi's shoulders and pull him to a stop. "What's out there?"

"Demons."

The sign was dark, but Ezechial could still make out the words, "Une Spezia Poco," written out in cold cathodes. The restaurant was tucked into the middle of the block, and as he'd instructed, the survivors were staying out of sight. A lookout, as Ezechial had explained it to them, would have protected them less than it would have acted like a beacon, calling the demons their way. Better for them to assume that the demons are ever-present, and treat each moment in the open as dangerous.

The boy had not complained once along the way. Since the pit, he'd managed to be somehow even more reticent. The sun was finally coming to rest, maybe only a half an hour or so of light left.

Ezechial padded softly up to the main entrance of the restaurant and slid a suddenly greasy, shadowy thumb down the reading edge of the door. There was a click, and then the door opened gracefully. He'd deactivated the lock when he first found the place, but decided it was better to keep it locked when he brought the first survivor back. Having come across no evidence of looting within the city, he wasn't sure it mattered, but he thought it was better locked than not.

He ushered the boy inside and closed the door behind them. Inside, the light was low, but Ezechial was Laterali, and going quickly in and out of the darkness was a requirement of the lifestyle, so he stepped forward without hesitation into the main dining area of the once-romantic establishment.

The tables were primarily two's and four's dispersed organically in the open portion of the room. Up against the walls there were a few cozier two's, and no booths. Candles of various heights, and tiny, single-flower vases made up the centerpiece of each, though the flowers had withered and died some time ago.

There was an el-shaped bar that served drinks nearest the entrance on the short side, and entrées on the long side, which went all the way to the back wall. The cooks and bartender were exposed to the patrons, but the preparation kitchen was hidden through a doorway in the back.

Ezechial gestured in the general direction of the kitchen and the boy went off in that direction, not exactly running, but with more exuberance than he'd shown so far. He hadn't really seen the *restaurant* before, but with the boy there, for some reason Ezechial found himself seeing the dining room as a place where people enjoyed themselves instead of as the buffer zone that protected—he hoped—the survivors from easy detection. He saw plates and drinks up on the bar, ready for pickup, and heard the pleasant chatter of a full restaurant bristling with the possibilities of the evening.

Ezechial remembered the last time he'd been in such a place: he had delivered a healthy dose of tetrodotoxin to a wealthy businessman's order of fugu. The chef, an aging Japanese woman, had reportedly killed herself afterward. The consensus was that she had been dishonored by what must have been her mistake, as she was responsible for butchering the fish that day.

The businessman had unwittingly extorted funds from a family that was protected.

The chef had an unnatural affection for young children, and a taste for torturing her food before she ate it.

Neither death had come under the slightest scrutiny of the Collective. Ezechial preferred that they knew as little as possible about the activities of the Laterali.

"Une Spezia Poco" wasn't much different from that restaurant, but as the boy explored, Ezechial felt differently about it. It seemed there was hope in this place, for a world without demons, without the Laterali.

Pallomor found a tiny bowl at the wait-station and walked over to one of the tables. He stood up on a chair and pinched a bit of powder from the dish, and then he sprinkled it on the candle. In a few seconds, the wick began to glow, and a few seconds later it caught flame. It burned orange, but only briefly, and then it turned white. Ezechial was opposite the boy, so that he could see his eyes sparkling in the candlelight, and the odd way that the features of his cherubic face were lit evil.

The candle flame gradually transitioned to green, and the boy's smile broadened. Ezechial walked up to the table and stood quietly watching the boy, observing and perhaps soaking up a bit of his joy.

After a few moments, the flame transitioned to red, and with his biggest smile yet, Pallomor looked through the flame directly at Ezechial. His prominent cheek bones cast shadows up his face, making his dark eyes even darker. The boy's breathing caused the flame to flicker, and the light shimmered and danced across his face. Ezechial, suddenly feeling uncomfortable, reached forward and pinched out the flame. For a moment, it looked like the boy's red lips were still aglow, but Ezechial thought that by contrast to his pale, almost colorless, complexion, the boy's lips always seemed to glow.

"We should get down into the basement with the others." Ezechial spoke softly, and thought that his suggestion had come out almost as a question, as though if the boy had said otherwise it would have mattered.

"Okay." He set the bowl down on the table and stepped down from the chair. He walked over to Ezechial and wrapped his small hand around two of the grown man's fingers, and started back through the curtain to a small hallway.

The wait-station was across from the opening to the prep kitchen. There was also a door to a restroom, and an unmarked door. The view into the prep kitchen revealed a large area with cutting boards and refrigeration units. There were several metro-shelving units set up holding a variety of serving plates and pans of several dimensions for the cook stations, as well as clean—though blackened from use—sauté pans. An opening to the exposed cook-line was the only other egress that could be seen inside.

Ezechial freed his hand from the boy, walked up to the unmarked door in the hallway. He slid a finger down the side of the door, but there was no response. Once, twice more, and the door finally opened.

Feeling the need to reassure the child, "The read on this side is unreliable, but from the inside, it always works clean." No reaction.

"Watch your step, that first one is farther than the rest." Then, lifting his voice and his attention, "I'm back, Keln."

No response.

"Keln?" Louder, "Oishi?" and louder, "Naddalia?"

Kneeling and taking the boy by the shoulders, Ezechial spoke gravely, "Go back out into the dining room. Hide under one of the tables, close to the entrance. If anyone comes up other than me, leave." He looked back down the staircase. Still no lights and no answer from below.

"You may have to pick your moment… don't run for the exit if you think they would see you running." Pausing to consider how much information the boy could handle, he decided it was too much already, "Go. Go now."

Pallomor's head tilted slightly, apparently unaware of the danger. Ezechial would have mistaken his expression for curious, or even patronizing, if he didn't think the boy was still in shock.

"Okay."

"Okay," and the boy took off running, through the curtain and out into to the dining room.

Ezechial tricked himself into the shadows. His steps were silent, and his body alternated between a shadow of itself and smoke and dust. It would have been difficult for anyone to see him, even if he or she knew where to look.

At the bottom of the stairs, he reached out into the darkness with all of his senses and found the survivors. Keln—a thick 300 pounds of hardworking construction—was inside the walk-in cooler, his face pressed into the door, which was open a slit. He was wielding a frying pan and a steel blackening plate as weapons, one in each hand. Oishi was crouched behind the storage shelves of lexicon containers, where he could easily hide his average size and still see the stairs. He held a tazer against his chest. Ezechial had advised him that it probably had no charge, but he looked ready to use it regardless. Naddalia was harder to find. She'd slid her slender build between a shelf and the wall. He couldn't see what was in her hands, but even if she held no obvious weapon, Ezechial knew that she had an advanced personal proximity guard that, if it was running active, would easily lay out an adult human cold, even if it was useless against the pack-like demons.

Ezechial couldn't guess what they were hiding from, because he'd entered the same way he always had. Something had clearly spooked them. Just as he was about to step out of the shadows and start asking questions, the stairs creaked behind him. Pallomor was coming down the steps and somehow Ezechial hadn't heard him or felt him until that moment.

At the bottom of the stairs the boy looked around casually, seemingly delighted. It was almost as though he was completely unaware of the last couple of days, totally oblivious to the world around him, and to Ezechial's urgent tone upstairs. Pangs of sadness gripped Ezechial, his heart reaching out to a boy who must have been completely broken by what he'd experienced. Saving him was probably a mistake, a thought he couldn't help but think. He didn't know what to do about it now other than break from the shadows and tension, and hope that the others might be able to help the boy cope.

As Ezechial allowed himself to be seen, stepping out from the shadows, he reached out to lay a calm hand on the boy's head. But all he touched was air as the child ran toward the walk-in cooler, toward the spring-ready Keln.

Keln screamed something incoherent as he kicked open the door, arms chambered to start swinging. There was a mix of fear and murder, kill or be killed, as he stepped into his first strike.

Reacting instinctively, Ezechial lashed out, a Devil's Tail ripping through the air and snatching the frying pan from Keln. But the immense man was already in full motion; waving air with that empty hand, he followed through with the blackening plate, and connected with the boy's face, sending him reeling across the floor. Oishi jumped out and fired the tazer at the boy, and even though no shock was delivered, the hooks caught Pallomor in the back and stuck.

Both hands white-knuckled around the small handle of the blackening plate, Keln stepped forward, winding up an overhead wood-chop swing, aiming at the boy's facedown head.

Ezechial broke from the shadows entirely and unleashed both Tails. The weapons were bound to him, bound to his desires. His conflicted feelings were foreign and sudden, but already loose in the whips. The right hit the plate hard, sending shivers down Keln's arms, and a reflexive shiver down his own. The left Tail snapped hard and cut clean through Keln's wrists. The plate clattered to the cement floor, one hand still attached. Blood spurted from the newly opened wounds, spraying the boy as Keln put everything he had into what he'd hoped would be a crushing blow that instead ended with the slapping sound of his other hand—half-attached—hitting the floor.

Keln blinked during the long moment that followed, in disbelief and confusion. Then the screaming began. Waving around his stumps, the dangling hand sprayed the walls and Oishi and everything, with blood.

Even through the screaming, Ezechial could hear the boy's labored breathing. He didn't know what to do to help him, or to help Keln. He hadn't expected any of this. Before he could think another thought about it, Oishi threw his tazer at him. Instinctively, Ezechial stepped to the side, and the tazer flew by. The two long wires that would have carried the current were still attached to the boy though, and they went taut for a split second before ripping the hooks out through his skin. A shudder roiled through his tiny body.

Oishi took two steps back to the nearby supply shelf and began hurling large cans of oil at Ezechial. The room was still pretty dark, and the cans were clumsy and awkward; he didn't connect with any of them. Ezechial tried to push his presence onto Oishi, to calm him down, but it wasn't working and Keln's continued screaming wasn't helping either.

There was a pocket of awkward inaction as Oishi tried to find something better than oil cans to throw, and Keln's screaming turned into silent shock. When Ezechial entered combat with someone, if he uncoiled his whips, he meant to kill. The choice had always been conscious, always deliberate. But not this one.

Ezechial felt like one of his marks—some were meant to suffer, to know death was imminent—desperate to negotiate with reality, to talk their way out of the situation. He'd always responded with silence, but he hoped—probably just like those marks—that somehow this time it would be different, "Oishi… Oishi stop." He turned, "Keln… Keln, what's…?"

At the sound of his name, Keln abruptly woke from his stupor. He faced Ezechial with murder in his eyes, and charged.

Ezechial slid to the side, and beneath Keln's flailing arms, then shoved him hard from behind as Keln ran by. Not able to contain the added momentum, Keln tried to stop himself with the hands he thought were there, and ended up stopping himself with his head hard against the brick wall. He toppled over backwards from the blow and hit his head again with a hollow thud on the floor.

Confident that Keln was out of the picture for the time being, Ezechial unleashed his Devil's Tails at Oishi. Wanting to just tie him up and incapacitate him, Ezechial looped his whips around the young man's legs and torso, but his left was slow to the task and both of Oishi's arms were free as his legs were pulled out from beneath him. He rolled over and struggled to pull himself away while Ezechial wriggled his Tail around to gain control of his arms. Oishi grabbed for another oil can from the bottom of the shelf and tipped it down to the floor where he was able to grab the handle on the top. Getting up to his knees, legs still bound around the ankles, he began swinging the can at the writhing Devil's Tail.

Yanking hard on his right Tail, Ezechial pulled Oishi back to a prostrate position, but as he came down, he finally landed a hit, and smashed the other Tail with the can. The throbbing ache in Ezechial's arm went sharp for a second, and then toughened. He felt the whips working together, his right coiling more up the young man's legs as it pulled him closer, the left giving up on the arms, instead looping around his chest, squeezing tighter and tighter with each wrap. His forearm was gripping, throbbing, and convulsing, and with each spasm Oishi's chest became more constricted.

Sliding along the floor toward Ezechial, Oishi grabbed at the coils around his chest and legs, and wriggled and struggled with all his might to get away. He clawed at the floor and reached for shelving impossibly far away. Then a coil went up around his neck and tightened. Ezechial's forearm was throbbing, but wouldn't let go. Instead, his muscle flexed even harder, cramping up his entire arm.

With his full concentration, Ezechial calmed himself and focused entirely on releasing his grip without letting go of the Tail. Letting go at that point would probably have been suicidal; the whips were alive in a manner of speaking, and this one was angry and blood-hungry. He could feel life slipping from Oishi as he weakened from the lack of breath. His heart would go first though, the pressure causing failure if Ezechial didn't open it up a little.

Pallomor tried to get up, a line of spittle and blood drawing from his lower lip to the floor. He looked over, and Ezechial could already see an eye darkening and swelling from where the plate had smashed his face.

Naddalia saw the boy getting up, too. She was on him quicker than Ezechial could react. She had a chef's knife, pulled from somewhere Ezechial didn't know. She jumped on the boy and stabbed at him once, and then jumped away as though she was scared of what she'd done. The twelve-inch knife was left behind, sticking out of the boy's back. Staring at the knife like she wanted it back, but wasn't sure how to get it, Naddalia backed away.

Concentration lost, a convulsion gripped Ezechial's arm and Oishi's heart stopped a couple of slow seconds later. Naddalia didn't last much longer. He lashed her throat and as the blood pumped out of her, she drifted down to her knees and then fell forward onto her face.

The Tails were busy lapping up the spill from the fight when Ezechial walked up to the boy. "Boy," it was a whisper. The blood was glowing strangely and steaming up from where the knife was buried in his back. It didn't make any sense to Ezechial. He looked closer, "Pallomor," this time louder, but still expecting the worst and pleading for a response.

Stepping even closer, Ezechial suddenly felt cold and breathless. Dizzy nausea sent the storage room spinning as he saw that the small creature bleeding out on the floor was not the boy he'd brought with him, but instead a child-like demon. Small and grey, it had features and stature similar to the boy, but also the unmistakable claws of a demon protruding from the end of each fingertip, scraping and twitching at the floor.

He knelt down beside the dying creature and reigned in his somewhat satisfied whips in the same motion, holstering them in neat coils within his jacket. Gripping the handle of the chef's knife, he yanked it from the demon's back without sympathy, and threw it to the floor. He rolled child-demon over. Its flesh was cold to the touch, though the blood was hot and glowing like liquid embers. The head of the immature beast rolled to the side limply, and coughed up a sulfurous spray of red-tinted breath.

"Is everything okay?" a quivering voice from the top of the stairs.

Half of the creature's face was smashed, broken cheek and nose, but it still managed to open its eyes at the sound of the boy's voice. Its split tongue wagged out and tried weakly to reach Ezechial's face, never quite making it there.

"Stay where you are." He wrapped his hands around the demon's neck and crushed its throat. So fierce, and so fragile.

Ezechial looked around, trying to understand what had happened. His forearm ached from use, from the unbearable cramping, but also deeper. As he inspected his arm in the low light with his eyes, gold discs reflecting brightly, he thought he saw the black cracks of the wound growing longer across his skin.

FALLEN SPIRE

The Den
Eleven

"The game is just too complex for us to understand?"

"No, that's not what I'm saying. I was wrong. It's not a game at all."

Mark and Marius had stayed through the night in Bradley's home, trying to develop an understanding of the library in the den. They finally slept just before dawn broke. Neither, however, could stay asleep long when the natural noon-light came screaming through the multiple panes of glass in the ceiling. They'd woken up and gotten right back into the discussion after heading to the kitchen.

Marius was at the Wall, manipulating settings deftly with his fingertips, "The premise feels wrong at this point," somewhat preoccupied.

Mark was at the kitchen table, staring mystified at Marius, "What are you…?"

"For the *supreme intellect* responsible for the end of the modern age as we know it, you sometimes have difficulty grasping the simplest of concepts," Marius pressed a button on the Wall, and turned around, "I think we have made some assumptions that have to be revisited."

Dark espresso dripped and then streamed from a silver tube protruding from a depression in the wall. The tiny porcelain glass beneath filled with rich fluid, and when it finally stopped there was a fine mousse of a caramel-colored crema on the top.

"No, no... ," Mark waved his hand admonishingly toward the beverage, "I mean, that. You aren't seriously considering drinking that are you?"

"Considering that I just made it, I had thought to drink it, yes."

Shaking his head, "Really? You know the manufacturer refused to take my advice regarding the necessity to vary the pressure and temperature according to the style of bean and relative ambient humidity, right?"

"I did not." He held the glass to his lips, closed his eyes, sniffed, smiled, and then sipped. "Delicious."

Mark tilted his head curiously, leaned over the table and pulled up a holographic display showing the current settings for the espresso machine, and repeated the order. A red ring appeared on the countertop beneath the dispenser. Mark cleared his throat pointedly.

Annoyed, but too tired to care, Marius responded by begrudgingly placing a new glass beneath the dispenser, and then the espresso began drizzling in. "I still believe there is another person, but not necessarily a player or a dealer."

The espresso finished and Mark stared at it, and then at Marius. The glass. Marius. Eyebrows raised.

Marius stared back at the one and only Mark, unblinkingly, raised his cup to his lips, and sipped again. "The premise really has been that whoever is operating the other side is a master of the device, or at the very least, that the person understands it. We assume that the operator is moving purposefully, but that seems," thoughtfully, "an inappropriate conclusion."

The tired and bedraggled Mark finally gave up and got up. He walked over toward his espresso. Marius gave no ground, forcing Mark to stand uncomfortably close to the much taller man. He retrieved his glass and sat back down, staring into the glass and swirling it a bit, examining the results.

Marius finished the last of his espresso, and then slipped it smoothly back into position beneath the dispenser.

"Right," thoughtfully, "The way we're using it…"

"Exactly."

"So, like us, there is a person on the other side of the library," he sipped more, "this someone is purposefully manipulating the positions and contents just like we've been doing, and is just as confused as we are?" he finished.

"Yes. Isn't that what it feels like?"

Mark smiled, "Whoever it is probably thinks that *we're* fucking with *them*!"

"Possibly… "

"But… then we're just chasing our tails?"

"Isn't that what it feels like?"

"Yes." Mark's disappointment was plain on his face and in his slumped and tired body. He couldn't help but agree with Marius. If he stepped back from it, most of the library's responses could be considered echoes of his actions, and those that weren't felt random and without purpose.

Marius walked out of the kitchen purposefully, leaving Mark alone to contemplate. He reached into his pants pocket and pulled out a single, red capsule. He stared at it. Rolling it around in his palm, he could barely feel its weight, it was so light. It was like any other gelatin he'd ever seen. Appearing small and innocuous, it was hard to believe it had so many secrets hidden within. He heard Marius' footsteps approaching from the living room, and abruptly returned the pill to his pocket.

Entering the kitchen again, Marius was immediately serious and suspicious, "What's the matter?"

"Nothing. Just confused."

Judging whether to pry or not, Marius evidently believed there was more to Mark's look than confusion. He observed a bit longer, and then chose to let it go.

They moved back into the den and looked over the library, wondering how to proceed. They tested the books half-heartedly, confirming that yesterday wasn't just a hallucination, and found that they worked in the same confusing way they had then. The closer they came to any kind of understanding, the farther away it seemed.

"What does this other person want, do you think?"

Sitting at Bradley's desk, Marius, "Let us assume this person wants what we want... to figure it out."

"Figure *us* out you mean, what *we're* doing to the library."

"Sure."

Each sat, lost in thought for a while. Then Marius, "The difficulty is that we have no way of knowing the level of intelligence operating on the other side."

"Well," Mark sounded helpless, "even assuming intelligence, how do we start to build a vocabulary from nothing? No common ground." He slid his hands along the spines of the shelved books, "I mean, maybe they aren't even books on the other side."

"You're right," stopping himself, "I don't mean about the specifics of your example." He waved his hand dismissively and then continued, "Imagining that whoever else is operating this device is just as confused as we are does nothing to help us proceed."

"Right." Mark moved on without waiting, "This was Bradley's work. He probably invented it."

"Invented or discovered..." Standing up from the desk, Marius walked over to the shelf opposite Mark, "Your point is that whoever is on the other end was working with Bradley... might even think we're Bradley, not knowing he died?"

"Yes." He dragged the word out, feeling confident that they were on the right track, but remaining at a loss as to what to do next.

"I think you touched on it a moment ago," *he's definitely touched*, "when you said we need a vocabulary. Bradley was busy developing a set of standards for communicating using a medium that operated over distance as though it was irrelevant. Quantum reflections, or echoes, or something similar. I confess that most of it was outside the realm of my expertise."

"I read through everything I could get my eyes on, but Bradley was damn secretive about this project. He kept everything about it off the…"

Marius waited. Then he waited some more, "The suspense is killing me," dryly.

"Well, he was probably communicating with multiple people. This isn't exactly a one-person project."

"So, who are we dealing with then?"

Mark went around to the desk again, plucked up the feather pen, and grabbed a book from the shelf, "Have you ever written anything with a pen?" He scratched something onto the outer margin of one of the pages.

Taking down a book from his side of the shelf, Marius opened it to a random page, "Do we have to look through all of the books?"

"I don't think it matters."

Leafing through quickly, he saw writing on the outer margin of a page, stopped, and leafed back. "Who are you?"

"Who are you."

"I actually read it and retained it. Do you think they got the message?"

Mark smiled, "Definitely. I think that is why you were able to retain it. Now, we have to answer it."

"I am Marius." The patronizing tone was tinged with a touch of vitriol, "Not terribly happy to have met you."

Throwing the pen, "Write it down."

Marius snatched the pen out of the air, and looked at it as though it was unclean. Feeling foolish for going down this path with Mark, he wondered if maybe it was time to part ways. The quantum library was the most interesting technology he had ever encountered, even though he still didn't understand it. He had been expecting the books to reveal something about the Spire, the demons, or Joshua, as Mark had suggested they would, but now he felt like they were just playing tic-tac-toe with a super computer.

"They, him, her, it, wrote the same question!" exasperated, "Answer it."

Marius played along, but if what he scratched on the page just appeared as-is in another book, he was done. He was tired of running around in circles.

As soon as Marius replaced his book, Mark excitedly snatched another from the shelf. Quickly feathering through his first choice, he went back and forth several times, not noticing anything peculiar. Disappointed, but still feathering through the pages, he started toward the shelf ready to try another book, but then he stopped.

He felt dizzy, processing, then reading aloud, "I am Bradley Falken."

Marius smiled.

"I am Bradley Falken!" practically bouncing, vibrating with excitement, "I am Bradley Falken!"

Convinced that they'd learned nothing new with the experiment, Marius placed a placating and patronizing hand on Mark's shoulder, and laid the pen in the open book in Mark's hands, "Yes, yes you are."

"This is the last thing I expected. What do you think it means?" his excitement somewhat more contained as his mind was distracted by all of the possibilities.

"Mmmm, well, it is precisely what I expected," nodding and smiling. The nonplussed look on Mark's face was priceless, and Marius was happy for it, "I am going to leave now. Bradley's project, whatever it is, is interesting, but irrelevant."

"But... ," Mark looked around apparently trying to grab something, anything at all, with his gaze alone, "Wait. What? I..."

"Please do not follow me."

Striding confidently and quickly out of the den, Marius located his trench and his gloves, donned them, and opened the front door without looking back.

Somewhat stunned, Mark wandered out of the den at the same moment as the front door latched closed. He ran over to the door, and had to remind himself to use the door knob in order to swing it open.

Already at the street, Marius was walking back toward the city, looking selectively at abandoned vehicles along the way.

"Wait!" yelling, but not leaving the doorway, "Wait! What did *you* write?! Did you write, 'I am Bradley Falken'?"

Marius ignored him.

"Why would you do that?!" staying in the doorway. Mark looked back inside, across the main room to the den, and then back out to Marius shrinking ever so slowly into the distance. Whispering to himself, "Doesn't he get it? Someone on the other side must have written that, too..."

Watching for a few more minutes, Mark thought about his options, about what he wanted. Right or wrong, about anything he'd concluded so far, he decided that the library was significant and related to Joshua, the demons, the Spire, everything... how could it not be? He needed to pursue it. He slid his finger down the side of the doorway, once and again, before remembering the door was actually beside him. Stepping out of the way, he slowly closed the door and turned the large heavy latch to the locked position.

Walking back into the den, he decided it was time to start over.

FALLEN SPIRE

A Collective Effort
Twelve

The boy was asleep.

It wasn't hard to believe that exhaustion had beaten fear and helped the child to blissful unconsciousness. On the other hand, what waited for him in his dreams might not have been much better than reality.

Ezechial had not been eager to travel in the dark with the child, but would not stay in the restaurant, not with all of the questions living there.

Whenever he closed his eyes, Ezechial saw himself dragging the body of the demon out of the basement and across the dining room floor. He saw himself through the eyes of Pallomor, who was waiting and watching from beneath a table, where he'd been instructed to wait. The slithering mass hissed on the floor as it slid. Even though the body was limp, its claws managed to hit and grab, and tug and pull, on every chair and every table on their way through the dining room. He was afraid and alone as the boy, and with his vision obscured by the table top, cloth, and legs, he couldn't see who was dragging the corpse, and couldn't really see what the corpse was. He only heard the sounds. He only saw the careless way the body dragged. He only understood the weight of the kill and the power of the killer. Ezechial was the monster.

111

He kept his eyes open as much as he could.

As soon as he'd seen Pallomor at the top of the stairs, he'd sent him into the dining room and told him to wait under a chair in a far corner. It was still unclear to him exactly how the demon had gotten into the restaurant, but that was one of the questions he had to leave behind by moving them to another building.

Using up the waning light of the day, he'd carried Pallomor several blocks, and finally arrived at a small apartment complex. He and the boy had then climbed the stairs to the fifth floor—the top floor—and chosen a room.

How had the situation gotten so out of control? One of the questions that followed him, one that he couldn't shake.

How could he trust himself, his vision, his judgment? Was another.

Seeing clearly was the first aspect of his training. Through tricks of light and shadow, tricks of deception and misdirection, a Laterali had to see clearly to understand and accept the consequences of his actions. Ezechial was a master.

What had blinded him? Was the most important.

Whatever or whoever had worked the wool over his eyes was powerful and subtle, and much stronger than he was. He had accepted a long time ago that many aspects of the world were out of his control, and that there were others who were more adept than he was at manipulating one aspect or another. Acceptance hadn't eliminated fear, but helped him to not be owned by it, helped him mature. The twisting deep in his gut as he contemplated his impotence made him feel like a child. For the first time in his life, he needed help finding hope.

The boy turned beneath the covers, which were up to his chin, and started from his slumber, "Ezechial?"

Sitting at the foot of the bed, Ezechial leaned in closer toward the boy, "Yes?"

The apartment was modern and furnished well, though sparsely. The clean lines of the living room were only broken by the comfortable contours of a couch, which divided it from the rest of the apartment. A simple round glass table and four chairs fit snugly into the dining room, or rather, defined the small space between the couch and the kitchen as a dining room. The kitchen had several counter-mounted appliances, everything necessary to prepare all manner of meals and desserts.

The bedroom matched the character of the rest of the place, though it felt a bit more lived-in, with some crumpled-up clothes not quite making it into the Closet, and a couple of dirty glasses, one on each bedside table. Also, the comforter was a variegated patchwork that looked as though it was made by hand, giving the room more warmth and personality than the others.

Pallomor rolled back over without another word, but Ezechial could tell that he hadn't gone back to sleep. He waited and eventually, "What happened?" The words were small, but clear enough.

Ezechial thought the question was too big for him, "At the restaurant?"

"What happened to everyone?"

The question defined was even larger than Ezechial first thought, but he took solace that it was less personal and tried to find a place to start, "How much do you know?"

"There were monsters coming out of the Spire," staring at the View set to look like a window looking into a lush forest full of playful nocturnal creatures, "and they were hurting people. We had to leave."

The bloody streams hadn't lasted long before all of the signals were lost, but someone had thankfully sheltered this boy from them. "Yes, those who reacted quickly enough fled inland away from the Spire, away from the monsters." Those with weak souls, though—Ezechial thought of the pit—just walked numbly to their deaths.

"So," the boy squirmed beneath the covers and righted himself so that he could look at Ezechial in the low light offered by the View, "Most people are okay? Living inland?"

"I don't know."

Pallomor took some time to digest that answer, "Why are there monsters?"

Ezechial thought about it for a moment.

He decided to start at the beginning, "I often find my answers in the prophecy." He glanced at the boy briefly to see if there was any recognition for the word, and then continued, "Our prophecy is a dynamic concept that is evaluated over and over again by all of us. Any Laterali, the people of my order..."

"Order?"

"A group of like-minded individuals." Then he continued, "Any one of us may contribute, and most of us do at some point." He found himself staring into the View, "It is a shared understanding of time and events... some events become inevitable even before they happen and other potential events fizzle into nothingness."

A toad on a patch of moss caught Ezechial's attention, its head a turret, moving smoothly to follow a mosquito-eater, just one of the numerous insects flying around it. "Always moving and changing, the prophecy is difficult to read and almost impossible to write." The toad's tongue shot out quick, but just as quick, a snake struck the frog, causing the tongue to fly wide of its mark. "But we tried, and keep trying. Some of our words have remained over the generations, and my order is charged with both guarding and challenging those words." As the toad's heart slowed, and its movement stopped, the snake repositioned itself so that it could swallow the toad, head first. The loose, dangling, sticky tongue held a grasshopper, struggling at its end, which must have been caught in the spasm when the frog was struck. The snake began its meal there.

"What happened? Why are there monsters?" Ezechial shrugged. "Some people think we tried to get too close to divinity, developing new genes, hybridizing technology and nature in a way that has called down retribution. They say the Spires are the manifestation, the embodiment of our arrogance, and so the punishment must start there, at the core of our evil."

"You're evil?" That odd, uncertain, crawling smile again.

"Well, that interpretation would have us believe that, yes. But I don't believe that... ," he stopped, feeling an ache in his arm; he flexed it, fist open and fist closed, and then wincing at it, he went on, "I don't believe that the judgment makes any sense. There is nothing more natural than a human being exploring the world, creating tools, and building. I would not say a beaver is evil for damming a river, though it dramatically changes the environment. Some species die from the change, while others become dependent on the change for survival... we might have brought this on ourselves, but we are not evil because of it. Nature is not so biased toward one species or another."

Pallomor was either too confused and too tired to inquire further or he was satisfied with the answer; either way, he said nothing.

"So, you asked what happened? I know that the Spire..."

"You said, 'Spires,' before. Is there more than one?"

"No matter how long the Laterali have stared into the future, or at the words, it is clear there is more than one. We don't really understand where or even *when* they are, or if they are all connected or simply coincidental. For the Laterali, it is a matter of philosophical discussion, but when it comes time to act, we act as though there is only the one."

Ezechial took his time before going on. He really couldn't read the child. He hadn't taken any time to think about it much, but the boy's inquisitiveness seemed odd to him. Though, he hadn't exactly spent much time with young children. More than his questions, Ezechial felt strangely comfortable—compelled even—to open up in ways that he normally wouldn't. Maybe he was more shaken up than he thought from the restaurant?

He had no reason to stop talking to the boy, and he even found it somewhat cathartic, so he continued, "I know that the Collective had many secret cells working for it. I know that one was working on an experiment to unlock human potential that was soon out of their control. They didn't really understand what they had in that first surviving test subject. They kept him in the Spire; or he allowed himself to be kept, anyway. The rest of their subjects were killed as far as I know. All but one other. I worked to keep him alive and out of the rea..."

Ezechial stood from the bed and walked up to the Wall. His fingers danced briefly on the interface, which lit up at his touch, and then the View changed to the roof of the building they were in. The night was clear and starry—the city contributing less light than ever before in Ezechial's recollection—and from their vantage, they could see splotches in the cityscape where city blocks had gone completely dark.

He activated the audio stream and waited.

"What...?"

Ezechial gave the boy a gentle gesture, a palm-down pulse, to stay quiet.

Looking deep into the scene, Ezechial examined rooftops and shadows in and around the buildings and along the streets. Then he saw them. Running, sliding, and stepping through the shadows, the Laterali were in motion together. It took several minutes for all of the greasy and smoky shapes to move through his panoramic view.

Ezechial became smoky and then opaque again alternatively a few times, following the motions in his mind. He suspected they were headed to the greatest concentration of demons—the blackened heart of the city—but their intentions were unclear. A force that large would do some damage, but certainly not end the demonic presence. The demons were far too great in number, and cared far too little for their own lives; they could throw themselves at the Laterali unreservedly. Ezechial couldn't imagine who among his order would have orchestrated such an attack or what the motivation might be.

He zoomed in and out all over the View, looking deeper for signs of the assassins and for an indication of their destination. The number of them working together was probably more for protection than anything else, so maybe the goal was something small.

It was odd to see so many shadows running together through the night.

As the minutes crept by and the distance between them increased, he was able to find fewer and fewer of them in the scene. When he couldn't see any, he gave up and zoomed back out to take in the whole city once again.

Though he still seemed preoccupied with the view of the city, Ezechial was lost in thought. He felt a momentary compulsion to join his brethren, but knew that he would not. The pull was strong. He didn't try to suppress it or ignore, he just felt it, and remembered that he'd chosen a different path. Ezechial had cast himself out of the order to play his part; his fate was tied to Joshua.

And now there was also the boy…

Ezechial looked back at Pallomor who was still nestled in the covers of the bed. He found that the boy was trying once again to articulate some semblance of a smile. It was an eerie and unsettling flexing and twitching of the muscles of his face. Shock? Delusion? Confusion? Despair? Madness? The boy held something back, some strong emotion, but what it was continued to elude the retired Laterali. Ezechial thought for a moment that the boy was trying desperately to be strong for him, "Pallomor, you don't have t…"

A buzzing whine started from the View and grew rapidly louder. A diamond squadron of mini-copters appeared in the sky, originating from behind the point of view. They flew over the apartment building, low and fast. Seconds later, two Carriers appeared, flying on the same trajectory.

The Carriers were a rare sight. Designed exclusively for the deployment of the elite airborne units of the Collective, it was generally unnecessary to employ such force, so the Carriers appeared mainly on holidays as a spectacle and as a reminder of the Collective's power. Even with all of the Watchers of the Collective working against it, it was still possible for an organized group to covertly acquire power and numbers, and a Carrier would be sent in to quell the uprising.

Ezechial had been witness to a live hostile deployment and it was an awesome display force. The entire state of India had become a home to the "Real People," a group of peaceful subversives who challenged the value of life within the Collective. Peaceful intentions or not, people are uncomfortable having their way of life challenged, and violence broke out all over the state. Who started it was irrelevant as the Collective ended it with a single, fully-loaded Carrier.

Two Carriers would be carrying forty airborne units between them, twenty each. The airborne units were monstrous specimens of human ingenuity. They were chosen and genetically enhanced while still within the womb. Engineered to be the largest and the strongest and the quickest that the human frame could withstand, they towered over even well-GEaRed C.O.s. They were enhanced for all occasions: Mantis, Compound, and light-gathering IOLs, spikes and scrubs for every chemical condition, and profound improvements to their inherent senses. Their body hairs were stiff and varied greatly in length, nerves at the base of each follicle that were one hundred times more sensitive than a normal human being's. Coupled with dramatically increased smell and taste, and sensitivity to changes in temperature, they possessed a sense of movement and space so vivid that it was rumored they could *see* 360 degrees, even without their spikes and vision enhancements.

The mini-copters, the Laterali, and the Carriers were converging on the center of the city. Once thriving with life and light at all hours of the day, the center was the largest and blackest of the smudges on the cityscape. It was where Ezechial assumed the demons congregated, where they seemed to have made their home, and appeared to be the focus of the concerted strike against them.

Before the mini-copters penetrated the outer edge, two jets streaked into view, overtaking them in seconds. The jets covered the distance in a blink, and as they flew over the apparent strike zone, they shot two bright red laser-like lights to the ground. The end of each light hit a target out of Ezechial's view, and stayed tethered to their respective targets as the jets flew, causing the red beams to sweep through the sky.

The beams winked out and the jets disappeared.

Two tall buildings began to shrink slowly down, descending into the ground and eventually out of sight behind other buildings. The sound arrived soon after. Ezechial wasn't sure if he heard it or felt it. It was similar to a sonic boom, but more concentrated, as the vibration passed through the dampening of the apartment walls.

The mini-copters zipped into action over the strike zone, and though Ezechial adjusted the zoom to show the entire area, they still appeared small in the View. Each was lighting up the ground with intense spotlights emitted from the nose and the tail. The mini-copters projected more than just the visible spectrum and projected them at varying angles in order to confuse and mislead targets.

The Laterali were likely hitting the outer perimeter as the mini-copters opened fire on targets Ezechial and the boy couldn't see. The entire View of the Wall was lit up with activity, in turn, lighting the bedroom. Streaks and flashes projected colorful displays on the walls, except where Ezechial blocked it, creating a shadowy cape over the bed.

A mini-copter went down, and another. Fiery light and smoke appeared, as one mini-copter flew out of control into a building of mirrored glass, pieces of it exploding out in arcs over the city below.

The Carriers flew into range and began depositing units all over the strike zone. The Carriers were capable of launching their C.O.s over a half-mile radius at their maximum height for deployment. Ezechial watched the fire-fight lights bend and warp around the dark figures as they flew at remarkable speeds toward the ground. There were sprays of distortion from rooftops as a few took up sniping positions.

One of the Carriers, having apparently spent its resources, began retreating from the fight, but it began moving and behaving erratically. Ezechial stepped back up to the Wall. Fingers playing on the display, he split it; one aspect zoomed in and following the flailing Carrier, the other steady on the strike zone.

Ezechial saw shadowy pools racing up the sides of the buildings nearest the Carrier, leaving smoky trails behind them. They accelerated rapidly to the tops of the buildings like shadows of rockets, but there were no rockets to be seen. At the top, the oblong pools burst open and demons leapt from them into the sky. They were running through shadows the way the Laterali stepped through them, or that's what Ezechial thought as he watched the demons launching into the air. Some missed, but most hit the Carrier in one way or another. Many exploded on the rotors while others went too fast into the body of the craft, breaking themselves against it and falling. A few managed to land though, and they began ripping at the fuselage viciously. On the side opposite his view, Ezechial inferred that one of the demons got in and killed the pilot because the Carrier suddenly pitched forward and accelerated, crashing into a high-rise just seconds later.

The other Carrier came under attack, and though the snipers responded quickly with supporting gunfire from the rooftops, they were not able to help for long. Eventually, the overwhelmed craft flew off erratically, out of range and out of sight. Although Ezechial didn't see it crash, he didn't expect it to return.

The mini-copters were much harder targets for the demons, but sheer numbers won out and the maneuverable fighters fell, one after another, until the combat zone was dark again. Dark, save for the glow of the fires.

Ezechial stood watching for a long time. No flares went up. No soldiers or Laterali returned. At least no one came back their direction that he could see. As the fires burned themselves out, he sat down on the bed.

Pallomor was looking at him, and although Ezechial wanted to comfort him, wanted to explain more, he just patted the covers with his hand, "You should sleep."

"But, what about the survivors?"

"There were none."

"You said there were two?"

"Oh?" He needed a moment to pick up the trail of their earlier conversation, "Oh, right." Tomorrow. Get some sleep, Pallomor."

Lonely at the Top

Thirteen

Marius put Mark, Bradley's house, and the den as far behind him as he could, as quickly as he could. The technology behind the books was fascinating, but not enough of a reason to stay, and there were so many reasons to leave.

He had never wanted to be without transportation, but at the same time, he had never wanted to be associated with any vehicle or agency of the Collective. So, he kept the necessary tools in his Glass to make any vehicle his, whenever he needed it. He decided to return to his office building in the city. Everything he needed could be found in the building. He hadn't been there since he dumped his old creds, but his new creds had the same access; it was always good to have a back door. Marius chose a fast but simple vehicle, and appropriated it.

None of the guidance systems could establish a connection, so he had to navigate and drive for himself. He wasn't accustomed to it, but with no one else on the road, it hardly mattered whether he looked like he knew where he was going or not.

Unfortunately, it didn't take him long to make it to some impassable intersections. Several miles away from his building, he found that he was driving around in circles, trying to find a way to penetrate the rows and columns of vehicles congesting the roadways. Although most of the cars were lined up to get out of the city, leaving the lanes into the city pretty open, the intersections were stacked against travel in all directions.

Marius finally gave up and started walking. He wasn't sure if he would find any of his employees in his building, and rather hoped he wouldn't. Not looking forward to any kind of conversation or having to explain himself in any way, he thought it would be best if he didn't encounter anyone in the building so that he could gather what he wanted, unhindered.

The situation had changed somewhat with the transportation difficulties. He could only bring with him what he could carry, and over several miles. Considering that most of the experimental weapons at his disposal were lightweight, they were the least of his concern. The problem as he saw it, as he passed around and between some creatively parked vehicles—apparently trying the sidewalk as an alternate route—was that he couldn't carry anything out with which he could bargain. He needed something to offer whatever form of civilization he found, something with which to barter.

Of course, there was always the option to simply stay in the building and live out his days there. They had several botanical gardens in which he could easily grow water-trees to create an unending supply of clean drinking water. Nutrient-rich gel packs— both standard and prototypical—were in vast supply throughout the building, and virtually inexhaustible for a single person. It might get boring to have no other food source, but he could definitely survive like that, which he could not say was true if he adventured into other territories.

On the other hand, there were the demons. If he was honest with himself though, he didn't consider them a real threat. In his former life as a Ghost, he required certain kinds of protection, so he'd expertly designed the building to blend in with all the others on the block, but with defense in mind. The structure was actually built to withstand the full force of a Collective attack, not to mention the numerous escape routes it had available. The demons would have to penetrate all of the defenses, and then get to him on the 27th floor before he was able to escape. The odds seemed to favor him.

Unfortunately, he probably wasn't the only person to reach the conclusion that one could survive within the confines of his building and he began to wonder who else might have taken up residence. Nevertheless, he walked on. He would deal with squatters when he arrived.

It took over two hours, but when he finally stood at the front entrance to the GlassTech building—his building—he was relieved, confident it was worth the effort. There were still several hours of light left, probably enough to get him safely back to Bradley's if he was wrong about GT functioning as a tenable hold against the coming night. He was a little surprised at himself for even considering returning to the house of madness, but at least it was a known, and safe as of last night anyway.

Although he'd left his old identity behind, Marius had ensured that he would be able to return as 'Jasper,' which is how the system would know him at this point. He stepped up to the door and it opened automatically, prompted by his proximity.

Entering the building from the front was always a pleasure for Marius. A typical office building entrance with a reception area, a security desk, and two banks of elevators, he was proud of how effectively he'd run a real business as a front for his activities as a Ghost. It was amazing to him that businesses like GlassTech could take up the entire effort and responsibility of a CEO, while he'd managed it in his spare time. The bragging rights were nonexistent when he was a Ghost, and completely irrelevant now, so the pleasure was short-lived.

He approached the elevators and stepped into the nearest one as it opened.

The elevator Wall lit up with all of Marius' destination floor options. His universal access was intact. "Fifteen." The inertial dampeners worked smoothly and the movement of the lift was almost completely undetectable. The doors opened a moment later and he stepped out into a long undecorated hallway.

There were several doors at irregular intervals along the hallway, but he was unconcerned with all but one. He walked swiftly to 1550 and opened the door. Inside were a Desk, a chair floating empty behind it, and several rows of storage lockers. Standing over the Desk, he placed his whole palm down on the surface and with a flick of his wrist, rotated the display to face him. He flipped through a few pages and made two selections. Two lockers slid open and Marius' IOL display lit up with a path to show him the way to each.

He arrived quickly at the first locker and selected two of the multiple guns from within. The locker door closed after he removed the weapons; then the Wall closest to him, as well as his IOL, began displaying pertinent information about them. They were Class 5 HDMAs.

Carrying one in each hand, Marius walked to the next locker. Within were several sling-style holsters, and he selected one. As he returned to the Desk at the front, the displays following him on the Wall showed information about the dual shoulder holster and the personal shield that it provided, in addition to the multiple configurations in which it could be worn.

Standing at the Desk, he set all of his newly acquired equipment down and flipped the display again to face him. He removed his trench, laid it carefully over the back of the chair, and started to adjust and configure the shoulder harness while he simultaneously worked the Desk.

He searched the building for any indication that other people were present by looking for tripped alarms and activity on the network. Pleasantly surprised to find no sign of interlopers, Marius finished adjusting his harness, holstered the HDMAs, and swept his trench back on gracefully. He hovered over the Desk for a bit longer, checked the power for the building—it was connected to a military grid, which was still running—and checked inventory of the supply rooms, which he found were nearly at capacity for most of the gel pack varieties.

Everything seemed in order. He left.

In the elevator, Marius thought about his options for a moment: Raid the supply rooms and leave, or plan to stay here for a while?

"Destination, please?" The elevator prompted with a female voice, and also began flashing an outline around the floor numbers. He pressed the '27' and the display, which would have changed to GlassTech propaganda for anyone else, went blank save for a red dash at the center. Marius waved his wrist over the dash, it turned green, and a couple of seconds later the doors opened onto the 27th floor.

It was dark in the foyer, illuminated only by the blue-tinted lines and diffusers, which ran along the floor and ceiling. An ornate rug ran along the hardwood away from him and across the foyer to a curved set of stairs, also minimally lit. The stairs led up to a landing and then continued up to a balcony that ran the entire perimeter of the room. The master bedroom of the suite and an indoor-outdoor observation deck were both accessible from the second floor, while his office, the kitchen, and dining room, were on the first.

Using the elevator to ascend to the 27th floor, to his penthouse, should have turned the lights on in anticipation of his arrival, but even as Marius stepped off the lift and took a couple of steps, the standard lights did not come on. He looked around suspiciously. The foyer was uncomfortably warm, even hot. Marius had set all of the values for his environment, and hot was not one of them. Even the Walls were dark and blank, and he'd had famous works of the impressionist era displayed throughout when he left.

A soft brushing sound told him that the elevator doors were closing behind him. When the sound stopped, he felt that he'd been very neatly trapped. If he would have had time to consider it, he might have cast the feeling aside as paranoid, but he didn't have the time as the door to his office opened. Trapped, he decided there was nowhere to go but in.

He walked across to the open door, and looked inside. Sitting at Marius' Desk, operating it as though it was his own, was a slender, bald man dressed in a loose shirt and pants. The clothes—made from a linen-like material—Marius recognized as the standard apparel for the Spire, but the man was a stranger to him.

Standing there in the doorway, he observed the Desk and the multiple displays, scrutinizing every detail for some clue to the man's identity. There were views of the Spire and satellite views of multiple blocks of the city. There were views of people, active and living, in places Marius did not recognize, but also, views of the upper-class residential that he'd just left. He wondered if this man had been watching him the entire time. Then he saw the stream of suite 1550.

Apparently outclassed—the man didn't even feel the need to turn and face him—Marius broke the silence, "Make yourself at home."

"It is interesting, don't you think?"

"What is that, exactly?" *That you talk over me, like Mark?*

"That there is still hope even after everything I have done." He finally swiveled in the chair to face the entrance, and the lights came up. His skin was dark chocolate in contrast to the clothing, but most remarkable were his bright amber eyes, which met Marius' evenly, unafraid.

"Everything that you have done?" Apparently, one way to survive the apocalypse was through self-delusion.

"The world has chosen me, Marius."

"Okay," Marius had had enough, "the world chose you. That's wonderful. I've been holding together pieces of insane, megalomaniacal ranting for weeks, so I'm quite done with it at this point."

The man's serious face became amused and curious, as though the conversation had taken an unexpected turn, and he wanted to see where it would go. He was casual.

Marius was nonplussed by the reaction, but forged ahead regardless, "I hope you have enjoyed the show," he nodded toward the displays, "but I'm not interested in continuing the drama. Am I dead, or not?"

"Clearly not, Marius." He clasped his hands in his lap, "Forgive me, I never did properly introduce myself did I? I am Deliah."

Deliah moved faster than Marius could see. He was standing half of a meter in front of Marius, one hand behind his back, the other outstretched to shake. Marius' brain caught up to the movement, and he twitched to reach for his weapons. He only twitched though, realizing it was too late before his hands even reached into his trench.

Marius swallowed hard, and realized he was unbearably hot. Even with the heat, Marius kept his gloves on when he reached out with his left hand to take Deliah's. They shook.

"There," Deliah brought his hand from behind his back and placed it around Marius', "Now, maybe we can talk?"

"Sure," though he was far from.

Marius could feel Deliah's strength radiating through his palms. He was positive Deliah could hold him there as long as he wanted.

"Good." Deliah patted Marius' held hand, and then released it slowly, clasping his hands together behind his back. "Good."

Eyes narrowed skeptically, "What would you like to discuss?" He watched as Deliah turned away and began pacing the office.

"You consider yourself a Ghost, Marius, do you not?"

"I, uh…," Marius was taken aback, "What?"

"Off the grid?" Deliah seemed preoccupied, as though he was warming up to something, "Untouchable?"

Marius' chest sank.

"I have a proposition for you."

Marius had once been comforted by the idea that this man needed something from him, but not today, "What sort of proposition?"

"You fascinate me. I know everything about what you've done, but almost nothing about you personally. I would like to know more about you." He half-turned toward Marius who still hadn't moved from the entrance, "You are unique in that there is a choice in your fate. I do not have to kill you."

"I tell you about myself, and you let me live?" *Seems unlikely.*

Deliah did not pause his inspection of the office, "Tell me about yourself. Then I decide."

"I'm not sure that is much of a proposition."

"Have faith in me, Marius."

His stomach twisted, "Faith," he was sweating fully, "is not something I believe in."

"You should have a seat." Deliah indicated the chair behind the Desk. "I'll turn down the temperature in here as well. Try to make you more comfortable."

Marius didn't see Deliah interact with anything that would change the temperature of the room, but it was cooler in the office almost immediately. Moving the chair to a corner, he sat down facing his interviewer. "What would you like to know? Why am I of interest to you?"

"You have no soul."

Afraid that he was captive to a much stronger and more frightening version of Mark, Marius prompted haltingly, "No soul?"

"Let us not have a discussion of semantics," shrugging, "Suffice it to say that you have spent no time in your life cultivating any kind of connection with others. You never even sought a deeper understanding of yourself." He looked fully at the steely-eyed Marius, "You were given this beautiful gift, this shining gift, and you did absolutely nothing with it."

"I'm not sure I follow."

"Your connection, your soul, your third eye—whatever your preference—is so withered, so shrunken and shriveled, that it is almost entirely useless."

Marius was not offended by the man's words, but he thought that, as interviews go, there were far too few questions. If his life was dependent on his answers, and there were no questions, he was surely going to die.

"At least the automatons have been useful to me, but you, you have nothing. No one would miss you if you were gone, in this world or the next. You are only here, in this one place, in this one time. You are completely untethered, and yet you live… you want to live…"

The last sounded close enough to a question that Marius took it, "Yes, I do."

Deliah was on top of Marius, moving again with that unfathomable speed. His hands were vices on the arms of the chair, crushing them. His face was too close, and the heat pouring off his body was suffocating, "Of. Course. You. Do." He was biting the words with unnaturally sharp teeth. "I will not ask any questions with such obvious answers."

The amber eyes were bright and unblinking, and Marius cowered beneath them. The heat became unbearable, like a fire burning close to his face. He couldn't breathe, he couldn't react, and the only thought he had was, *This man is going to kill me.*

Then Deliah slowly released the chair and stood fully upright, hands once again behind his back. Marius thought the man was somehow smaller than he was a second ago. Deliah seemed to have a way of diminishing his stature when he wanted to be less imposing. It would have impressed Marius, under other circumstances.

"You want to live, even though you are the only entity that exists in your world. You are supremely selfish, so much so that you are entirely alone."

The once regal-looking Ghost looked aged and beleaguered as he slumped down into his office chair. His salt-and-pepper hair was mussed and still somewhat wet with sweat. He could think of nothing to say. Thinking it through, it was probably for the best that he said nothing.

"Do not misinterpret; there have been many weak souls along my journey, and I have dealt with all of them." Speaking to the room, "The automatons have been giving away their souls for generations without knowing their worth. They parted with them for a promise."

Locking eyes with Marius, "I think they are happier now, honestly. You would likely agree."

Deliah walked over to the Desk, turned off all of the displays, and then sat on the corner facing Marius before he continued, "Then there are others of course, the few who struggle to stay connected, despite great adversity. I respect their determination even though their resistance is an exercise in futility. They cannot undo centuries of decay with nothing but hope. The idea of it is absurd. Unfortunately, they are at odds with my purpose, which brings me to you." He gestured toward Marius casually. "What is your purpose? What do you want?"

Feeling as though the questions were loaded, Marius sat more upright in an attempt to regain some dignity before dying, "Those are difficult questions. I would suggest they are unanswerable," he found a sarcastic tone naturally working its way into his manner of speaking and stifled it quickly, "But, but, I would have to say there is no purpose. No one has a purpose." Sensing that Deliah considered the global version of the answer a dodge, he specified, "I have no purpose.

He swallowed hard again, "I wanted to be entirely invisible, but remain immensely influential. I wanted to control as much as I possibly could for as long as I could."

"And now?" Deliah did not quite disguise his disappointment. It was difficult for Marius to tell if the disappointment was in the content of his answer, or in the fact that he'd answered in the past tense.

"Now," he thought better than to state his obvious desire to live again, "I'm considering my options," he indicated the office, the entire building, "Guaranteed food and shelter here, or venturing inland."

"Why inland?"

"Well," gesturing at Deliah, "I'm now just a tad concerned about the security and safety of living here." Deliah's ambers sparkled a little brighter at the comment, but he made no move toward Marius.

"There might be some remnants of civilization inland, and I could probably set myself up well."

Deliah nodded his head and stood up from the Desk. Marius prepared himself, sliding his hands across each other and into his trench. Maybe the man from the Spire had seen him get his guns, maybe not. Either way, he was going to try.

"At least you are consistently selfish," Deliah's lips curled up, "Would you like my advice?"

Marius couldn't speak, mesmerized by the moment, expecting to draw.

"Of course you would," Deliah turned his back to Marius and began walking toward the exit. He looked over his shoulder as he went, "you should stay here Marius. Live out the rest of your empty life. You are of no consequence to anyone."

Marius drew his guns as he stood. He took aim and fired. No flash. No sound.

Deliah continued his way out. At the elevator, the doors opened for him, and he got on without ceremony.

When Marius finally went to check, he found that the doors would no longer open for him.

FALLEN SPIRE

This is Mark

Fourteen

Bradley's den.

He began again. He simply took out a book and tried to read it, taking notes on his Glass. Even though everything he wrote was static, it was gibberish and it felt nothing like what he had read in the book.

After a couple of hours looking through countless more books, he realized that he wasn't alone in starting over. He had not seen any evidence of his earlier attempts to unravel the inner workings of the books. There were no torn pages. There were no words scratched into the margins of any of the books he'd pulled. There was no indication that the books were in any condition other than when he'd first arrived.

It was possible that he simply hadn't pulled any of those books again. He couldn't deny it was possible, but to not pull a single mangled book after all of the pages he'd torn, dog-eared, scratched, or written on? He didn't believe it. No.

The library had reset.

There was no information being conveyed, nothing being communicated.

It was exactly what he wanted as a starting ground. Not one dog-eared page, so he retrieved a book, flipped it open to a random page and folded down the corner, and replaced the book.

He wanted to ensure that he pulled a different book, but he knew it was impossible for him to tell one from another. Thinking he should just walk to the other side of the room, he turned, but didn't move; he was pretty sure he'd just switched sides. Smiling, he turned back around and grabbed a book and flipped through it.

There. Deep in the book. The folded-down corner.

He flicked the edge of the down-turned corner, making a soft and satisfying tap against his fingernail. Playing with the fold between his fingers, he felt the texture and thickness of the page, single and doubled. It worried him for a moment. as he smoothed out the corner. that it hadn't been there when he pulled the book, but he remembered the feeling of confusion that he felt whenever he played with the books and trusted that he had actually completed the test.

He returned the book.

The den was still and quiet. Every movement he made created a pronounced vibration: his inner thighs swiping each other as he stepped, the books sliding in and out against one another, his breathing. He imagined hearing his heartbeat. He imagined he was alone.

Walking around the desk, he went to the other side of the library and selected a volume. He retrieved it and carried it over to the desk. He tossed open the hard cover and several pages shuffled over with it. He left it there like that while he retrieved more books from the shelves. After arranging all of them in various ways on the desk, he plucked the feather pen from the desk and stepped up to a shelf. Opening a book, he scrawled a quick, "Hello World," into the margin of a randomly selected page and returned it. Then, he drew out another book, held it open, and began thumbing through the pages quickly.

"Hello World."

Retrieving one more book, keeping the first, he looked at the next, "hello world."

He walked over to the desk, carrying both books, and sat down. Setting them on his lap, he looked at the open books on the desk. They were free of any markings as far as he could tell without touching them. After several minutes, he decided to open one of the other books that had been closed on the desk, and there were the words, strange but clear, "Hello, World." He placed that book with the others on his lap.

Lifting one of the open books with both hands, he examined it closely, and then with a snap, he closed it tight. Carefully, as though he was nervous about moving too quickly, about what he might find, he opened the book.

"hello, world."

His heart was pounding in his chest. Okay, okay, he thought to himself repeatedly, assuring himself. Same as before, he put that book with the others on his lap, and lifted another open book with both hands. This time though, he leafed through the pages without closing the book. Back and forth, he was almost convinced the words were not there, but then, "Hello, world."

Palms sweaty, he pressed his face closer to the book until his nose was practically touching the page. He traced the words he'd written there with a shaking finger. It didn't matter that he'd seen inexplicable behavior from the books numerous times previously; this was different. The words weren't written the way he'd remembered them.

Clearing the space immediately in front of him on the desk, he put the book down, open to the page with the words written in the margin. He grabbed the book that was on his lap and opened it until he found the words, "Hello, world."

Leaning forward, he retraced the letters with the pen. Several times, darker and darker, he wrote. When the pen was running dry, he dipped it in the ink well and pulled up on the lever as though he'd used a pen like it his whole life.

He flipped open all of the books on the desk to the blank lead-in pages. Pen fast to the page, he wrote in all of them. Scooting the chair closer to the desk, he leaned and wrote haphazardly, and turned pages when needed. The pages were blank until he filled them. The pages were blank.

His heart was racing. He couldn't breathe.

He stood. The books on his lap fell to the floor, but when he looked there were no books. Propping himself up, he leaned over the desk onto his hands, hanging his head down. He squeezed his eyes hard against the sweat and feverish heat building inside of him, and tried to calm himself down.

He tried to think about anything else but the library. Imagining himself at his Desk, observing the world through a thousand windows, he thought of the calm and regular movement of information across his displays. He thought of the poetic shirts that filled his closet and of his favorites among them. He thought about tamping espresso and the consistency of temperature and pressure applied. The smell. He thought about the smell. Breathing in deeply, he smelled an espresso.

He opened his eyes as a drop of sweat from the tip of his nose fell into a tiny porcelain cup of espresso beneath him.

Looking up and looking around the room, he saw the shelves were full. There was only one book on the desk, and it was closed, next to his espresso.

He was calm. Exhausted though, he slumped back down into the chair and looked around the library, around Bradley's den.

Reaching forward, he slid the cup away and pulled the book closer. He scooted all the way into the desk and grabbed the pen from its holder, opening the book at the same time.

"The books don't do anything." He wrote it. He read it.

"It's not the books." He read it.

"It's the room." He wrote it.

"It is me."

"I am in the room."

"I am in the room."

He read it and wrote it, several times, or thought he did. When he eventually paused, he read over the page again. Finally, he very slowly wrote, "Who are you?"

He waited for several minutes. Reading over the page, the words began looking like random assemblages of curves and lines that illustrated nothing in particular, the drawings of a poor artist. Reading the last words, as though for the first time, he wrote a response beneath them, "This is Mark."

He tried desperately to remember the last few hours. There was a version of his past where Marius had left, after which he'd gone back into the kitchen, made a new espresso, and then went into the library to sit down and start over. There was a version of the memory that, instead, had him return directly to the den. He remembered writing madly into all of the books. He remembered dropping books, and throwing them across the room. He remembered picking them up and putting them back.

Goosebumps formed on his arms as his mind wandered over the words written before him. It's the room. It's the room.

A knock came from the front door.

Mark almost pissed himself he was so startled. He thought that it must be Marius, and the thought made him extremely happy. He needed someone to help him think through what he'd learned. It's the room. He was excited to share the idea. Thinking that Marius would think that he was insane though, he considered revising some of what had happened, or what he thought happened anyway.

The knock was repeated, though louder this time.

The echoes of the knocks pounded through the quiet library. Mark stood up from the desk and was at the doorway to the den before realizing that he wanted to grab the book he was using and keep it separate. Even though he was confident that the books themselves were irrelevant—that the room was doing something to him, or perhaps to many of him—he couldn't help but think the book was special. It was superstitious, but he embraced it.

More knocking came from the front door, the same rhythm as each time previous. Only knock, knock; nothing more and nothing less.

Hustling back to the desk, he took one last look at the page he had written, or read. There were lines he recognized, but didn't understand until that moment:

"Don't answer the door."

He reached into his pocket and took out the candy-looking gelatin. Mark was scared and he shook the pill around in his hand. There was no time. He read the words one more time, and the knocking immediately followed, startling him into action.

He swallowed once and ran.

A Watchful Eye

Fifteen

Sleep—if it could be called that—came to Ezechial as the sun came up in the early morning and only lasted a couple of hours. He spent those hours in a lucid dream, floating through shadows of time gone and times to come, feeling as though he was sliding between realities. It was a method that he'd used for years to help him find his way: a consideration of possibilities framed by his experience, unfettered by the anchors of time and space.

It didn't help him this time.

The boy was still sleeping when Ezechial got up from his place at the foot of the bed on the floor. Pallomor's porcelain face was serene sticking out from beneath the covers. He was a beautiful child, and in sleep, seemed unmarked by the recent hardships of his life. The unwrinkled covers were still tucked up neatly beneath his chin, adding to the picturesque quality of his slumber; he must have slept without moving at all. If not for the full, sanguine lips, Ezechial might have thought the boy was in his final repose instead of sleep.

Just as Ezechial started to wonder if Pallomor was breathing at all, he stirred, "Ezechial?"

"I'm right here."

The View was set to watch the morning as the early morning light cast long shadows out over the city. They couldn't see the breaking light from the current point of view, but the effect on the dormant city was sobering. Ezechial thought it looked like an odd nature reserve that had been emptied for cleaning, the habitat neglected for too long.

The boy's eyes were clear, as though he didn't even need a second to make the journey from sleep to wakefulness. Ezechial thought it was a gift of youth to be so quick to transition. He stared at Ezechial expectantly as he propped himself up, "I'm hungry."

Right. Ezechial had almost forgotten that it was a child in front of him, "We can find a restaurant or a grocery and get something for you as soon as you are ready to leave."

Pallomor hopped up out of bed, slipped his shoes on, "I'm ready now," excited.

"Good. But I think we both could use a wash," he thought it might be the last time the boy would have it this easy. Venturing inland, even if they plotted carefully, they probably wouldn't find as much life support in such great density as in the city again. Moreover, Ezechial couldn't shake the urge to investigate the attack area, which could mean that Pallomor would have to take care of himself for a day or two.

The boy dashed into the master bathroom. Ezechial left him to it. After a few minutes the boy appeared, "I'm ready." For the first time since Ezechial found him, the boy was acting his age, and he found it a surprising relief.

"I need a minute as well."

Ezechial went into the bathroom, found a tooth-stick, formed it, and chewed it. While the chems worked in his mouth and on his teeth, he pulled his shirt off and threw it over the shower door. When he turned to splash water onto his face, he saw himself in the Wall—apparently the boy had been using it. The black fissures crawling up his arm had made it around his shoulder and were running down his side. He stretched his left arm over his head to inspect the spreading branches more closely, and winced at the tightness of the muscles. Looking closer, he found signs all the way down to the top of his hip and partially across his abdomen and chest, though the markings were less prominent there. At the rate they were growing, it wouldn't be long before the cracks spread over his entire body. He reached down to the counter and fluidly adjusted a few settings so that he could look at his back, and found the marks there, too.

Having seen enough, he turned off the Wall display and ran the water. After splashing his face and his chest, he felt refreshed and reached for his shirt. He pulled it over his head as he turned toward the door and there was the boy staring at him. The door had been opened and Pallomor had come fully within the master bathroom without Ezechial knowing it.

The boy stood there with a reversal of the strange expression he sometimes wore; instead of barely holding onto a smile, he was barely frowning. It was as though he had a giggle beneath his sadness that he could barely stifle.

"Are you okay?" The boy started the question just before Ezechial, but they both finished it.

"I'm sorry you saw. I was… wounded."

"But, how were you wounded?"

"I share more than I should with my whips," he stared off, wondering how much longer he would be able to protect himself, much less a defenseless child, "Let's just leave it at that."

"How bad is it?"

"Strange. Tight." He flexed his fist and twisted his hand and arm around, feeling out the range of motion. The arm felt even slower to react than before, and he wasn't sure about the strength of the muscle, which seemed ready to cramp if he stressed it at all.

"You're probably just hungry, like me," the boy offered some encouragement, or perhaps oblivious to the seriousness, just restated his own needs. Either way, Ezechial thought that food would probably help.

"I'm ready now. We can go."

Ezechial—years of trained movements evident—swung on his harness, ensured that his Devil's Tails were secure, and threw on his jacket, "We should find you a jacket as well."

"Okay." And then, "One like yours?"

"Sure."

Out on the street they only walked a few blocks before they found plenty of food options. Among the small restaurants and conveniences, there was a Thai restaurant that caught Pallomor's attention. They went in.

In the kitchen, as Ezechial arranged supplies and pots and pans, "I may need you to take care of yourself for a day or two."

The boy was sitting up on the butcher's block across from the six-burner, gas range behind Ezechial, "Why?"

Starting some water boiling for the rice noodles he found, "I need to travel back into the city," he placed some dried spices and herbs beside Pallomor, "Maybe even go back to the Spire." He looked at the boy levelly, "It's dangerous, but I have to go," pausing, hesitating, "I may not return, but I expect to return."

"I'll go with you."

Ezechial stepped away to gather more items from the near shelf, "It's more dangerous with us together than with us apart." He grabbed a couple cans of coconut milk and placed one after another into the opener mounted on the wall.

"I'm going with you."

The top of the second can was gone like the first when Ezechial removed it from the opener, "Why?" He continued preparing lunch for breakfast.

"Because you want me to go with you."

Ezechial stopped what he was doing briefly, taken aback by the certainty with which the boy spoke. When he started moving again, carefully, "What do you mean?"

"Try to go without me, you'll see."

He momentarily felt like he was sinking, like a bobber on a fishing line when the hook is struck. It was a sickening sensation. Turning from what he was doing, sauce-covered spoon still in his hand, "I'm going into the city without you."

The boy listened like Ezechial was the child, and responded with nothing but a slight tilt of the head and a placid expression. There was no sense of confrontation, just an overwhelming sense of knowing.

Ezechial felt less like the bobber and more like the fish now.

He put the feeling aside and continued to cook. It's only a boy. He would leave Pallomor at the apartment they'd stayed in last night. Ezechial would set the View to follow himself so that they boy could watch as he went. He thought it would help comfort the boy and make it easier for him to stay behind. If he put up a struggle, or a fight, or threw some kind of fit, Ezechial would just knock him out. Simple. Safe.

Thinking that he had a handle of the situation, Ezechial reached for his sauce pan and felt his forearm twitch and burn uncomfortably. He snatched it back from the pan as though he'd placed it into the fire.

"Does it hurt a lot?"

Thick tension wound around his gut. He set the spoon down in the sauce, leaning the handle against the lip of the pan, and turned around slowly. His eyes darted to his jacket—harness and Tails tucked within—which was laid out beside the boy on the butcher's block, and then to the boy.

"You have to eat something. You'll feel better."

As he stood there staring into the boy's unblinking, unyielding eyes, he felt an itching in his healthy forearm. It was an urge—momentary and ephemeral—but if he'd had his whip in his hand, he would have snapped it out at the boy. He didn't want to just injure the child, he wanted to tear his head off. But it passed. It passed, and he noticed the shaky smile returning to the cherubic face of the helpless boy.

Ezechial couldn't trust himself. If he travelled with the boy, he would probably kill him. He couldn't risk it. "You're right. I need to eat. We can discuss the arrangements later."

"Okay."

When everything was ready, they ate in the dining room. They sat across from each other at the table without talking for several minutes. The boy forked spoonful after spoonful of the saucy noodles into his mouth without paying much attention to Ezechial. Eating slowly, Ezechial never took his eyes off the boy.

Pallomor finished his serving when Ezechial was half done with his own, "Yummy!"

Gesturing to the large remainder in the bowl at the center of the table, "I made extra so that you would have something to eat later today and possibly tomorrow." Almost as an afterthought to maintain conversational civility more than to express gratitude, "I'm glad you like it."

Scooping up the remainder, Ezechial went into the kitchen again, leaving Pallomor to finish his portion. He found a vacuum packager in the back and dumped the contents of the bowl into the opening, causing a clear plastic bag to start descending out of the bottom. Once half of the leftovers were in the bag, Ezechial slid his finger across the front and the bag was sucked, sealed, and cut. It dropped into the catcher a short distance below, and then Ezechial repeated the process.

Ezechial swept his harness and jacket back on, and then grabbed both bags. He went back out to the dining room. Pallomor was waiting for him at the entrance. The boy seemed older to Ezechial, as though the last hour or so had aged him unnaturally. "We don't have to go back to the apartment do we?"

Ezechial crossed the dining room, "I think we should. Drop off the food. Get you settled for my absence."

"We don't really have to go through all of that. I can stay right here." He spoke flatly, as though he had no commitment to it.

"You want to stay here?"

"Sure."

It seemed unreasonable to believe that the boy should stay in the restaurant. He thought Pallomor might be right about his inability to leave him behind. Doubts and hesitation swelled up from somewhere deep inside of him at the prospect of leaving Pallomor behind, but he knew it wasn't about the location: the hesitation was with regard to leaving him at all.

Ezechial was feeling less and less comfortable as the seconds crawled by. He didn't even notice that he was clawing the bags of food until Pallomor eyed one expectantly. Falling apart, he was losing his control and self-awareness, and it disturbed him to acknowledge it. If he cared about the boy at all, he should probably put some distance between them. At the same time, he couldn't help but be unnerved by the child.

Unnerved by a child.

Setting the packs down on the nearest dining table, Ezechial flexed his cracked arm and wondered how many fractures were growing in his brain.

"There isn't a bed or anything comfortable to sleep on."

"I don't mind. I like the floor."

"It's only a couple of days." Ezechial scrutinized the boy carefully and could find nothing to indicate whether he was happy or sad about the situation.

"Yes. You'll be back." He was sure beyond sure.

Ezechial thought he was supposed to say something like, "Be careful," or, "Don't venture out at night," but even in his head the phrases sounded ridiculous. Instead he went with, "Right. I will be back."

Pallomor didn't move, forcing Ezechial to walk around him to get to the door. The door opened with a sliding finger, and Ezechial stood at the threshold; but when he went to take a step, he found he couldn't.

Ezechial stood there for a long time. Staring out into the daylight of the street and at the vacant businesses, he searched himself for the reasons why he couldn't walk out into it. It seemed so simple, and if he had to be realistic about it, there was no reason why not. Nevertheless, he couldn't do it. He couldn't leave the boy there to fend for himself. He couldn't leave him all alone. He couldn't.

Finally, the boy walked out ahead of him to stand on the sidewalk, "Can we bring the food? I really liked it."

Ezechial went back in and gathered up the two bags of noodles, putting them in a long-handled shopping bag he found behind the register that he thought to wear as a backpack. Everything bundled, he met up with Pallomor on the sidewalk.

"You'll have to keep an eye on me."

"I already do."

Author's Notes
Sixteen

Deliah stood outside the door to Bradley's home. His hands were at his sides, unmoving. The shirt and pants he wore flowed around him when a soft breeze passed through the affluent neighborhood. He dominated the fragile landscape, a constant as the world moved around him uncertainly.

Deliberately, and with the utmost control, Deliah knocked on the door. It was forceful but patient. His hand returned to his side, and he returned to his statuesque appearance. He waited.

In any other modern home, the knock would have been recorded and reproduced in all the rooms of the house that contained conscious occupants, but not this one. The door wasn't just a functional piece of the entrance; it was a work of art. The wood was unique. It had been worked with sand and sweat to a polish like thick, dark glass. The finish was the result of pressure and time, and created an illusion of depth. Staring into that depth, observing the character of the door reflecting the craftsman who made it, you could see each subtle layer as it was revealed over time. The progressively finer-grained papers must have ended with a sheet of a texture that most people would have mistaken for silk.

There was only one imperfection—hidden from casual eyes, present only for someone who cared to know or who cared to prove authenticity—a burned and tastefully scripted capital 'K.' The flourish after the letter might have represented a few trailing characters or not, it was difficult to tell.

Again, deliberately and patiently, Deliah knocked on the door. There was no change in his posture otherwise. He gave the impression that he would be happy to stay there for an eternity, knocking at regular intervals until there was an answer. There was no answer again, and after an appropriate delay, he knocked another time.

His face was composed and his amber eyes were wide, bright, and unassuming. Deliah was easy look at, but impossible to read, betraying nothing of his inner thoughts to the world. Placing a palm on the smooth surface of the wood, his entire body stock-still, he pushed gently.

The door flew inward, splinters of the frame and surrounding structure buckling from the force. The heavy metal hinges stayed locked firmly in the door, but were ripped clean out of the weaker wall. Remaining upright, the door slid into the living room at great speed until it hit a coffee table and finally impaled the far Wall. A loud crunching sound accompanied the destruction of the Wall, which broke into fragments. The gaping wound was surrounded by inky black shards and rainbow-colored trails.

Stepping in, his hands behind his back, Deliah inspected the living room. He looked up at the balcony. He walked over to the entrance of the kitchen and peered in, then continued over to where the Wall and former front door met. Stopping in front of the odd, but beautiful design of the destruction for only a moment before moving on, he eventually arrived at the open doorway to the den.

There was no one inside. His eyebrows arched up slightly, as if in surprise. Then he stepped inside. As he crossed the threshold, his surprise became obvious as he turned quickly around, walked out, and then back in again. He closed his eyes, as though looking for an explanation that he couldn't find within the room. When he finally opened them again, they betrayed a sinister glint of disapproval. The room was not identical to his at the top of the Spire, but it was irrefutably similar, too similar to be a coincidence.

Walking around the den, he ran his fingers along the spines of the books tucked neatly into the shelves. He stopped to stare at the painting behind the desk, and almost seemed to admire it. He spent several minutes tracing the connections on the canvas with his eyes before he was finally satisfied.

He sat down in the chair and looked over the desk. Arranged neatly on the surface were a feather pen, a Newton's Cradle, and a compass, as well as one book, which sat closed before him. There was also a half-empty espresso-sized porcelain cup beside the book. Leaning forward, Deliah pinched the edge of the hardcover book and opened it.

Reading:

There are tunnels or nodes. There are intersections of two and of many. They may be people, they may be places, but no matter their form; they connect this universe with the next. The stronger the connections, the closer we are to the center of all things, to all times and all spaces.

People are the strongest connections. People may be the strongest of all connections.

Apparently bored, Deliah flipped the page:

… the Apple is an open doorway into each of you. It is a way to carry a connection with you, to communicate with all of your selves, the way I am communicating with another self right now. Most people cannot live with it. It is too much to see all of the possibilities that exist in each moment…

Next page:

… links are broken. Too few people seek understanding to temper their intelligence. The metaverse spirals; and swinging out away from the center is our universe, your universe. The threads that tie us together are thin and stretched. It is a normal behavior though; it is not special. The metaverse continues regardless, and sheds the universes that are nothing more than a dying burden pulling from the core without giving anything in return.

Those who only exist in one place in time, they are the ones who experience no significant change! They are the empty vessels who have become the entropic...

Next:

... has happened before. This is happening right now. This will happen again...

Several pages of repetition later:

... choosing to stay connected. The universe, your universe, our universe, isn't done yet. There is hope...

Deliah began leafing through the book quickly, looking for the end, for the last notes of the handwritten scrawl that was all over every page. Finally, he arrived at some blank pages, and turned back a few until he found a few more scratches of the pen.

The books don't do anything.

It's not the books.

It's the room.

It is me.

I am in the room.

I am in the room.

Don't answer the door.

He is close.

Run.

Deliah's eyes burned intensely, amber irises swallowing pupils and whites alike until only gold existed. Beneath the line 'Run,' was one more line, "Sorry, Deliah, you just missed me."

He stood and slammed the book shut, leaving scorched fingerprint marks on the cover. His skin blackened to coal and heat gradients appeared around him. The painting behind Deliah began to melt and smolder, and it caught fire as he walked away from it. The books and shelves caught fire moments later as he walked out of the room.

In the living room, he stopped to put his hand directly onto the door that was wedged into the Wall. Smoking almost immediately at his touch, it only took a few seconds to catch fire. The couch and the balcony lit up suddenly as a breeze blew in through the open entrance.

Deliah walked to the entrance and looked out into the street as the blaze rose up behind him. There was no one in the street. There was no sign of Mark. He strode back across the living room into the kitchen, spreading flames with each step.

In the kitchen, he moved without hesitation to the porch door, which exploded out into the yard at his touch. Again, there was nothing to see.

Deliah stayed until the house was burned completely to the ground. It was dusk when he finally left.

FALLEN SPIRE

Spies

Seventeen

She only had one goal, and tracking Ezechial and his little friend wasn't it. Still, they were headed her way, so she had followed them.

Eve had spent the last couple of days in the Spire looking for some kind of explanation for what had happened to everyone within. She suspected that whoever killed the Leader was likely tied to whatever or whoever was responsible for the rest of the dead and missing. The Leader's assassin was really the only lead she had and she hoped it would lead to answers. So, she had searched through everything that Leader 127 was working on.

There were files that contained references to the Laterali prophecies, Ezechial, Apple, Joshua, and of course, Eve. Most of the information she already knew.

The prophecies were being scrutinized by a variety of departments, and in particular, there was a request for the Leader to devote a resource to tracking an aging Laterali who had recently seceded. Ezechial was put on a Watch-list for the Collective at that time, and as a courtesy to the Laterali, the Collective would protect him if he got into any kind of trouble. That was actually how Eve had decided to contact him in the first place, so there wasn't much more for her to gather.

The files on Apple were nothing new to her either, for the most part. There were several reports and requests, however, that had apparently languished with the UpperS, eliciting some castigating messages from the Leader. Of course, those messages had been about as effective as the original reports.

She knew more about Joshua than anyone, so reviewing files on him offered her little at first, but then she'd stumbled onto his activities since she'd lost contact with him; The Collective hadn't been handling him well. She'd been unable to stifle her smile throughout the multi-stream of the diner and the attempted apprehension on the street. It seemed that she was right about him after all, although that was pretty much where her understanding of him ended. Still, she was drawn to him, compelled to help him survive and succeed. She didn't know exactly what it was he was supposed to do, but she knew it was important.

Having spent many hours with almost nothing to show for the effort, she finally found a lead when she queried who else was reviewing the same sets of files that she had been. Eve didn't even have to add up occurrences; Secretary Deliah was on all of them. She was not able to unlock any of his personal documents when she searched directly for him, but Eve was able to access some of the other files that he'd been reviewing, those she hadn't known about already.

Most of the documents were indecipherable; but nevertheless, they consistently connected the dots. Deliah linked all of the players that she knew, including Gabriel and Marius, as well as Demetrius. They were all there. Also though, there were references to a unique room at the top of the Spire—a communications structure from what she could gather—critical to Deliah. There was an odd mix of science and prophecy in several of the files, all of which were beyond her comprehension. While she understood the jargon, it was more that the writers seemed baffled by their findings, and more speculative than specific.

At the highest level she could access, she found all of the references she could to Deliah and the number was smaller than she'd hoped. The accounts had tapered off completely over the last couple of months, which had piqued her interest. Even though she couldn't actually view the documents, she saw a steady decline in correspondence of any kind coming down from the Upper Spire, and although she couldn't be sure—she assumed there were circulations of communication completely out of her reach—she noticed that there was less and less visible review across the board. Leader 127 wasn't alone in sending formal complaints up the ladder. It was difficult when no one above you was listening.

Eve stared down at her unwitting companions. Ezechial and the boy were moving pretty slowly, but they still seemed to be heading to the center of the city, so Eve continued to follow. They stopped to eat and Eve was surprised by the way Ezechial seemed to cater to the child. It wasn't obvious, but there was something strange in his demeanor, an inexplicable deference to the boy. Watching them chopstick their way through a bag of noodles together, she ripped open a gel pack and enjoyed a refreshing blast of fruit-flavored meal ration. It was delicious and immediately made her feel charged and ready.

She crouched down low and away as the boy looked skyward. Eve moved back from the ledge of her skyscraper, though she was confident that the boy couldn't see her. Instead, she was worried that Ezechial might follow the boy's gaze up, and she knew that Ezechial could see things with his natural vision that most couldn't see at all. She wondered how much the assassin could hear, and with a flicker of her eyes, adjusted the volume of her hearing, filtered for human voices. She only caught bits and pieces of the dialog below, but thought it was odd that the boy seemed to be convinced that Ezechial still hadn't eaten enough. It was less a disagreement between the two, and more a misunderstanding, as though Ezechial had no idea what it meant to eat as the boy understood it.

There wasn't much spoken between the two beyond that, and Eve still couldn't discern the relationship, or guess at Ezechial's interest in the child.

Sitting there waiting for them to get on the move again, she tuned them out and thought over her plans. That was when she realized why she was following them; she didn't have a plan.

There was Deliah, but there were no leads to help Eve find him. She hadn't even been able to find a picture or video of the Secretary, his profile was too neatly locked up. It was difficult to imagine. Everyone in the Spire had a three-dimensional profile pic, even the UpperS. If Deliah was still alive he probably had answers about the Leader, the demons, and whatever had happened to the Spire, but she might not even know it if she found him.

Access to so much information, but not the information she needed, she wasn't any closer to understanding how the world had been flipped upside down. Eve knew that she'd seen more of the big picture than she ever had previously and that she'd fit the pieces together correctly. The problem was that the big picture was a big mess.

She looked back out over the edge and found the two still sitting quietly. Ezechial seemed to be staring off into space, and the child was playfully moving around him. He was energetic, demonstrating anticipation, like they were on their way to somewhere he desperately wanted to go. The boy's face—all of his visible skin— was snowy white, and even though she couldn't see his face, she was uncomfortable looking at him. So she let her eyes fall back onto Ezechial, an attractive and powerful presence, even if it was somewhat diminished then. Something was wrong with him, and that was another reason why she continued to follow them. She respected Ezechial a great deal. Although she didn't entirely trust his motivations, or share his beliefs—whatever they were— she would try to help him if he needed it… if she could without compromising herself.

Eventually, the two packed up and moved on again. Eve stuck to the rooftops as usual. She leapt across the gaps between buildings, and descended when the gaps were too great. She did her best to avoid detection, moving through the shared foundations of the buildings instead of running out into the street. It was an effort to stay with the two, but not much of one, so she kept at it.

She felt a sense of destiny as she followed them—maybe that was just the way Apple made a person feel? Eve didn't know. She was still alive though, and still had things to do.

It started getting dark, and Eve knew she needed to get inside. The demons would be out soon. She was compelled to hide somewhere that would not draw their attention. She had seen very little evidence that the demons had entered buildings out this far from the Spire, but that didn't put her off her guard. It was strange, though; it seemed at some point that the people had all gotten out, or the demons had gotten lazy. As far as she could tell, they mainly stuck around the heart of the downtown area. The strike zone of the attack she'd partially witnessed the night before seemed to confirm that as well.

She thought about it briefly, about what she would find when they got closer to where the Collective had felled the buildings and dropped troops. It was only coincidence that she'd seen any of it. Last night, she had gotten up to walk around a bit after a lengthy reading of secure files. She'd gone to the Wall and set the entire display to show her favorite view of the ocean. At first, the scene was serene and calm. After only a few minutes though, a Carrier had flown into view. Erratic and distressed, it eventually crashed down into the ocean not far from shore. She had looked closely, but seen no sign of survivors as the airship sank below the surface. She'd searched other perspectives until she found the fires of the fight burning, and the last of the mini-copters crashing.

It was that attack—having exhausted her abilities to decrypt the archives—that pushed Eve out of the Spire. She wanted to investigate the strike zone; if there was a reason for the Collective to be there, maybe she should be there, too. She had taken a variety of gel packs and left the building. The ferries weren't running of course, but not knowing who was looking, she thought it was better to walk the bridge anyway. It wasn't long after she'd made it back to the city proper that she'd spotted the odd pair walking together.

Ezechial and the boy took longer than she would have liked to find a spot to hole up for the night. She looked up at the sky turning purple and felt a breeze kick up strong from the east. It was going to be a windy night, though the clouds were few.

She watched as the boy—fearless or heedless of the demons— confidently went from building to building, before eventually deciding on an apartment building with an art showroom on the ground floor. Surprised, she saw that they didn't go in the side stairs up to the apartments, but instead, went directly into the business. Ezechial didn't protest, or even lead the way in, inciting even more curiosity in Eve.

Not able to see much more of the two after they left the street, Eve decided to move in closer. First though, she needed to find a place for herself. Across from the art showroom was a cheesesteak place with a few residences above it, and she found a small place within that would do well for the evening. Folding up her clothes and leaving them behind, Eve activated her dermal cloak and went down to the street.

She observed through the front window of the showroom for several minutes. Her eyes were thick and dark, filtering spectrums of electromagnetic energy to improve her fine vision. Unfortunately, there wasn't much to see, even as she magnified. Accessing her IOL interface, she dumped the Mantis filters, opting instead for a sensory array detecting heat and scent. Sensitive, but not sensitive enough from where she was standing, and with the security glass between her and her targets, there was no way for her to gauge their positions. Her infrared feed was direct from SENTRy, a satellite hook-up through the hive, which was down, so she was going to just have to get closer.

The entrance to the showroom opened before Eve left her vantage. The boy was coming back out. He looked back inside for a minute, seemed satisfied, and then ventured out onto the sidewalk on his own. Not wasting any time, the boy immediately started off down the street away from her, continuing in the direction they were previously headed.

Even though she hadn't seen him for long, she felt uncomfortable about the child, and the image of him lingered in her mind long after it should have passed. It was something about his face, or his expression, that made her want to look away from him. She waited until the small boy was far enough down the street that she could confidently move across the street undetected. Quickly looking inside the showroom, she still couldn't see any sign of the assassin.

She couldn't imagine how the small child could have done anything harmful to Ezechial, but how had he snuck off alone? She felt an urgent need to know more about the strange boy, so instead of entering the showroom she followed him.

Fully rested and fully stocked, she didn't hesitate to spike adrenaline as she evaluated the surrounding buildings. She tuned in and cranked her senses, gathering and compositing information to form a flowing vision of the world that was rich and alive, even in this desolate city. Her nails grew long and sharp to aid her grip as she free-climbed the outside of a building. She was aware of some pain in her shoulder from where the Leader had attacked her. It seemed so long ago now, and although her arm wasn't as strong as it should be yet, she found it comforting to remember 127's power, and held to that.

She kept the boy in sight as she moved. The dermal cloak that she'd designed and implemented was a mix of known technologies. Her version was undetectable by the Collective, but was a little slower to adjust to dramatic changes in light than the alternatives. The few working cathodes and streetlights rippled through her silhouette as she passed by them, but for the most part, she was silent and invisible.

After several blocks, Eve sensed several demons congregating in the street not far ahead of the boy. They were milling around, aimlessly. There were more than she wanted to fight—maybe more than she *could* fight—and the boy was walking directly into them. The demons hadn't caught the boy's scent yet, but they would, and Eve had no idea what she would do when they did. The boy was unnerving, and the way he interacted with Ezechial was more than a little suspicious, but he was still just a boy. She'd had to make tough decisions before, but leaving a child to die wasn't one of them.

There was another smell mixed in with the demons—a human—and one with hints of the Spire in his clothes. Eve was overwhelmed with anxiety at the thought of a human being standing among the demons. Compulsion gripped her to run and protect, to flee, to kill… but there was no attack. The demons wandered around the man like they were his pets. She focused and calmed her initial reaction as best she could, but a creeping sense of fear remained—not for him, for herself.

Fear wasn't enough to keep her away. She spiked chems to keep her hands steady and her mind focused, and then climbed to a position above them. The man met the boy in the middle of the demons, who had become docile, kowtowing to the two humans. Despite her chems, chills ran up and down her spine as she watched.

Exchanging no kind of greeting Eve could understand, the two stood closely together facing one another.

The tall man was dark-skinned, and wore the garb of the Collective. She found herself wishing he was Deliah, and then wishing he wasn't. If it *was* him, the little hope she had to get answers from him was dwindling. And what if he was responsible for 127? A man who could control demons certainly seemed capable of hurting Adam, but what chance did she have of exacting vengeance against him?

The two spoke in hushed tones, and even with her hearing maximally enhanced, she couldn't make out the words from her vantage so far above. There was wind carrying away their voices, too, making it even more difficult for her to understand what was happening. Eve had spiked everything she could to overcome the urge to run, but still the need to get away, far away, was buzzing along her nerves. It was a force of pure will that allowed her to make her way down the side of the building.

As she descended, the stench became much stronger than she'd expected. Her perception took an extra second to catch up as she slowly turned her head to the side and saw the pair of eyes staring back at her. Two sinister, jaundice discs floated in a shadow-shrouded, emaciated face.

Eve was stone-still. Her heart pounded thick and heavy with the weight of the moment. The demon stared right at her, and then focused through her; it didn't quite know *where* or *what* she was.

Eve could smell the demon and feel the currents of wind deflected by its body. She kept her breathing slow and silent, and held herself rigid to the wall.

The demon wagged its tongue around, lazily at first; it randomly sampled the air, and then its tongue suddenly became rigid. The demon must have picked up something from her because its temperature raised a few degrees, and the grey tongue began probing the air and wall purposefully.

The space of a Glass between them, the demon licked Eve's bare hips and smiled. Or at least, if she lived to tell the story, she would say that it had smiled.

It howled and the metal-on-metal grinding whine broke the silence. The sound almost pierced her eardrums before her autonomic responses turned down her enhancements. She lashed out with a handful of laser-sharp nails cutting up under the chin of the smiling, howling demon, silencing it instantly and setting it free of its grip on the building.

The body fell, and the reaction of the crowd below was almost simultaneous; the man, the boy, and the demons jerked up in unison. The demons smoked into the shadows and the boy and the man stared up to where Eve had been only a second before; she was already racing along the wall, heading up to the roof. She didn't think that either of them could have seen her, but the demons—shadowy and smoky like she'd seen Ezechial sometimes—were running up in a wide net, and would find her whether they saw her or not; they'd run right over her. So she crawled, ran, and leapt at GEaRed-up speed, with no consideration for distance or height.

The world swam past her in a dream as endorphins and serotonin helped her cope and accept the insanity of what she was doing. Eve was well-trained though, and she was thoroughly experienced with the effects of all the chems that were being dumped into her system. She could see everything and she felt as though she could fly. The chems allowed her to move without doubt, where hesitation might have cost her; but her senses were sharp enough to keep her from choosing purely fantastic and fatal actions.

She'd left a scent trail. The wind and the jumping from building to building would slow them down, but they would find her eventually. She continued at high speed until she got to the apartment across from the showroom. Gathering her stuff up and bursting a gel pack in her mouth, she dressed quickly and fled the building.

Out front, she thought about Ezechial. He might have answers, an explanation for the boy. Maybe the child was supposed to be his captive instead of his charge? There were so many possibilities. Sampling the air and listening closely, she decided she had time.

Eve entered the showroom carefully, quietly. No reason to set off alarms, security, or Ezechial. Most of the artwork on display was structural, physical. There were a variety of materials, both natural and synthetic, bent and shaped and stretched into all manner of compositions. Eve worked her way around the various pedestals and backdrops until she arrived at a set of offices at the back that were partitioned by free-standing, translucent Walls. Ezechial stood with his back to Eve, his shirt off at one of the Walls. The left half of his back was black, almost necrotic-looking. She would have looked closer, but Ezechial was already using the Wall to examine himself.

The display was a magnification of three separate sections of Ezechial's skin, all which showed a branching network of cracks going from greater to lesser density from his left to his right. The lines were three-dimensional, as wide as his skin was thick. He stretched his arm carefully, as though the lines were razor wire wrapped around his skin, and then he saw something that surprised him as much as it surprised Eve: the cracks faintly and briefly glowed the way near-dead embers brighten with breath.

Ezechial reached up and touched the Wall, navigating a variety of panes, but apparently not finding what he wanted. The Hive was down, and along with it, all connections that were not independently maintained. It looked like he was searching for medical archives and was coming up with nothing.

He looked down at his arm one more time, and then flexed until it hurt, and then more. The branches along his arms and across his back and chest burned to life. The glow was no longer faint, but a bright red. A long, thin note sounded out, and where the Wall was displaying the cracks, the Wall itself cracked.

Eve stepped back cautiously. She couldn't understand what she was seeing, but she was sure it wasn't good. One of the free-standing Walls suddenly shattered as though it had been punched. She took another slow step back.

"Ezechial?" a whisper as she placed her hand on the hilt of her sword.

He turned toward her. She saw the red elements lighting through the skin of his chest, and those steely, grey-blue eyes staring back at her. Then he looked at something, some article of clothing that he had folded over the back of a chair. It was a couple of meters away from him, but she recognized his look and she knew his weapons.

"Ezechial, don't." A moment of sympathy, "What's the matter with you? What happened?" But he slid, leaving a trail of greasy-charcoal behind him, and made for the chair. Eve was already gone.

She didn't look back, she just ran.

FALLEN SPIRE

Pathfinding

Eighteen

Slick with sweat, Joshua ran hard through the streets of the city.

He'd had to wait for the demons to disperse after their cannibalistic frenzy. It wasn't for several hours that Joshua had an opportunity to escape. Tentatively, he'd stayed within a nearby building for a while, ransacking apartments for food and clothing. When he was confident that the demons were out of range, he took to the streets and pounded the ground, legs burning from the effort. There was nothing chasing him, but he ran anyway, straight for the Spire.

There were lights and signs in the road, pointing and explaining where to go, but for all their colors and lines, they depicted nothing. Weakened and feverish, Joshua looked at them differently. He realized they had only been helping him go around in circles. He needed to connect the dots himself, to give their directions meaning; he had to have a destination to give them context.

He didn't know for sure that the Spire was where he should be going, but there were breadcrumbs he'd dropped into the watery echoes of his fugue. The crumbs were dissolving, softening around the edges and losing their details, but still they all pointed him to Eve and Ezechial, and inevitably, the Spire.

The Spire loomed in the distance, close enough now that he knew he would be there soon. Joshua looked at the black obelisk, standing like a shadow of a building cast against nothing, and wondered about it. He had always just accepted the building as part of the landscape, and given it nothing more than a casual glance now and again. Even by the light of day though—it occurred to him for the first time—the tower was intimidating and ominous. It was several seconds before he realized that he'd stopped moving. He was standing idly, staring up at the top of the Collective building, mesmerized by it.

Joshua shook himself and stretched.

He focused on the road, and started again. The businesses on either side of him could have been anything, the facades were so lacking in character. Without people present to define them, the buildings were just tall boxes stacked neatly beside and on top of one another, blocking out the sky.

Joshua could see the shadows of people who had been there without consciously trying anymore. The disturbances were simply there all the time, pushing apart the lavender dust that was thick in the street. But there was something wrong with the impressions, because they seemed to have lost a dimension; they seemed thinner. The dust flowed through them instead of around them, making them difficult to see. Some were more defined than others, but most were wispy phantoms, shapeless and faint disturbances in the dust. As he ran, he saw one impression after another float away, as if a breeze had swept them up and carried them down the road together.

No matter what was wrong with the majority though, there was something dramatically wrong with one in particular. Joshua first saw the strange figure crawl out of a building and into the street. It flickered sharply and its edges were jagged, but it looked like a man on his hands and knees. Moving slowly, Joshua came up beside it to look closer.

The impression it left behind was breaking and reforming, but it was definitely a short stocky person crawling on the ground, on hands and knees. Joshua scrutinized the figure, trying to understand it as it jumped ahead of him, apparently walking, and then broke apart and appeared behind him, crawling again. It seemed to move forward and backward in time, always along the same path, but never making up its mind where it should be.

Joshua followed it, becoming more curious with each jump the man made. And the jumps were increasing in frequency as they travelled together. Sometimes the being would dissolve, but other times it would shatter or collapse when it disappeared. When it reappeared, sometimes it came with a flourish, pushing back the dust dramatically, but other times it just faded in subtly with multiple faint impressions merging. It came close to Joshua, appearing almost inside of him, startling him even though he knew that the man wasn't actually there in that moment.

The frequency of the jumps became so rapid that the man appeared to be in many places at once, and Joshua had to stop moving in order to follow the movements and not become dizzy. And then all of the motion stopped.

The background of faint impressions moving along in their lives stalled out, even as Joshua's lavender ash continued to swirl and fall. The man—the once crawling, sparking, schizoid figure—was standing in front of Joshua holding back the ash strongly. Joshua thought to himself that the negative space the man held was almost solid, and he was compelled to reach out and touch it. Before he could stick his hand into the impression though, the man faced him as though he could see him. The ash swirled and fell around his head and shoulders, making the man appear to be cloaked, except when he moved, creating eddies that would show his arms or his legs.

Joshua walked around the figure, and the figure spun in place to follow. He was close enough now to see that the figure was not only definitely a man, but short, overweight, and middle-aged. And although the eyes only appeared as blurry impressions, the man was staring at Joshua.

They exchanged curious movements, testing the truth of what each was seeing. Joshua stepped left, the man followed. The man raised a hand, Joshua mimicked. After a few more tilts, each convinced himself that he wasn't insane, that he was seeing something real.

The man spoke. Joshua imagined he spoke anyway, because of the movements of his face and hands, but if there was sound, Joshua couldn't hear it. After several seconds, Joshua raised his hand to the man, indicating that he should stop, "I can't hear you. I don't understand."

The man starting talking again, apparently not caring that Joshua couldn't hear him. Joshua thought the man might just be talking to himself after a while, because he seemed to pause for responses and then go on. Joshua tried again to interrupt, raising his hand, waiting for a break in the man's gesticulations, "I need to get to the Spire."

The man stepped back, and then sadly nodded, seeming to accept the inevitable, though he didn't seem sure he agreed with it.

Plaintively, the man stepped back again. Joshua stepped toward him slowly, hands raised, but the man just began shaking his head. The man's posture metamorphosed from sadness to fear and then he ran, almost through Joshua, in the direction opposite from where they were previously travelling. Joshua turned around to follow, but before he could take a step he saw the man had already stopped a couple of meters away. Along the ground, a shadow moved toward the man, burning up the falling ash as it went.

The burning shadow raced by Joshua and joined others coming from every direction. The man cowered and shook, looking as though it took all his strength to stand there. Joshua couldn't understand what was happening. He wanted to help the man. He wanted save him from whatever the shadows were doing to him. Joshua stomped on the shadows, but seemed to do nothing to them. The burning ash reminded him of the demons, but these weren't the demons he knew.

The burning edge of the shadows grew up and took shape, outlining large beasts with long grasping hands. They reached for the man, and through the man, and he writhed in agony at the touch.

Something flew at the man, dark and low. It might have been a bird, a raven, but it was moving too fast for Joshua to tell what it was. When it hit the man, he fell to his knees, and Joshua heard him scream. He heard him scream and he ran to him.

The man was shaking on the ground and Joshua stood beside him, trying to protect him from whatever would come next. But the flights came in waves, moving up and down as they flew, and they crushed the man down to his hands and knees. Joshua was hit too, and he heard them, voices shrieking out words he couldn't comprehend. The noise grew to a cacophony as he was inundated by flight after flight. But Joshua stood through it. The voices weren't for him.

He looked down at the man and saw him turning slowly around, and although he couldn't be sure it did anything, Joshua tried to help him. He leaned down and attempted to hug the negative space that was the impression of the man. Trying to lift him up a little, he thought he felt the man's weight shifting in his hands. The waves of shrieking sounds diminished, and the grasping wraiths gathered at the man's heels, but no longer touched him. Finally, after crawling for a bit together, the attack seemed to be over.

Joshua whispered into where he thought the man's ear would have been, "Rest." He didn't know why he said it, but he did. And the man responded with a mumble, "… the top of the Spire," before collapsing, and the ash rushed in to fill the void.

The impressions of the people of the city began moving again, but Joshua barely noticed.

Eventually, he stood up and started on his way again. Once in a while, he thought he caught a glimpse of the fractured man, but most of the time he could not be sure.

As he travelled, the impressions of people became fewer, and the stains on the streets and sidewalks increased. There were no bodies mixed in with the wreckage of the buildings and vehicles, not even bones. The demons had feasted on everything, and left nothing behind. When Joshua finally arrived at the shore, the sidewalk was as black as the asphalt, but not as black as the Spire.

Walking the bridge slowly, Joshua didn't take his eyes off the building again until he entered it. The lobby was full of ghosts, the impressions so dense that it was hard for Joshua to distinguish one from another. The demons flowing out looked no different than the people—so many people—coming and going. There were a few that stood out even in the masses.

Joshua was sure that he saw the fractured man. He saw him entering and leaving, breaking more with each step. His time came and went, and then Joshua saw her. Eve's presence was distinctive; she might have been there that day. She was defined as clearly as he remembered her from the bar where they'd met. There was no fluctuation as she floated through, and Joshua thought he could even see her feet touch the ground. She had also already gone. But another already had his attention.

The new impression was stronger than the others and as he walked, he swallowed them up. His presence absorbed and erased the others. He walked up to Joshua and stopped, and then he seemed to grow and thicken. At the edge of his silhouette the ash started to burn. Each particle of dust that touched him sparked, and then ignited two more. The fire spread rapidly, accelerating to the extents of the enormous lobby, immolating all of the dust, and with it, all of the people.

The room was empty and quiet, and Joshua was completely alone. He walked up to one of the elevators, it opened for him, and he got in. On the Wall of the interior, the accessible floors stopped at eleven.

Joshua closed his eyes. He filled his lungs slowly, as his veins turned black and bulged beneath his skin. If his eyes were open they would have been opaque and blue, broken down the middle by pitch slivers.

The fractured man appeared in his mind. He knew the man had been at the top of the Spire not long ago. He imagined him there, and how he'd been able to get access to the floor, how the floors must have all lit up for him and then he opened his eyes. There were no lighted floors on the panel. The doors opened.

The lobby floor was gone; instead, there was a long unlit hallway, at the end of which was a large wooden door. Joshua stepped out and behind him, the doors of the elevator stayed open, offering some light, though he felt he didn't need it. The wooden door, something behind it, was tugging at him so strongly that he could have found his way to it blindfolded. The pull grew stronger the closer he got, but never so strong that he couldn't walk away.

At the door, Joshua placed his hand on the wood and felt warmth. There was also a soft vibration, as though some enormous, heavy engine was running on the other side. Joshua lifted the latch and pushed open the door.

The elevator doors finally slid shut behind him, leaving him in total blackness. He blinked his eyes several times; unable to tell whether they were open or closed. Unsure, but unwilling to turn around, Joshua stepped inside the room.

The floor conducted the same hum as the door. He could feel the vibration through his shoes. It was a soothing feeling. The room seemed to resonate with him, comforting him like a heart beating in time with his own. Still though, he couldn't hear it, only feel it. The rest of his senses were deprived as well.

He walked farther into the room—he couldn't tell how far—and sat down, crossing his legs beneath him. The floor was the temperature of his body, and it disoriented him to push against it, causing momentary vertigo. After a while, he thought he heard the door close, but he couldn't be sure, and he didn't move to check.

There was a strong sense of familiarity in the room, but he thought he was probably just filling the emptiness with his memories. When the singing began, he assumed it was only his imagination. He couldn't make out any words, but the sound was mellifluous and enjoyable. He wasn't actually sure there were words to hear, but the cadence reminded him of choral music.

Joshua listened for a long time. He never fell unconscious, but as the minutes ticked by, he was lulled into a state similar to his frequent dreamy-knowing state. His last thought before the visions appeared was that the room felt like he had on and off since taking Pez.

He saw Sara in a small town with several tents set up, and people moving hurriedly from one to another, and in and out of buildings. Some were worried and confused, while others were angry, perhaps vengeful. She spoke with a group of people, away from the rest, and when they were done talking—though Joshua only heard the choir—every one of them, save Sara, tricked into the shadows. Then she turned around and spotted Joshua staring at her hypnotically, mesmerized by her. She pointed at him and he ran.

He ran across the street, in front of car after car, headlights turned on him, drivers and passengers alike, staring. He kept running though, dodging cars and glances. There were eyes—large, luminous and cat-like—staring back from one car, so he pulled his hoodie up over his head and around his face.

A motorcycle almost ran him down, a fancy bike that he didn't recognize, but knew that it was custom-fast nonetheless. When he looked at the driver, he couldn't see anything but the silhouette of a lithe figure as streetlights and headlights alike bounced and bent around it. He kept running. He ran hard until he felt sweat building up beneath his hoodie and then he jogged. The cars were stopped, all the way up and down the streets, bumper to bumper. It became difficult for him to get through without touching them or even vaulting over them. He didn't worry about it though, because the cars were all empty, just like the sidewalk as he stepped up on to it.

He immediately walked up to the intercom of the apartment building in front of him and selected Demetrius' room, even though the building looked nothing like his. The connection lit up, but the apartment was empty. A howling sound, like an engine rattling and winding up, ripped through the choral music and Joshua turned back to the street, busy with people and cars and motorcycles and heavy construction equipment. A man—odd because he wore spectacles—leaned on a jackhammer like it was his cane and stared at Joshua. Joshua stared back, and the man waved him over with his free hand.

Joshua looked back at the view into Demetrius' apartment. Demetrius was there at the Wall in his bedroom, a woman under the covers behind him was sweating through the sheets. With a serious posture and tone, he spoke with someone. Two men walked out of the Wall with medical equipment. They put on rubber gloves while exchanging small talk with Demy. One drew back the sheets, revealing the slender red-haired woman with thoroughly freckled skin. The other man strapped a mask over her mouth and nose, while they argued about who would dress her and attach the tubes.

Standing back as they worked, Demy slouched into himself, but couldn't look away. The men held the woman between them, her arms draped over their shoulders. She was conscious, but she dragged her feet languorously, slowing them down. As they passed Demy, he mouthed, "I'm sorry," and she looked up at him. Her eyes were swirling green and blue, and she grinned as she strangled the men and pushed them down. Her skin was charcoal black as though she'd been burned badly. She stood taller than Demetrius, and appeared considerably stronger. Walking up to the frozen Demy, she put her hand on his chest and cut through his skin with her nails. She pulled out one rib, and another, snapping them off loudly.

Joshua turned around, and the construction site had grown up around him. He heard the loud snap of flat wooden boards dropping on top of one another, and straps pulling taut across them. The man with the spectacles was gesturing for Joshua to come over and take a look at the ground at his feet. The asphalt was unlined and smooth, a pool of black beneath the man.

The man leaned on a sledgehammer, as though it was a cane.

Demy was on the floor, back against the Wall of his apartment, his hands wrapped around something sticking out of his chest. A man was bent over him, arms behind his back, examining him curiously. The man was obsidian black, and he turned to face the camera, his amber eyes glowing brightly. He walked toward the camera with his hands behind his back. But there was someone behind the man walking up to Demy that the man didn't know was there, and couldn't see. Joshua saw her reach down to Demy, just before the stream went completely black. Joshua couldn't discern whether he was looking at the dark color of the man's skin or at a blank glassy display, so he stared, waiting to see if the man would move out of the way, or if the stream had died.

The ground vibrated and the display cracked. The world vibrated and the walls of the building cracked up the sides, fissures all the way to the sky. The cracks were branching red veins, glowing from within the black polished surface.

The vibration—deep and heavy—came once again and Joshua followed the cracks all the way around the inside of the cave. At the center of the room, the spectacled man held a tiny bell by a string. He gestured for Joshua to come over, and he did. The man's glasses were cracked, and behind the cracks were soft, apologetic blue irises. He pointed to the ground, and Joshua looked down.

"I opened it."

At the man's feet, Joshua could only see the perfect sheen of a black pool reflecting back. He looked back up at the man, and saw him flick the edge of the little bell.

He looked down.

Joshua looked down.

Ripples started at the man's feet, and became waves by the time they reached the walls of the room, then came back. Joshua and the man started sinking into the tarry black water. Slowly, the wetness grew up over Joshua's feet, over his knees. When it reached his chest, the water was heavy and thick, and made it difficult for him to breathe. He looked up and saw that the spectacled man was already completely submersed. Joshua reached out and strained to hold him up.

Black water dripped off the rims of his glasses, off his nose and ears, and sprayed from his lips as he spoke, "I opened it to drown us all. For me. For mercy. All of us, quietly into the dark… but you struggled to hold on."

The man was too heavy for Joshua to hold up, and the water was rising and growing thicker. For several long seconds, head completely beneath the surface, Joshua could see nothing, could feel nothing. Then, faintly, he heard the choir.

Their voices rose up and carried through the heavy water. More and more individuals joined, and strengthened the song. One voice steadily demanded to be heard above the rest. It was pure and healthy, connected and sure. It was a man's voice, one that he recognized, familiar and comforting from his past. And as he heard it, he felt an overwhelming sense that he could do something. That it wasn't too late. That there was hope.

Joshua reached out and took the bell, and felt his blood pressure rise. He felt his veins bulging and throbbing beneath his skin, and the pounding of his chest. He felt himself growing out to the edges of the ovular room. The pressure built up as the water pushed back. The heavy dark would not compress or give ground, and neither would Joshua.

He put the bell in his mouth and crushed it with his teeth. From his mouth, echoing within his chest and through his bones, the vibration went out through the water. The walls cracked and broke. As the water exploded out from the building, Joshua expanded to fill the sudden drop in pressure. He grew up against the walls and they cracked open like an eggshell. Unfurling himself, stretching himself out, he looked out over the city.

Pieces of the tower fell around him, tumbling down through space to hit the ground at the bottom. Joshua shook all of the loose pieces from his body and watched them plummet with the rest. He tested his large, clawed hands and feet, standing up on all fours, uncoiling his tail. He grasped the edges of the building, his body taking up the entire top floor, or what remained of it. His claws cut easily into the building, his grip unwavering. Unfolding his wings out from around him, he batted at the air.

Joshua jumped from his perch and flew.

The wind startled Joshua. He opened his eyes and saw the night sky all around him. He was still sitting cross-legged on the floor at the top of the Spire, but the walls and ceiling were gone.

By the light of the stars, Joshua looked down at the center of floor and saw glowing red fissures extending out from him in all directions. They grew even as he looked at them, and he stood and followed one to the edge of the building.

The view was unlike anything he would have imagined. The city was lit up by thousands of specks of light. There was a dark patch though, standing out against the rest as a place with absolutely no illumination. A sudden wave of dizziness hit him as he stood there, nearly causing him to lose his balance. With nothing to hold on to, he got down on all fours and realized he wasn't dizzy at all; the building was listing one way, and then the other. The effect was nauseating as Joshua tried to keep his balance.

A vibration—irregular and jagged—started up from beneath his hands and feet. The feeling was not at all soothing or comforting; the Spire was coming apart. Joshua stood and ran for the side of the building where he thought the elevator would be. Running on the top of the building in the open air felt exactly like he was on the deck of a cruise ship out on the open ocean during a storm; his vision disagreed with his inner ear, wrenching at his guts, causing him to lean when he wanted to do the opposite.

At the elevator, he dropped to all fours again at the lip of the shaft. There was nothing but an empty drop into the black as far as he could see. He swallowed hard and tried to focus on the here and now. So many dreams and memories were rushing through his mind, all clamoring for his attention, while the world shifted uneasily beneath him. And then, although he couldn't understand the words, he heard the one strong voice calling out to him, singing to him again.

His brother's voice was joined by the voices of all of the people who struggle each day for a way to connect to one another, to connect this universe to the next, and they resonated with him.

Joshua felt his veins thicken, but this time without heat or fever. He felt his eyes grow wide and gather up all of the light around him, so that he could see everything as clear as if the sun were shining down instead of the moon. But he saw so much more than that as all of his senses stretched out, unfettered by doubt or confusion.

Listening deeply to the choir, he found his voice, and joined them. Loud and clear, Joshua could feel each of them and he resonated with every one of them. There were so many universes so close to his; all he had to do was reach out, grab one, and hold on.

Joshua—his fingers buried deep into the cracking top floor of the Spire—grinned widely and remembered what it felt like to fly.

FALLEN SPIRE

Seeing Things
Nineteen

"Are you okay?"

Pallomor walked in on Ezechial who was standing at a Desk, staring at a display with his chest bared.

"No," gravely, as Ezechial straightened up and pulled his shirt off the back of a nearby chair in the same motion. "Did I wake you?" He didn't look at the boy.

"I wasn't sleeping. What's wrong?"

Ezechial secured his weapons harness and wrapped himself in his jacket, "I'm seeing things."

"What do you see?"

"Demons," there was a heavy weight in his voice.

"There *are* demons," the boy looked at Ezechial with a disarming concern and an almost patronizing curiosity.

"There are," Ezechial turned back to the Desk and swiped it, causing it to go dark. "And there are angels," shaking his head, "Prophecies… they are never clear, but there was a time when at least *I* was clear…"

The boy watched as Ezechial clenched and unclenched his fist, but said nothing.

The free-standing Walls around him were shattered, debris scattered at their bases. Each emitted a fractional amount of the ambient light that it would have had they not been broken. They were still powered, bleeding light out of their exposed edges, and displaying erratic patterns of colors and shards of black.

Pallomor waited through a heavy minute for Ezechial to gather himself and continue.

"I saw a friend. She was here... right about where you are standing now," he continued with calm acceptance, "I was examining my... injury." He finally looked at Pallomor, "Did you hear the Walls break? Did you hear her or see her?"

The boy offered nothing. He gave no hint as to what he might be thinking.

Ezechial shrugged slightly, "If I'm losing my mind, how would I know?"

Pallomor looked back into Ezechial's eyes with a knowing glint, but Ezechial was too lost in introspection to notice. The boy waited patiently for the assassin to work through his thoughts.

Ezechial shook his head again, "I'm even starting to think that the Prophecies are about me," he smiled softly, eyes shining, "denying it seems foolish... whether I am mad," he flexed his arm again, "sick, or otherwise."

Returning the same soft smile, "Otherwise." Pallomor continued curiously, "Did your friend hurt you?"

"No." He adjusted his jacket and came back to the present situation, to the boy. "No, she just stood there. She looked like a demon, but she wasn't a demon. Then she hissed at me, and...," His shoulders sagged a little, and he went on sadly, "I was going to kill her, but I was too slow."

"You wanted to kill her?"

Ezechial lifted himself up. Digging deep down into the heels of his shoes, he stood up tall and resolute, "Yes and no. I felt both ways at once. I hesitated to act because I couldn't see clearly. I didn't know for sure if it was Eve, or just a demon that looked like her." He walked over to the boy, "I can't trust myself."

"Trust me." There was no wavering in Pallomor's face this time, no fidgeting or strange convulsions.

"I don't know if I can," Ezechial reached out like he was going to touch the boy's head, then thought better of it, "You weren't asleep, but you didn't hear her?" he breathed deeply, and whispered to himself, "Everything is unclear."

"Would you trust me if I said I *did* hear her?" he asked as though he already knew the answer.

Ezechial hesitated, "This isn't about trusting you. You can't be my eyes and ears. If I can't tell the difference between Eve and a demon, you're not safe with me."

"You'll never hurt me," it was the confidence of absolute knowing.

Ezechial scrutinized the boy's expression. When the boy spoke confidently like that, it was unnerving. It was the same when Ezechial tried to leave Pallomor behind. He'd convinced himself that it was compassion that wouldn't allow him to leave the boy alone to fend for himself, but was that it? Maybe he didn't trust the boy.

He thought it was the wound messing with his perception, but he couldn't shake the feeling that the boy was dangerous, and here he was confiding in him.

I'm paranoid. Not a good sign.

"I might not know it is you," Ezechial held back his distrustful thoughts, wishing he had never mentioned his encounter with Eve to the boy. He wished he hadn't said quite so much. He felt spread so thin, his consciousness bifurcated, living in two disparate realities. Pallomor was his charge or Pallmor was in charge.

The boy reached out and put his hand in Ezechial's. He tugged the retired Laterali closer and looked at the cracks cutting up his forearm. Pallomor traced the branches with his fingertips. The gesture calmed Ezechial at first, but after a few seconds it disturbed him. The boy acted as though there was a kinship between them and Ezechial bristled at it.

The boy, apparently sensing Ezechial's discomfort, stopped tracing, "It's beautiful."

Ezechial pulled his arm away and slid down his sleeve. *This is madness.*

Sighing, "We should sleep." He couldn't stay up all night trying to see what he couldn't see, "I'll go with you this time." Looking at Pallomor like a child, "Was the office comfortable, or did you want to look upstairs…"

Excitedly, "Let's go to the top!"

"Sure."

Looping his small fingers around two of Ezechial's, Pallomor led them outside and around to the apartment entrance. Ezechial tricked the lock and they went up the stairs together. On the top floor, they made their way to an apartment that Pallomor chose, went in, and made themselves comfortable for the evening.

From beneath the covers, "Can we look outside again?"

Thinking he knew what the child meant, "Another forest view, or something else?"

"I'd like to see the Spire."

The apartment was small, but had the usual amenities, including a full-sized Wall in the bedroom. Ezechial walked up to the Wall and navigated the menus quickly. The city appeared, though the view certainly wasn't from the top of the building they were in currently, but rather from a much taller building. Nevertheless, the Spire was there, tall and dark, blotting out stars, and obscuring the view of the ocean. The glow from the fissures running up and down it seemed brighter to Ezechial, but he was unsure.

They watched together for a while, Pallomor tucked into bed, and Ezechial sitting at the foot as they had been the night before. Ezechial thought to himself that if he only ever saw the world through a View, he'd have no idea what was real.

He remembered the names of the survivors he'd rescued and later slaughtered: Keln, Oishi, and Naddalia. As he remembered their names, he remembered conversations they had and how peaceful but strong they all were. He had never relied on streams and news feeds to define his reality, but he desperately wished he had access to a stream from the restaurant now. If he could see the events over again, examine them, maybe he could see what really happened.

Everything was upside down for him. Media could not be trusted as memory, so he had trained and practiced to see more with his own senses, to understand more experientially. It wasn't that he avoided technology—it was an extremely useful tool—but he didn't allow it to replace skills he could cultivate for himself, skills that he could always trust. But he couldn't trust himself now, and the desire for a recording to substantiate and make real what had happened back at the restaurant was powerful. It was probably the first time that he really understood the allure, and why the technology was ubiquitous. If he couldn't trust his eyes, he needed to manufacture some to see for him.

The boy's eyes were closed, and he looked peaceful. Ezechial took the opportunity to examine his own body again. He snuck off into the bathroom, which was tiny but serviceable. This time, he stripped down entirely, and although he didn't have as many perspectives available to him on the small Wall display, he was able to see in enough detail to note that the growth had slowed considerably. Although a few branches found their way across his center line, most were held to his left side. His left leg and arm were completely covered, and the left side of his chest was thick with the flat black elements, thinner as they spread right. He wasn't sure the branching would ever recede, or what other permanent effects might result, but he thought that at least for now, it wasn't getting worse.

Ezechial stepped into the shower stall and set the temperature before activating the two-minute cycle. The glass door sealed shut as the atomizers kicked into life, filling the space with a surprisingly floral mist. There were three vertical atomizing poles—one at the center of each of the walls—so the stall was filled in seconds. By the time the cycle ended, he decided that he liked the smell. A blast of air swirled up around him, and then down, and the door clicked open.

Stepping out, he examined his body again before getting dressed, but there was nothing new to see. He walked back into the bedroom, his trained eyes adjusting quickly to the change in light as the bathroom brights turned off automatically as he left.

Pallomor was standing at the Wall. He looked surprised, which was a look Ezechial hadn't seen before on the young boy's face. Ezechial walked over to see what he was seeing.

The top of the Spire was gone.

The jagged edges that defined the new top partially blocked the view of the floor that was now exposed. Even with their somewhat distant View, Ezechial could see that more pieces were breaking off and tumbling down toward the earth below.

Then, the Spire collapsed.

It was faster than either of them would have imagined. The tallest building in the city collapsed in on itself, all the way to the ground. The black dust that it created exploded up into the sky, steadily billowing up, higher and higher. A second later, Ezechial felt the force of all that mass falling. The apartment was vibrating. He wasn't sure he heard the sound of the actual fall or if he just heard their own building shaking as a result, but it was both deafening and shocking.

Ezechial ran out of the bedroom, out of the apartment, and down the hall to the rooftop access stairway. He leapt up the stairs and slid through the exterior door as soon as there was enough room for him to squeeze through. Standing on the rooftop, he found the Spire—or where the Spire used to stand—and watched as the dust expanded slowly, growing up and out over the small island and over the water.

The night sky was perfectly clear. There was a bitter wind buffeting his face and eyes, but Ezechial was unbothered. He didn't think. He could only be there. Then, from out of the bottom of the ever more slowly expanding dust cloud, a very large and dark figure appeared. It flapped its wings once, creating visible eddies at the tips as it accelerated out of the cloud. Then it shot up at incredible speed until it was above most of the buildings that Ezechial could see. It sinuously leveled out, and swept itself down into the city where it flew in and around buildings until Ezechial lost sight of it completely.

It was a dragon, but not at all like what he'd seen Joshua do before; it was *real*—not ethereal or insubstantial—but a physical creature. Still, Ezechial thought it must be Joshua… it had to be him.

"Interesting." Pallomor was standing beside him.

FALLEN SPIRE

Soul-Searching

Twenty

"Are you okay?"

Mark had hacked his way to the top of the GlassTech building, only to find Marius despondent and drinking at his Desk. Mark wasn't expecting Marius to be in the GT building; he figured Marius had gone as far away from the city as he possibly could. He chose the GT building because it was well-equipped and seemed like a good place to plan out his next move. Regardless, he found Marius in his office with a bottle that looked a lot like he did: empty.

"I'm fine." He sipped from a glass filled with milky green liquid. There was a tiny sieve-like implement, a box of sugar cubes, and a lighter beside the old and empty bottle.

"You're sure you're okay?" Mark had to ask twice. As far as he could tell from his access to the system earlier, the top floor had been closed off, both from within and out. The system reported that no one was inside; nevertheless, Mark had arrived and found Marius inexplicably imprisoned in his own home.

"I was happier when *you* weren't here, but yes, I'm fine," the Wall in front of Marius was dark. Mark was only aware that the display was running because of an occasional, indecipherable movement, as though there was something dark moving against an even darker background.

Marius' speech was clear, though Mark could tell that the man was less than sober. His usually confident demeanor was replaced with a jester's version of nobility, apparently in mockery of himself. Mark pressed on, "What are you doing?"

"Does it matter?"

"Probably not," Mark thought there was little point in explaining what he'd learned from his time in the den. He knew that he didn't understand all of it, but he thought that Marius didn't care to understand any of it.

"Then why. Ask. The question?" increasing sharpness with each word.

He was sure that Marius didn't give a damn, so Mark stood up to the Ghost this time; he needed to work and he needed Marius' equipment to do it. "If you aren't going to help, you need to leave me alone. I need your Desk."

"Apparently, everyone has control over me... except me," he sipped, "You guys need to get together, though, and decide where you want me. It's annoying, being shuffled around like this. Because," he leaned intimately, "one soulless bastard to another, this is bullshit."

"Marius, what the fuck are you talking about?"

"You weren't visited by an angel of death?" he waited, "Tall, mean fellow, with dark chocolate skin? Striking amber eyes? Beautiful man, really," he paused again, "No? Well, he stopped by—you know, before I was even here—and we had a nice chat. He removed my credentials from existence. No amateur there. You'd like him. He mentioned something about me being soulless and alone." He gestured emphatically at Mark, "But look! He was wrong! I have you."

"I haven't seen anyone like that, but someone came knocking for me at Bradley's," Mark decided to take a risk and explain a little bit to Marius, or at least try, "I didn't see who it was, but I was warned..." unsure how to continue, he eventually decided to just say it, "by another Mark, another me. Many of me. I learned how Bradley's quantum communication works, or something he stumbled onto anyway."

"Oh please, tell me Mark, what ever did you learn? Talking to yourself must have been so terribly informative. Did you find a way to cure whatever disease is rotting your brain?" he became more agitated with each word and leaned ever closer to Mark, "Well, I learned something, *Mark*. Let me tell you. I'm in the middle of an un-fucking-believable nightmare and unless you can wake me up, I don't give a fuck!" Spit followed the last. Apparently satisfied with himself, he took another sip.

"You *are* alone," Mark felt sorry for him, "but you don't have to be. And you don't have to leave either. I mean, just give me some room. I need to see if I can contact the Collective, and… and look into all that stuff about Bradley's den you don't care about."

Marius twittered then laughed. It was harsh, and without joy. He got up from his chair overly quickly and knocked it back into the Desk. Gathering up the empty bottle and his paraphernalia, as well as his half-full glass, into his arms, he walked to the door of the room. The door took much longer to respond than it should have— at least a whole second—eliciting an awkward kick. The motion caused him to drop the little silver sieve, and he looked at it with disdain as he walked out of the room.

Mark immediately sat down at the Desk and went to work setting the Wall up to display as much as he could. He had his own satellites that he hoped he could still reach, but he still wouldn't be able to access anything held outside of his network. It had never occurred to him to attempt to hoard duplication of all the data in the world, and right then he thought maybe he should have. It would have been easy enough for him to set up a system to mirror… but that was past. He needed to stay focused.

He needed to stay focused if he was going to remember all that he'd learned. Marius was at least partially right; he had spent a lot of time talking to himself, and it was pretty enlightening.

The metaverse.

The connections.

Mark wasn't sure the picture made sense, but he saw the metaverse as a spiraling column of universes, collections of time and space, and his universe had drifted too far from the central core. He knew from his time in the den that the connections had not been maintained, and that accounted for the drift. So many disparate images were conveyed in an attempt at explanation; so many similar, but different Marks—maybe not all were even Marks—had been trying to contact each other, trying to solve and describe the model together. The connections seemed like gravitational threads among people. Within a single universe they added a kind of mass, which helped increase the magnitudes of all of the connections across universes. The inter-universal threads had their own values as well, pulling and holding stronger when they were maintained. There was an abstract notion of distance, which affected all of the forces. A person could be both literally and figuratively closer to another, and that had been the crux of Bradley's research: quantum-level communication, disregarding distance as we understand it, but nonetheless affected by proximity. In the den, Mark was *close* to the others. It wasn't enough though, for one man to be close. This universe needed more connections, closer connections, stronger connections, to survive.

He had no idea how to create inter-universal connections, but Bradley had done it with the den. Mark thought it was a kind of node where multiple quantum aspects converged. He thought if he created more of them—or maybe found more of them—then maybe they could be used to keep this universe from flying off into nothingness. They were drifting farther away from the axis and if they went much farther, Mark thought they wouldn't be able to get back.

One man though? On one planet, in one galaxy? Maybe I am *losing my mind*, he couldn't help but wonder. But he had to try.

The Collective had obviously known a lot about Bradley's research, even if Mark had never gained access to all of the information. And they were still alive and attacking the demons. If he could make contact, maybe he could find out more, or find out how to access the Bradley files, assuming they had some emergency protocols in place.

Mark didn't understand the demons, so he didn't think about them except to recognize them as a threat to his plans. He knew they were related to their universal drift away from the core, and if he could get everything lined back up, he thought they could be dealt with.

He went to work at the Desk, diving in with both hands. His hands were agile, and he was able to bring up numerous displays with visual information about the city to begin attempts to usurp other satellites and conduct a worldwide search for the Collective, and eventually, for nodes. Mark began combing through Marius' files and access, dropping in several tools that he used for navigating data at high speeds in unfamiliar environments. At some point, almost unconsciously, he secured a look at Bradley's house—the only node he knew existed—because he would need to start breaking it down for analyses soon.

It was shock that stopped his fingers. Then, slowly, Mark removed overlapping displays until all he saw were the remains of the house. Remains were an exaggeration, because there was nothing left but a hole where the house should have been standing. Scorched earth and burned-out houses at the perimeter, Bradley's home was a crater in the earth. Even the street had melted and hardened again.

"Bradley's?"

Mark jerked back from the Desk, startled. Marius had come back into the office only to retrieve the little implement that he'd dropped earlier, and was walking over to the Desk when he spoke.

"Yes," settling his hands back onto the Desk, "Unfortunately, yes."

If Marius had thoughts, he kept them to himself. He silently watched as Mark navigated the available perspectives. Mark—his environment fully in place—began several video-analysis programs. Both current and deduced temperatures appeared on the display, along with material analyses.

"What's that?" Marius pointed to his original display, which was behind several others at that point.

Mark brought the stream into the foreground and they both watched as the Spire fell. The GlassTech building shook violently and they were both stunned. When the shaking diminished a few seconds later, both were still staring blankly at the display.

There was no way to process what they were seeing. The Spire had fully collapsed into itself, and the dust and debris of the destruction were floating up into the atmosphere, obscuring an already dark view. As Mark started to come to, as he finally realized the magnitude of what he was seeing, he wondered what it meant for his universe. It could be a good sign, it might be bad. He didn't know.

As if in answer to Mark, "I never liked that place."

Mark was unsure how to respond, or if there was anything to say at all. He felt as though he couldn't move, as though he was incapable of controlling anything, including where he was sitting, or where his hands should be.

Eventually, Marius leaned in and manned the controls. He zoomed out a bit, making it easier to see the entire island and where the whole Spire originally stood. Seconds later, Joshua flew out through the dust, and again the two men were dumbstruck. There was nothing to say or do, so they watched silently until there was nothing more to see.

Changing Course

Twenty-One

At the top of a tall skyscraper, Eve watched the city for any sign that she was being followed. She was fairly confident that she'd lost the demons that were hunting her, but she wanted to be sure.

Not a shadow moved, but she continued peering into the night regardless. She looked for demons, she looked for Laterali. Her robe billowed around her in the wind, flapping occasionally around her rigid body, even though it was tied down around her waist and chest.

Ezechial was an adversary not to be taken lightly. She'd witnessed the assassin firsthand, and had no reason to get into a fight with the man. But there was something wrong with him. He recognized her, while simultaneously mistaking her for someone, or something else. And she knew he meant to kill her when he dove for his Devil's Tails. He didn't uncoil those serpents unless he meant to feed them. She ran before giving him the chance. He was slower to react than she remembered, but that just confirmed for her that he was sick or hurt.

The markings on his chest were foreign, strange designs that she didn't recognize. Maybe they indicated some kind of illness or infection, or perhaps something else she couldn't imagine. She couldn't be sure; she only knew that the markings weren't there the last time she'd seen the Laterali assassin.

And the boy... there was no way he was to be trusted. Every part of her body ached with a need to get away from him. She thought that Ezechial should have felt the same, but apparently he felt something else. He treated the boy with deference just like the demons had, which unnerved Eve. She felt like she wanted to save Ezechial, or kill him. The two results might have been the same.

Instinctively, she'd dug her long nails into the concrete wall along the roof of the building. The wall was a barrier to keep roof-walkers from falling off, but Eve just used it for greater height and vision.

It took a conscious effort for her to calm down and retract her claws. Thinking about Ezechial didn't help. She smelled the air and thought about how much her life had changed since she betrayed the Collective. She also considered the likelihood of her suffering the same fate as those who lived in the Spire if she'd ignored the impulse to help Joshua. But the consideration was as irrational to her as deciding between love and friendship.

Thinking about the past, the consequences of her choices, and the alternatives wasn't something she'd done much, until she was assigned to the Apple project. In that moment, Eve suddenly realized the real reason why she craved heights. It was true that heights gave her a vantage that helped her tactically, but the impulse was deeper than that rationalization. She climbed buildings and observed the city from up high because it was peaceful from that distance. Everything came into stark perspective, backgrounds and foregrounds. Able to sift through what really mattered and what was just temporary confusion, she'd always been able to find answers from great heights. There were no answers tonight though, only questions.

Her world was upside down.

The fissures in the Spire began radiating brighter than before. Eve couldn't be sure at that distance whether she saw new cracks forming, or if the fractures were always there and had finally become visible. The tower was cut from top to bottom by crisscrossing, jagged lines, but it held together regardless.

The intensity of the bright red cracks increased until Eve thought she was looking at an enormous shard of volcanic glass, lit from within by super-heated, liquid metal.

The top of the building expanded and contracted, like the floors were breathing together. The cracks in those upper floors widened with each inhale and narrowed with each exhale. Finally, the seams burst, and pieces of black metal were pushed out into a vaguely spherical shape. They were suspended for a brief moment before giving in to gravity.

The secrets of the Upper Spire were revealed to the world, but as far as Eve could tell, there was nothing inside. The dark metal of the building was replaced by the black of night.

Eve looked on, unafraid. She teetered for a moment on her perch though, and dug her claws into the concrete wall. Her balance was fine; it was the Spire that was swaying. The entire building had listed a little to the right and then back to the left.

Then she saw a man running along the top floor. He fell, then got back up and ran again. She recognized him—the way he moved— and then she zoomed in and immediately recognized the odd eyes. The last time she'd seen him like that was through her SPYder, recording him as he fought off the feverish effects of Apple.

Joshua! She peered so hard she thought she could touch him with her vision. Not able to guess, or even consider why Joshua was in the Spire, or how he'd gotten there, Eve plotted her way back to the building. The fastest route would take her toward Ezechial, the boy and the robed man, and the pack of howling demons she'd escaped not that long ago. She'd have to risk it.

Even though she'd burned some of her resources fleeing the demons, she'd already mostly recovered. A quick glance at her intraocular display revealed her that she was close to clean after the adrenaline and serotonin spikes. A GEaRS check showed that all of her enhancements and replacements were responding positively.

With the exception of her shoulder—she'd been trickling proteins and emollients directly into the muscle for weeks—her body was ready for the full spectrum of augments. She slipped her fingers into a pocket within her robes, pulled out a gel pack and sliced it open with one of her fingernails before placing the small pouch into her cheek.

Dopamine, serotonin re-uptake receptor blockers, cortisol, amphetamine, hydrocodone, oxycodone, paracetamol, and adrenaline: over the years she'd mixed up her own doses, release orders, and durations in order to achieve various effects. To get to Joshua quickly, she needed balance, burst strength, enhanced visual acuity, and a little insanity.

The surge hit her, and like always, no matter how serious or life-threatening the situation, she smiled. It was playtime. Her ego quieted down into nothing more than a whisper in the background. The usual chatter of what needed to be done next and what had happened before was completely extinguished, leaving only the present.

Eve fell off the side of the building. After a second of free-fall, she began running down the building, pulling herself to it with her claws. She used window sills and pipes, and dragged deeper to create a gradual arc in her descent, slowing herself as she approached the ground. Turning herself upright as she controlled her fall, she was hang-dragging her claws and jumping more than falling. By the time she hit the street, she was moving fast and level, having transitioned to a full run.

Obstacles appeared, but she saw them as parts of the terrain. At that speed, she had to believe that there was always another safe place to land her feet, even when she couldn't see it. She ran along the tops of cars and buses, and used walls of buildings whenever she needed. As she rounded a corner, she had to dig in hard, and cut at a hard angle to the right to avoid crashing headlong into a jackknifed truck.

As she covered the distance to the Spire, she moved faster, but covered less ground. Eve wasn't tired, but the orderly lines of vehicles had turned into wreckage, and although she continued fearlessly, she had to evade and recover as often as run forward. An overturned car teetered beneath her as she landed on it; when she tried to jump from it, the hood crushed and gave in, shrinking the distance of her jump to less than a meter. She stumbled into another car, but rebounded off to a near wall and carried on.

Suddenly, the world started to shake. There were buildings, light posts, and vehicles that were barely holding their positions from when the first wave of demons had rolled over the city, and they all began to settle. The wall of a building slid off beside her and ate up half of the sidewalk as it kicked up massive amounts of debris and dust. Eve's terrain had become slippery with the vibrations, but she scrambled to keep on.

She broke free of the last proper block, buildings behind her, a small green before her, and the bridge to the Spire. But there was no Spire. In place of the building, floating out over the water and obscuring more than half of the bridge already, was a billowing cloud of black dust. Eve continued to the edge of the green, where there was a safety wall before a cliff-like drop off to the water below. She jumped up the wall with only one touch and a graceful lift.

The black dust cloud continued to grow, but slower, as though she'd missed the peak of its greatest force. She found it beautiful and strange. Peripherally aware that her fascination was primarily the result of her spikes, she couldn't help but think how amazing, how awesome it was to see the ocean-scape. And the black cloud of debris and dust was a ghostly apparition floating over the corpse of the building, the spirit of it unable to leave the body. She was enchanted.

Inside the cloud, something disturbed the dust. There was a strong breeze blowing off the water, climbing the wall and cooling Eve's sweating face. It might have been the same breeze pushing around the cloud, but Eve saw something dark and solid through the more diffuse billowing mass. And then the enormous serpentine head appeared. Its wings swept down, catching and pushing a ridiculous volume of air, and launching it forward to clear the smoky mass entirely.

Joshua flew straight toward Eve a second longer and then flew up
and slithered into the sky. His body was long and slender, covered
by mottled deep blue and green scales that might have appeared
black to anyone without Eve's light-gathering vision. He had two
pairs of wings. The front pair was tip-to-tip as wide as he was long.
They were broad and thick, like a peregrine's, and like the back
pair, they were covered in silvery feathers. About half the size of
the front pair, the rears began just before the front pair ended,
overlapping a little. The rear wings were more diamond-shaped, but
other than that, and the difference in size, they were like the front.
She had noticed thick, scaled arms tucked in beneath the shoulders
of his wings, at the sides of his chest. Eve saw the enormous paws
at the ends of each arm as Joshua pulsed up and down over her
head, and wondered how much damage he could do with the talons
buried within.

He was magnificent.

Eve watched as he looped in and around the buildings dreamily.
She wanted to follow him, but before she could start running, she
heard the metallic howl of the demons. They weren't close, but she
was decidedly up-wind from them. She had the instinct to hunt
down the sound and investigate, but as more voices joined the first,
she felt more like finding someplace to hide and watch. Neither
reaction was helpful.

Slinking down the wall, she prowled the green stealthily, listening
and watching the buildings with all of their ominous hiding places
staring back at her. Demons were in all of the windows, poking
their heads out of every alley and around every corner, or so she
imagined anyway.

When she was sure she had a clear path, she started to run again.
Eve headed to the city center. It was probably just her primal lucid
state, but she felt that overwhelming sense of destiny again.

Eve followed a circuitous route, moving carefully and slowly.
She still had hours before dawn though, when she made it to
the outskirts of the blacked-out heart of the city. The demon
presence was stronger than she'd ever felt before; sulfur and heat

were pervasive and oppressive. She found a nearby inconspicuous apartment building and bundled herself into one of the inner-most rooms, not only for safety, but to get away from the heat. Even with more than a couple of meters of concrete, insulation, climate controls, and complex air-filtration systems, the smell and the heat still managed to affect her room. The filters were cooked, so she consulted the Wall. Systems were shutting down and requesting repairs.

The diagnostics display on her intraocular lens showed that her systems were doing the same. Nothing that couldn't be scrubbed clean in a few hours. Eve curled up on the bed and went to sleep.

FALLEN SPIRE

Raising Hell
Twenty-Two

Deliah walked along the tracks of the subway. He was unhurried, stepping lightly between ties and sometimes walking along the rail. Agile as he was, he appeared to stick to the ground wherever he stood, unwavering. If he had stopped on a single tip-toe, it would not have looked any different than seeing him stand with both feet firmly planted underneath him.

The tunnel was dark. The trains had been disabled since Deliah unleashed the demons on the city. The bioluminescent blue glow of the tubes running along the center of the ceiling and along the walls at waist-height offered some ambient light, which increased in spots via focusing lenses. Several series were empty from unrepaired leaks and breaks over the years. Deliah didn't need any light though, so the occasional stretches of darkness were not an impediment. He stopped at a glowing pool that had gathered from a break in the ceiling lights. The bacteria responsible for the glow had either encountered a new food source or mutated, because the pool had turned purple except where the fresh drops of viscous fluid landed. It only took seconds for the fresh drop to be eaten up completely. Deliah stepped around the bi-colored pool and moved on.

The temperature steadily increased as Deliah walked, but he was not fazed by the change. Not a bead of sweat formed on his brow, or on his polished bald head. Even when the temperature exceeded one hundred and forty, he appeared cool and comfortable. It was hot enough that in some areas the bio-lighting pipes burst from the increased pressure, so that Deliah continued in almost total darkness for a few hundred meters. Eventually, a ruddy, diffuse light became apparent, but before he arrived at the source, the tunnel shook powerfully.

The quaking lasted for several seconds, shaking loose some debris from the ceiling. The rattling of the rails against the ties and spikes sounded almost like a train was right there on top of him, running him down, but Deliah was steady. In fact, he was the only thing in the tunnel that appeared unaffected by the deep vibration. He stood easily, unshaken.

A booming sound followed the shaking and the event ended abruptly after that. Deliah did not move for several seconds, seemingly far away in thought. The only change was in his eyes, which were now large and round ambers. Eventually, he closed his eyes and continued.

Deliah veered from the main track off to the right into a one-track tunnel. He followed a soft curve in the smaller tunnel for quite some time, the ruddy light gradually casting austere shadows at harsh angles. Deliah's shadow followed him like the tail of a great cloak, darkness behind him against every surface. The shadows began to move on their own, scuttling along in various directions, but mostly staying close on his heels.

The tunnel opened up to a great expanse of subterranean architecture. The ceiling was high and a rough hole was bored out of it all the way up and through the street above so that the night sky was visible through it. The walls of the room carved out an immense cylindrical volume of space, more than sixty meters in diameter. There were artisanal touches to the room, including green marbled tiles and carved stone bricks. The floor might have also been crafted, but it was difficult to tell because only the lip of it still existed around the perimeter. There really wasn't a floor anymore.

Heat gradients roiled up from below, distorting the architecture with a liquid movement of air. The room was bathed in a muddy red glow. Deliah walked up to the edge of the hole and leaned over, looking down into the depths of the heat. At the bottom, meters below, was a swirling maelstrom. Bright scarlet lightning streaked across dark grey clouds so thick they were liquid. Peering down through the storm was disorienting because it appeared endless, but it also had a surface. It was a pool of heavy hot metal, charged and translucent, mixing energetically with the walls of earth that contained it. A chunk of earth broke off and was swept into the storm, where it burned brightly for a moment before bleeding into a smear, scarlet lightning sparking from it to the walls.

Deliah erected himself gracefully. Several shadows slid in from the tunnel behind him and the black pools began to boil and churn. Shades began to break through the surface tension, their wraith-like bodies swimming around in the air, but still tethered to their shadowy pools. There were other forms in the pools, though: large and cat-like beasts charging at the surface, but never breeching.

The shadows and Shades flowed around Deliah and around the lip of the maelstrom. A body fell from above and hit the surface of the maelstrom, sending ripples through it before it was digested and extinguished. Another dropped in, and another. Then a gray-skinned hand appeared at the edge nearest Deliah. It dug into the surface and hauled the slick, hairless body to which it was attached, up out of the pool. As it rose up and stood fully, it was taller than Deliah, well-muscled and slavering. A Shade passed into it, and it jerked back its head violently, letting loose the tell-tale metal-on-metal shriek of a demon. It scaled the wall easily and ran out and up into the night.

One after another, slowly, the silvery claws appeared at the edges of the maelstrom. Boiling shadows flowed endlessly into the room and into the demonic bodies of the horde.

Deliah leaned over the edge of the bottomless hole into the maelstrom. The surface of the pool had risen several centimeters. He watched as the ruddy gaseous liquid swirled and burst, and charges arced from cloudy smear to bloody smear.

FALLEN SPIRE

The frequency of bodies and Shades eventually slowed and Deliah left the same way he'd come, out through the tunnels and back into the world. Dawn was close and he wanted to see the sunrise.

Self Help

Twenty-Three

Mark gathered information. Sitting at Marius' Desk, he watched
and navigated as many overlapping streams as he could handle.
Several were text consoles, but the language display was a kind
of shorthand that few others could have understood, and even
fewer could have read at the speed that Mark did. He picked the
important bits, skipping most of it, and answered prompts when
they appeared. Multiple windows flashed and flickered, brilliantly
dancing before his eyes. Some of the streams appeared only for
a frame, but that was enough for Mark and his multi-threaded
consciousness.

There were displays showing Bradley's crater, the fallen Spire, the
city as a whole, and the GlassTech building. The last was a paranoid
precaution against the return of Deliah. Marius had divulged more
specific details about his recent interaction with the man from the
Collective at Mark's insistence. Mark didn't have time to comb
through the compromised security system, and he was unwilling to
trust it, so he kept a display dedicated to the top-down.

Mark found working cells of networks and invaded them. His
tools, like his satellites, were hidden in the system. He sifted data
for anything that might give him a clue as to where the remaining
Collective might be gathered. Mark was diligent about being

discreet; not wanting to tip off Deliah and the Collective that he was looking for them. He wanted to know their intentions before contacting them.

Mark described his work briefly to Marius, who was looking over his shoulder at an unobtrusive distance.

"Deliah was from the Collective, but he's certainly not working for them now," Marius had replaced his absinthe with water and he took a sip, "We won't find them together." He was disheveled, but uncharacteristically unwilling to do anything about it. His hair was unkempt and the stubble on his face was more than he would have ever allowed normally. "Deliah was... one of my clients... the only client who remained out of my reach throughout our business together. He was always one step ahead of me. If he doesn't want to be found, you won't find him. If you think he's still looking for you? After Bradley's?" continuing with strong resolve, "It's probably too late."

"No reason to believe he isn't still looking... but, what else can I do?" Mark turned away from the Desk and rubbed his eyes. He'd done nothing but stare at the Wall for hours. Finally, he looked up and focused on Marius. He raised his eyebrows, "You're looking healthy." Mark meant it, but his words came across sarcastically, regardless.

Marius stared back at the remark with patronizing tolerance and said nothing. He sipped more water and waited.

For as long as Mark had known Marius, or even known of him, he had never heard of him lacking a composed countenance. The Ghost rarely went out into public, but when he did travel in the world, he presented himself with conscious intention as untouchable business class. He was far from presentation now. Mark thought the haggard look suited the man. He was like a hungry and tenacious animal. It seemed like a more genuine portrayal—an accurate projection of the man, not the Ghost.

Eventually, Mark shrugged and went back to work at the Desk. Marius continued looking over Mark's shoulder, not really trying to follow everything that he was doing, but observing nonetheless, and gleaning whatever he could. Mostly, he watched the video streams. They were easier for him to understand and he found he could easily filter out the multiple text overlays as noise. Even if the text scrolling by had been in English, Marius would have been hard-pressed to do much with the information. It was outside of his area of expertise.

Mark was linking up to satellites outside of his clandestine set. He was burrowing past their defenses in order to obtain more feeds, and at the same time, searching for the Collective archive. The search was not going well.

The Hive had been disabled, but the data was still out there. The expansive network existed in clusters all over the world, and there was even a local cluster built exclusively for archiving. He didn't question the integrity of the physical storage, or the redundancies, his problem was getting access to them.

Mark didn't know *where* anything was because his programs did everything for him automatically, surreptitiously. Network traffic supplied all the 'where' and 'how' to traverse the Hive, but now, there was no traffic to follow.

So, Mark decided to search everywhere.

He accessed large silos around the world, powering them up, and sifting through their data. He was building a multi-factor search key to accurately identify the Collective archive when he hit it. Without a key, the magnitude of data would be impossible to search. But, he couldn't even test his key against a known Collective databank. So, with a combination of logic, and guess and check, he struggled on.

At the same time, Mark was trying to find the remaining Collective. He waited for another call to action—anything with human chatter—to light up his listeners, but there was nothing so far.

"What's that?" Marius indicated the Wall, non-specifically.

"Huh?" Mark cycled through all of his streams at seizure-inducing speeds.

Dizzy, but patiently, "The city view. Pull it to the front."

The stream of the city, a map-like top-down, came to the center of the Wall. Mark made the window opaque and expanded it. "What is it? I don't see…," he drifted as he thought he saw movement. It was dark and difficult to see anything. His other views had night vision, but not this one.

"Can you get closer?"

"No. This sat only has the stock camera," he shrugged, "It wasn't intended to do more than store and link." After a moment, "I could blow the image up, but the missing bits will be filled in algori…"

"Please don't."

Mark couldn't tell if Marius was asking him not to explain, not to talk, or not to blow up the image beyond the actual visual data available, so he did none of the three.

They stared together a while longer, but Mark didn't see the movement again and thought it was just a trick of his imagination. He was itching to get back to his key construction, and to evaluate the hits from his previous attempt. When he turned to face Marius to tell him that he needed to get back to work, he saw a look that made him stop.

"What is it, Marius?"

"There are people out there."

Mark gazed into the window and thought he saw movement again, doubted it again, and then he was sure. He blew out the image a little, not needing any kind of definition, but to see the movement without losing it. "People? Or demons?"

"It's not the Collective," Marius held his stern look at the display, trying to bend it to his will for more information, "They're moving too slowly."

Hands going to work at the Desk, Mark ran one of his multiple utilities and lines appeared, "Velocity vectors." The lines moved and changed length, and sometimes winked out completely, but a pattern emerged regardless. A few short lines were all moving generally toward the center of the display, while the longer lines appeared to move outward from the center. All of the short lines terminated at the origin of the longer, faster moving lines.

"The blue lines represent an adjusted scale for easier reading. All of them are below five kilometers per hour."

"The yellow vectors are significantly faster... not just a little faster," Marius' inflection suggested he understood, and was just testing the statement.

"Well, more than the comparative length would indicate, but yeah, more than twice as fast, and some of them..." Mark's fingers slid and tapped on the Desk, stopping the stream, "move very fast apparently, even if it is only briefly." He circled two long red vectors, "Definitely not human."

"They could all be demons."

"I don't know. Maybe? But something is definitely happening right here," Mark wiped the screen clear of his highlights, and displayed the last several minutes of video simultaneously, overlapping the frames and displaying the vectors.

The image was a starburst with an obvious center. Just then though, the display's opacity dropped to 30 percent, and a flashing dialog appeared, prompting a response.

"Found somebody," urgently, proudly.

Mark flashed a text display that told him everything he needed to know, but left Marius in the dark. Then they heard a woman's voice, "... handle it. It was suicide...," garbled for a bit, "... partial information only. No idea what hit the Spire...," noise.

Pulling another satellite display to the front, Mark pointed to an area just outside the city, "I'd guess it's a reconnaissance team reporting back. That attack went pretty badly... We're losing the signal because whoever is transmitting is on her way out. They're using dedicated short-range communications..."

"Can we reach them?" interrupting quietly.

"Maybe? I'm connected to several relays around the city. They're all remotely configurable.... and most are capable of transmitting and receiving at that frequency…," Mark paused, trailed off into deep thought, and then continued, "Yes." He was confident. He faced Marius, skeptically, "But do we want to reach them?"

"Yes."

"What should I tell them?"

"We're here to help."

Contact

Twenty-Four

"I have a message for the Leaders," a woman with brown eyes made wise by smile lines. Lesha was barely forty, slight of frame, and less than one hundred thirty centimeters tall. Dark shoulder-length hair framed her tan, freckled face. At a glance, her body might have disguised her strength and agility, but her graceful movements and posture revealed both.

"They're meeting with the Laterali right now, and asked not to be disturbed," the high-ranking C.O. who was posted as the door guard offered the information as an advisory, not a dismissal. Amo was younger and equally slender, but taller than Lesha.

The business district of the outer borough was busy, even before dawn. Low-level Collective Officers and civilians were in the street organizing supplies they'd gathered throughout the night. They moved with purpose and spoke sparingly, but everyone contributed.

"It's important. I was contacted by two survivors located deep in the city. They want to help us," Lesha's words were visible as her breath condensed in the air. Her voice suited her well, a silky timbre rounding the edges of her serious intent.

"Contacted how?" curious, not skeptical, Amo stepped toward the entrance to the office building.

"They've managed to reconnect some local systems, brought a remedial network online. They were listening in, heard my chatter as I reached the outskirts, and said hello," Lesha followed the younger woman respectfully as she slid open the door and they went inside.

The two inner guards nodded at their superior as she passed, and watched Lesha closely.

"They want to help?" Amo strode confidently through the lobby, opened an interior door, and entered the office proper. They were in a hallway with doors on the near side all the way down to the right and left. Directly in front of them was a room defined by Walls, glass all the way around. Inside, several men and women stood in conference. One was fast at work on the far Wall, but whatever he was working on couldn't be seen from the outside; it looked like he was finger-painting with invisible ink.

The two women continued together around the conference room. From inside the Walled enclosure, a few eyes followed their progression, and one woman smiled at them briefly.

"Yes. They already identified an area of unusual activity. Said they were going to continue activating and connecting networks, and gathering intelligence. I was pretty impressed with what they knew."

Amo stopped short of the entrance to the conference room, "*You* were impressed?" familiar and teasing skepticism. The young C.O. furrowed her brow.

"It does happen, you know," Lesha managed a smile that expressed both thanks and goodbye simultaneously.

Amo touched the Wall, and a blue outline appeared to indicate the location of the entrance. She opened the door, announced Lesha's arrival, and then departed. At the lobby entrance, Amo glanced back briefly and caught a knowing look from Lesha, smiled back and waved goodbye with two fingers.

Back at the main entrance, one of the inner guards found the courage, "What was that about?"

Running her fingers through her medium-length black hair, Amo turned it blue, and sighed, "Lesha's done. Whatever she learned out there convinced her to slide."

"That can't be good."

"Well, it's tough to say what it means. Lesha plugged and scrubbed more people than anyone should," Amo drifted away in thought, and then came back, "She knew some of them... made promises, before she cleaned 'em. Lesha's going to fulfill those promises. It's who she is."

She opened the door, but before it closed she looked back in, "She might have promised *you* something," Amo winked, and the door closed.

"That's unsettling," the guard turned to his partner who raised a single eyebrow and shrugged.

"How can we trust you?"

"You don't have to trust me. Check it out for yourself," Lesha addressed the conference room full of Collective Leaders and Laterali.

The Walls were full of detailed plans and maps of the city. No satellites were feeding them though; it was all static data streamed from the archives.

A Laterali stepped forward, and she addressed Lesha directly, "I mean no disrespect. It is just that the weight of your position has always been a burden deserving of certain, uh, dispensations. Those allowances have made you more than a few enemies, and worse, made you beholden to specters."

A Leader spoke up in agreement with an edge to his voice, "We scrub people on purpose... to erase them. But you, you persist. I don't want to commit the Collective or the Laterali to anything..."

Lesha interrupted him gracefully, and in a room full of the commanding elite she held her composure, "You're making this personal, which is understandable, but not helpful right now." She continued calmly and firmly, "Move trusted units into the field to solidify communication with the civilian contacts at the GlassTech building. You can decide for yourselves what to do next."

The conference room was silent for several seconds, windows on the Walls flashing for attention that they wouldn't receive.

"I'm sorry, I have to go. I have a promise to keep."

"The nature of which you won't divulge?" A man at the back.

"You know the answer to that."

A woman, who she could tell was Laterali by the way she moved even though she wore civilian clothing, "What would you do? With all of your secrets and all of your knowledge?"

Lesha took a moment to consider and then spoke clearly, "I once had the privilege of meeting one of your greatest Leaders," she gestured toward the Collective side of the room, "and one of your most skilled assassins," toward the Laterali side, "I heard them both say something to the effect that in war you never have time to choose between battle and retreat. You're at war *because* time has been taken from you. The decision has already been made and you're just unwilling to admit it."

She felt her words sink through the room, and when they hit bottom she walked to the exit. "This fight is already happening, I'd fight back before it's over," Lesha, opened the door and left.

Living with It

Twenty-Five

Pallomor walked ahead of Ezechial as usual. There were four lanes in each direction on the main thoroughfare. Ezechial had avoided it previously, but it seemed fine now. Everything seemed fine now.

The two had left the roof of the apartment complex not long after Joshua had flown out of sight. Ezechial immediately understood that they were continuing to the center of the city, and it didn't bother him at all to get moving. It was the wrong time for sleep anyway, and the boy didn't seem to need rest at all.

It was still dark, and the farther they walked the fewer the sources of light. Some were broken out, but many blocks simply had no power. Ezechial found the growing darkness comforting. He felt at home within the blackness. In fact, he even felt strangely more at ease with the boy. He would have expected Pallomor's skin to glow like the moon in the low light, but instead, he seemed to absorb whatever ambient light existed.

Ezechial stopped checking his thoughts, and just let them go. Probably another result of the perpetual shadow he was walking into; he felt as though it didn't matter that he was irrational at times, or unable to see clearly. Actually, his doubts about his clarity of thought and vision were ebbing along with the waning light. It helped that he couldn't see the cracks on his arm anymore.

The branching lines had stopped growing at the point where they split his body in two; they appeared thin when they weren't glowing red, like their width was buried into the thickness of his skin. He knew the lines had spread onto his face as well, but hadn't seen them; he felt them. The infection seemed to matter less now that the tightness in his muscles had gone away. He couldn't even remember the pain and he was confident his body would be deadly responsive when he needed it.

They stopped. The boy turned around and looked up into the assassin's steady grey eyes and smiled. It was a genuine smile, without edginess or confusing quirks. Ezechial knelt down and Pallomor placed his palm again on the stubble of his cheek, on the infection-scarred side. It was a warm and soothing touch.

"Are you feeling better?" genuine concern.

Ezechial nodded his head forward and back slightly, a subtle affirmative nod.

"Good," he lowered his hand and looked up into the night sky. Even the bright red of his lips seemed to have turned grey. His eyes were pits of blackness, open and taking everything in.

Standing up, Ezechial followed the boy's gaze to the sky. It was a beautiful night. The steady, salty breeze filled his nostrils and elicited an even deeper inhale from him. He had noticed the changing temperature, the environment warming as they walked, but right then he enjoyed the polarizing effect of the breeze against his back as he faced the warmer air ahead of them. He imagined in a few blocks the effect would be gone entirely, ephemeral, like all things.

"You need to eat."

Pallomor had said it before, too often. Ezechial felt uncomfortable each time, thinking that the boy was seeing him falter. But, he didn't feel weak or tired. He couldn't imagine what the boy was seeing in him.

"I'm going to watch," the boy spoke plainly. Then, as though he was Ezechial's patron, "Don't worry about me." Ezechial felt some pangs of regret and anxiety, uncertain for what he was being prepped.

Pallomor turned and ran to a building—V&B Financial—and opened it on his own. It was odd to see the child defeat the lock so easily. He would have thought about it longer, but the whining and grinding began, the unmistakable cry of a demon.

There was one standing alone, twice the size of any he'd seen before, not too far down the street. It slowly lowered itself onto all fours, and Ezechial thought he saw it smile. Letting loose one more harsh, ringing growl, it moved forward. And then the others joined in.

He could see them as they closed the distance. They thought they were hidden from him—he could tell by the way they moved; some of the demons were crawling up and around behind him to flank his position. He saw them all though, and he knew it this time. He knew that there was nothing outside his vision in this blackness. The darkness was his domain, and they were trespassing.

Reaching into his jacket with both hands, he slipped the clasp and grabbed the handles. The coils dropped to the ground at his feet. Ezechial pulled his hands from his jacket and flipped his wrists, sending a ripple through the long black whips that stirred them into action. They slithered out and away from him, slowly and fearlessly exploring their surroundings.

Ezechial marked each of the demons as they approached, noting their respective smells and details, so that he would know them. He would not lose track of any of them. As he tagged more of them with his senses, he stopped counting and just allowed himself to open up and see them all, focusing on no individual, but instead, seeing the attackers as a single, many-limbed organism.

His wounded Tail flicked at the ground and alternatively swept the air anxiously. Distantly, he recognized that the markings were now running up and down the length of that whip. They started to glow, and as the Tail flicked and swept, the motion set his retina on fire with brilliant trails.

There was a moment of quiet uncertainty. The demons were not expecting Ezechial's composure. His confidence gave them pause, so he struck first.

The one on the truck is ready. Ezechial slid forward, lagging the whips behind like sledgehammers, and then hauled them forward. His right wrapped the demon's forelimbs, and his left went around its neck. Ezechial pulled back as he continued forward and sheared the creature's head off. He pulled the body down and off the roof of the truck at the same time and landed there himself. Then they came for him.

One after another, they climbed, jumped, and raced toward him, toward their deaths. He dispatched them cleanly. If they met him, they met death. The more there were, the stronger Ezechial became, moving faster than he'd ever moved before, sliding through the darkness effortlessly.

The slaughter continued without slowing for what seemed like an eternity. Time stretched out for Ezechial to see everything. He was flawless, but he thought his body would have to tire eventually... *wouldn't it?*

For a moment, he thought he had become the darkness. He could feel them moving on him and through him. His nerves were directly connected to everything as far as the shadow of total darkness was cast. The moment passed though, as he ripped a demon down from over his head. He swung the demon up and over his shoulder, and down and through the roof of a nearby car. He had felt the weight of it, and knew that the rush was leaving him. He might have been one with the darkness, but he still had his body, and it couldn't fight forever.

There weren't many left, but the large one was still at the back, still smiling.

Ezechial ran, sliding through the darkness like a greasy smoke specter, whips rippling behind him in the air. He jumped onto the roof of a car and dove down toward the hulking demon. Stopping short, he snapped his Tails forward to spike the bone quills through the beast, rather than grapple with it. Missed. His whips penetrated nothing but smoky residue. It had shifted through the lightless street, just like Ezechial.

The demon lunged at him from the right, and he became aware of it just in time to avoid it. The snapping sound of its teeth clamping down on nothing was so close to him that Ezechial's head rattled. He rolled and whipped out, and the beast shifted again.

From the left, before he fully had his feet beneath him, the demon charged. Ezechial scrambled beneath a taxi, whip handles still in hand, Tails writhing for purchase. The demon hit the taxi, sliding it along the ground and over the top of Ezechial, crushing it into another car. Ezechial unwound his Tails along the ground, over his head, and looped them around the belly of another vehicle. He pulled himself out from beneath the taxi just before the demon buried it into the asphalt.

Ezechial popped up on the other side and felt the demon slip away. Two other demons ran up to him from either side, and then slowed to stalk him. He killed them both where they stood; the ends of his whips like bullets through their chests.

He looked around. He listened. He crawled through the darkness trying to find the shifting demon. There was nothing. The other demons were gone. If he stretched, he could still feel the others far away and going farther.

It was suddenly eerily quiet. His Devil's Tails wanted to feast, but he held them back. They were lying on the ground, meters of linked 'S's in either direction.

A warm breeze pushed up the hairs of his neck as though someone was breathing over his right shoulder. He twisted himself around and away and unfurled his whips, but the demon had anticipated and already moved. The whips flew by the demon's face, and the red glow glinted off its wet fangs and drooling lower lip. It reached out and caught the Tails.

The demon pulled hard on the whips and yanked Ezechial off his feet. The Tails were stretched too far, too fast, and nerve pain shot through them, echoing up Ezechial's arms all the way to his shoulders. The assassin's brain went numb from the neural flash burn, and the whips went limp as Ezechial stumbled back down to the ground.

Ezechial held his head up on his own, but his sagging arms were held up by the towering beast holding the ends of his whips. The demon brought the whips close to his face to smell and inspect them. The Tails' quilled ends flicked and snapped, but couldn't reach the monster.

Ezechial's face was flushing with blood, and the cracks all along his left side were hot from the surface of his skin all the way down to his bones. Pressure was building inside of him, invigorating him.

Tightening the whips between his hands and the demon, Ezechial tested his arms. The demon fidgeted angrily. Frustrated by the resistance, it pulled back and tightened its grip. Clenching the cracked Tail in its hand, it squeezed the end of the whip turgid, and another surge of pain came down the Tail to Ezechial's arm, driving him down to one knee. He was barely able to hold on.

The demon held the ends close to his mouth again. It flipped its wrists and bicep-curled the soft, exposed portion of the whips to his face. The ends were split apart so that the dangling bone quills couldn't reach opposite hands.

The pressure and heat continued to build in Ezechial and he allowed it to control him. The cracks and fractures of his infection opened up and he shadow-slid forward, still on one knee. He jumped toward the demon, and the cracked whip curled and looped as Ezechial fed it forcefully into the demon's mouth. The whip filled the beast's mouth and throat with thick coils.

Ezechial flicked the right Tail in a wave around the demon's forearms and neck, and thread his entire arm through the eye of the loop. He used his arm like a crank and wrapped the whip around it quickly, tightening it.

Ezechial landed on the demon's chest with his knees tucked beneath him. He looped the remaining slack of his left Tail around the demon's neck, and opened both arms wide. He pulled with his back and arms while burying his knees harder into its chest. The coils tightened viciously, trussing the demon's forearms to its face.

Ezechial continued to flex, bringing him even closer to the demon, while at the same time he pushed away with his knees. He curled his back like a cat and put his face in the demon's face. Ezechial saw the hate-filled, eerily human eyes, and his own hate reflected in them.

The demon let go of the Devil's Tails, and tried to claw Ezechial's face. But Ezechial was too fast, and held his face just out of reach. He pulled even tighter.

The grinding whine that rose up out of the demon was muffled and choked out. Ezechial bared his teeth and hissed at the demon, promising inexplicable and unimaginable violence. The freed ends of his whips snapped their quills, making promises of their own.

Ezechial retracted some of his left Tail, and the quilled end was pulled back along the path of the coils, down into the demon's throat. The coils rubbed over each other wetly, ominously, and a second later blood burst into one of the demon's eyes. The other burst with blood too, and then its face went slack. Both eyes rolled back, and the standing corpse finally collapsed.

Ezechial crouched on the crumpled hill of demon for a moment before his Devil's Tails urged him from it. They thoughtlessly sliced and carved and punched through the demon flesh until it was nothing more than a pulpy mess. Ezechial stomped one of the demon's hands and was satisfied by the damp, muffled crunch it made.

Turning and walking back to where the fight began, Ezechial left the Devil's Tails unfurled. They slurped and slid around ecstatically as they were dragged behind him. He did not stop for them, but he didn't recoil them either. His face was calm, though it was splattered sulfur and red, and heat waves roiled off his body.

Back where he began, Ezechial knelt down and let his whips continue to absorb the remains of all the demons they'd killed. Though his shoulders were hunched somewhat, Ezechial stared straightforward, expressionless. He noticed that the cracks in his body had closed back up, although there was still a soft glow emanating from within.

He might have closed his eyes. He might have fallen asleep. He had no idea how much time had passed. He had no idea how long Pallomor had been standing there in front of him.

"What's happened to me?" his own voice sounded like it was coming through thick glass.

"Nothing. You are who you've always been."

Ezechial stared into the boy's eyes without judgment, but he did not move. The Devil's Tails were coiled and clipped beneath his jacket, though he didn't remember when he'd done that. He didn't even have to check for them, because they rubbed and slid against his sides to let him know they were there. They'd never done that before.

"You have brought death with you for so long," Pallomor comforted, "that it is as familiar to you as life." He waited, looking for Ezechial to have some reaction.

He didn't.

"You're finally embracing it." Pallomor's eyes grew wide and deep, and he smiled genuinely, "I'm glad you're here." The boy wrapped his small arms around Ezechial's neck and hugged him.

Dawn

Twenty-Six

The sun rose, unobstructed for the first time. Nothing could hide within the shadow of the Spire anymore. Eve had always considered the vista from the top of the Spire to be one of the most magnificent she'd ever seen. It was her favorite. Whenever she'd had the pleasure, she felt like she was floating in blue. Floating so high up that she couldn't see the land beneath her, she could convince herself that there was no land, that only her body, and the limitless sky, and the endless ocean existed. Whether sunrise or sunset, from Leader 127's office you could see it all, take it all in at once. The view swept her away every time, made her feel whole.

Today though, she saw the sun rising up from the ocean while standing on the ground. Instead of taking her away, the view attached her to the earth, and deeply rooted her. It was just as much fantasy as anything, but she was closer to the work she needed to do.

The Spire had shown her great things, and given her strength, but it also detached her from the world. She had worked in a vacuum, executing orders and people as required. As a high-ranking C.O. working for a legendary Leader, she was given some of the most challenging tasks and knew that she was shaping the world with her actions. But they weren't really her actions. Without ever being able to see the big picture, how could she place herself within it? She'd just trusted in the Spire and in her Leader.

Saving and hiding Joshua was the first time she'd worked without the Collective's approval in her career. She was proud of herself for going forward with her plans, for operating within and without the Collective as she wanted. Eve had put all of her tools and skills to the test and believed firmly that she was in the right. If she hadn't intervened, Joshua would have been owned by the Collective. Maybe they would have dissected him, or lost control of him, but she thought whatever they intended, it would have ended badly. Considering the demons came from the Spire, she imagined the Joshua version would have already eaten the world. Although she didn't know for sure how it happened, she believed that Joshua had destroyed the Spire and her gut told her that was the first step to stopping the demons. The next step was causing her to sweat.

The heat gradients rising up from asphalt were fluid and thick. Still, she had to carry on into the increasing temperatures. She knew that she was going to find something very important at the source of the heat. It was the target of the Collective strike—although they'd missed the mark considerably—and it was where all of the demons were congregating. Whatever the significance, the heart of the city was the obvious destination if she wanted to understand more and stop the demons.

She was worried that the heat was going to stop her before she had the chance to do anything. Eve's GEaRS were reporting temperatures and she was quickly reaching the safety thresholds of some of her compositions. Full burn was out of the question. On the other hand, some aspects were enhanced. If the ambient temperature didn't rise too much more, not only would it be survivable, but her muscle tissue response would go up. If she remained hydrated, she could expect herself to be faster and more agile.

It was several more blocks, but only a few degrees hotter before she found the hole. It wasn't where she expected to find it, down a cross street a hundred meters or so. She kept her distance at first, but without her satellite feeds, she needed to get a better perspective if she wanted to figure anything out. Surveying the surrounding buildings, she picked one that would provide at least a partial view through the hole—she hoped. She knew she was near the main line of the subterranean public transit system, because it followed the main street all the way across the city. In fact, Eve knew the hole was somewhere between the 'L' and the 'T,' but she had no idea what would be down there.

A few minutes later, she was looking down into the hole that extended from sidewalk to sidewalk across six lanes. There was so little for her to see. The caved-in portion of the road went down for a few meters. Conduit, pipes of various sizes, and fluid were spilling out from the broken cross-section. Beneath that though, there was darkness rimmed by a feint muddy-red light. Eve couldn't even get a read on the depth. Assuming the hole didn't continue through the center of the earth, she'd basically learned nothing except that her GEaRS couldn't penetrate it from where she was perched. At least there was some relief from the heat at her height, but it was still stifling being positioned directly above the maw.

Then a demon clawed its way up and over the lip of the hole. She leaned back a bit, and waited. Confident it hadn't seen her, Eve leaned back over the edge again and tried to watch the beast as it ran down the street in the opposite the direction she had come. It disappeared behind a building and she looked back down the hole again. She had to get closer.

Eve lowered herself down off the roof of the building and carefully descended half the height, nearly twenty floors. Running spectral analysis came up with nothing but mud. Her GEaRS should have been able to tell her something about the heat source, but there was only superficial information about the surface materials reflected in her IOL display.

She hugged herself close to the building as another demon surfaced. It clawed its way up a building on the far side of the hole and eventually went out of sight around the side of it. Eve hesitated for a while longer, not wanting to be found out before she could see what was down there.

Eventually, she decided to climb farther down and stopped only ten stories up from the street. The Leader's robe customized to her body and flowed around her, revealing every contour as her muscles flexed and held her to the wall. The outfit was designed for the rigorous training and exercise of the elite Collective, and it worked extremely well in the field. It held close to her when she needed, went loose when she didn't. And somehow, the material rarely caught on any surface. Eve knew she should just cut it off and activate her cloak, but she hesitated. The robe offered protection, of course, but she also just wasn't ready to take it off yet. Emotional decisions were rarely good, but she'd been making them a lot lately, so she went with it and stayed visible.

Directly beneath her, she heard footsteps. The building to which she was clinging opened up at the ground floor and spit out a person. She watched as the man slowly approached the hole, apparently oblivious to its existence. He got closer and closer and showed no sign of stopping. Eve had no intention of sacrificing her position for the stranger, and in the forefront of her mind, she didn't believe the man would just walk off the edge. It simply didn't occur to her that it was a possibility.

The man walked off.

He didn't scream.

Eve didn't hear him hit bottom. She didn't hear anything.

There was a brief flash. And then it was as though the man had never been.

Eve stayed tight against the wall and waited. She couldn't make any sense of it. When the demon rose up from below, she only watched and wondered. After it was gone like the others, she decided to risk the street.

Crouch-walking up to the edge of the hole, she placed her feet carefully, making sure she had firm ground. She looked down and saw the maelstrom. From her position, she couldn't see any walls or identifying architecture beneath her; she could only see red, clouded with mud, swirling like a storm beneath the surface of a lake as thick as oil. Dry hot air exhausted from the hole and reminded her of her escape from the Net.

She pushed herself up and away from the edge and saw another man—larger in all ways than the previous—walking toward the edge. *Fuck it.* Not wanting to watch another person fall in, she ran over to him. But she didn't have the effect she thought she would. The man was not startled by her presence, or even remotely interested in her. It was as though he saw through her. She recognized the look, and had to check to see if she was cloaked. Of course she wasn't, but, "Sir," an urgent, harsh whisper. Eve put her hand on his chest. It was fever-sweat chilly, but she held her hand there regardless. "*Sir,*" added desperation to the whisper.

"There is nothing you can do for him."

Eve dropped to all fours and instinctively activated her dermal cloak—though her robe was still plainly visible—and several spikes, careful not to use anything that she had previously thought unwise in the heat. The tall, bald man standing not more than ten meters from her did nothing to hide himself. She uncloaked like she was releasing a tensed muscle.

It was the man she'd seen talking with demons, and with Ezechial's strange companion.

Her scans went to work immediately—passive and active—and the strangest thing she found was that he was normal. Blood pressure, heart rate, and the surface temperature of his skin were all completely unaffected by the heat. His GEaRS didn't show up on her scans either, but that wasn't entirely uncommon among the highest ranking Officers.

His posture suggested he thought she might be skittish, so he didn't walk toward her. Instead, he pointed helpfully toward the man she was attempting to save, "He's already dead."

Eve glanced out of the corner of her eye and saw that the man was already walking over the edge. The moment was drawn out torturously by her heightened awareness. She only learned each of the ways that she couldn't cover the distance in time to grab him, to help him. And then he was gone.

"Eve, you're responsible for all of this."

Not able to think of any response that made sense, she shifted herself into an attack posture while contemplating escape routes. The man was a complete unknown to her, "You're Deliah," to stall for time. She needed to run. He knew her and probably knew most of her capabilities, which was a pretty extreme advantage. But she felt the truth… the decision had already been made for her, as the Leader would have said.

"I am," he seemed to weigh his next words carefully, "I meant what I said. If you hadn't hidden Joshua from the Collective, and ultimately from me, this could have been avoided."

Talking to him couldn't possibly give him more of an edge over her, but maybe she could learn something, "*What* could have been avoided?"

"Consciousness."

Hive Minds

Twenty-Seven

Everything was in place. Mark had been able to network components throughout the city, and the results were live streams of every square mile. Thermal imaging was in place, as was street-level audio-capture in many places. The short-range communications band was available continuously over the central part of the city, losing density from there to the outer boroughs. Mark also kept the velocity vector overlay in place; the clearest images he could gather were still 400-500 meters from the ground.

Most of the streams were background though, as Mark focused his attention on the center of the largest city in the world.

"We're sending you everything we have…," Marius spoke to the Wall at Mark's left. The responses were sent directly to Marius' ears. Though the office was easily large enough to accommodate multiple Desks and effective work stations, Marius attempted to spare Mark the noisy line. "No, it's still not clear what's happening in that area…"

Mark flipped a small console to the front and noticed that the words displayed were incoherent nonsense. Mark opened a console on Marius' Wall:

Send 2 room
v2t fail on primitive

Marius touched the Wall and made the adjustment. Garbled, static noise filled the room.

A voice came through, "Affirmative." Several seconds passed, "You... relay... directly...," more noisy seconds, "Copy?" They made out the words, but only barely.

"Once you're in range, everything will connect up... like the Hive," Marius opened up a console on Mark's Wall, front and center:

"Clean this up?"

"Source"

Mark turned around in his chair and shrugged.

"Fuck"

"Did you get that? Everything will connect up exactly like the Hive. Your systems won't know the difference." Marius waited.

"Affirmative," something followed that sounded like a question, but neither man could be sure.

Marius was still looking at Mark when he noticed a window flashing in Mark's stack. He pointed to it and Mark turned around and brought the window forward while they heard, "... gathering assets. Do *you* copy?" It was the window displaying the center of the city.

Marius noticed it a second before Mark, "Are there two people standing there?"

Noise came back across the room, and Marius quickly silenced and muted the connection, though he left it open.

Mark switched to thermal imaging. It didn't help much, but there were two bodies close to each other near the hole. One was hot, affected by the environmental temperature, but the other one was cold. *Well, not cold, normal*, reflected Mark. He immediately checked his tools to see what had prompted the window to flash. He'd set numerous trips trying to guess at what changes in the pattern would warrant inspection.

Two criteria had tripped. The first was that a slow mover—identified by minimum duration of existence, average speed, and topped max speed of less than 5kph—had stopped somewhere other than the hole. The second was the intersection of any two vectors. Both alerts specified the same targets on the display when he set them as the focus.

"I... I'm not sure...," Mark's nose was almost touching the Wall, as he leaned over the Desk.

Another trip flashed, this time it was a proximity warning for congregating vectors. Mark focused the alert and found another *normal* temperature body. It wasn't far from the other two.

Marius stepped up behind Mark and stared over his shoulder, intensely trying to put the pieces of the image together. They both watched as the blue vector grew out of the cool body toward the hole. It was brief, lasting only a few seconds, and then it was extinguished.

"Shit," Mark's fingers danced on the surface of the Desk.

"What?"

"I forgot..."

"Eve, you're responsible for all of this," a man's voice interrupted Mark.

"... we have audio," Mark finished, and then, "Eve?"

"Deliah," Marius' voice, thick with venom.

The conversation continued, but another man's voice broke in, "Marius?" it was crystal clear, and it pushed the audio from the street to the background. It was the Leader Marius had spoken with earlier. He was requesting a full-open connection.

Mark accepted the request, and several systems came online all at once. A window appeared negotiating and aggregating all of the information, while a new window appeared dedicated to each connecting unit. Used to receiving and parsing overwhelming amounts of information at once, Mark dumped all of the new windows to the right Wall, grouping and aligning them for later examination. He had *borrowed* several of the Collective's tactical-analysis programs, as well as unit maps, years ago. The programs were overkill for his use—managing the numerous Marks—but he had the originals fully intact, regardless.

"Leader," Marius stepped back to his Wall and opened a video interface. The man who appeared had shaggy grey hair down to his ears and charcoal, multifaceted orbs for eyes.

Marius considered himself on the bleeding edge, but the multifaceted eyes unnerved him. It wasn't the aesthetic that bothered him. It was the amount of neural-webbing added to the visual cortex—one layer per facet, per eye—in addition to the inhuman amount of training it took to simply function, that bothered Marius. This Leader did not think visually or spatially the way humans did. He probably never slept either.

Mortality rates for that replacement were high, and Marius had never heard of a Leader who'd had it done. Still, it told him a lot about the man. Marius didn't even have to review the Leader's GEaRS to know everything he had was to support his vision.

"Good," the Leader, "Now, we know each other."

"Yes," a nod.

"Our force will be completely inside your Net in moments," his hands worked at his console, and he continued, "I've connected you directly to the archive."

Mark was immediately excited by finally having access to the archive. He tested his search key as a matter of curiosity and it hit. He executed all of his tools for traversing and gathering data about Bradley and his experiments. He also went after tactical information regarding the city center, the surrounding area, and Secretary Deliah. Finally, he navigated the Hive's combat simulator, synching it with his unit map and individual unit interfaces.

It only took seconds to get everything started, and it would only take minutes more to establish that everything was running smoothly. He'd need time to sift through it all.

"Impressive," the Leader addressed Mark, "It seems we're fully functional again."

Marius interjected, "I'm glad we could help. But you should take a look at this," he opened a display showing everything on Mark's Wall and grabbed the thermal stream showing Deliah and Eve. He dropped it on the Leader's face and it disappeared. "That's Secretary Deliah's current location... right beside the hole."

"I hate that guy," the Leader, flatly.

Marius and Mark exchanged a surprised glance.

The Leader's silver-grey eyebrows raised slightly, "What?" and then, "I really do hate that guy."

Perfect. "We agree," Marius motioned toward Mark, "We'll send you the audio stream as well."

"Excellent, we're mobilizing all units to the area of the GlassTech building now. We'll be in touch." The display went black and text appeared indicating that the stream was discontinued as an action by the source.

Mark was in three places at once, but he still managed to assimilate some of the information he had in front of him, "Marius, the majority of the Collective's forces are foot soldiers. There are enough transports to carry them all, but if we assume that all of the things coming out of the hole are demons... the Collective force is only one-fourth of what we saw last night."

"When they arrive, we'll open up the arsenal to them," he navigated the Wall while he was talking and eventually landed at a security prompt. He input complex characters with several gestures. "See for yourself."

"Good idea," Mark nodded. He'd seen everything in there, but he hadn't thought to arm the Collective with it. He wasn't in the habit of giving the Collective access to anything that wasn't measured very carefully.

"Now, what are our two friends talking about?"

Consciousness

Twenty-Eight

"Consciousness?" *Who the fuck is this guy?*

"Yes, consciousness," Deliah bowed his head slightly, and gestured forward, taking a single step, "May I... come a little closer?"

"I'd prefer it if you didn't," Eve edged herself back, aware that there wasn't a great distance between where she was standing and the edge.

"Ah," Deliah seemed a little disappointed, but he stood still and continued, "This world was arrogant and ignorant. It was drowning in emptiness. But none of you *knew* it. Well, I shouldn't say *none of you*, because clearly there *were* tethers from our universe to next," he opened his hands out in front of himself, shrugging somewhat guiltily, "I was the one severing the ties."

"Is that what you call murdering the Collective?"

Deliah laughed. It was genuine, and natural. "The Collective? Almost all of them went happily into the abyss." He folded his hands neatly together, "They were the first demons across the water... appetites on those... they were something special."

Eve shook her head, "What do you mean, *happily?*" trying to stall. Eve tried to pick an escape route and found she had access to the

Hive. *What the…?* But she didn't hesitate to connect. Something wasn't quite right though; she used to just think about what she wanted to see and she'd see it. The closest she got to a bird's eye of Deliah was much too far away to use.

"Most of them were unhappy," he moved slightly closer, "All I did was offer them a way out, an escape."

"An *abyss* is a way out?" she shrugged sarcastically, "You'll have to explain that to me."

Deliah slowly nodded his head in affirmation, "I'll start from the beginning then. Each of us is given this brief moment, this life, to do something miraculous… to find ways to reach out to each other and to open ourselves up." He spoke with his hands, moving them with graceful emotion. Eve noted they seemed delicate; all of him seemed delicate as he moved. She tried not to let it distract her.

He continued, "I know it sounds immature, but these are the words that centuries of people chose to describe the interconnectedness of all things—the way life is at the center of the multiverse," drifting toward Eve as he spoke centimeters at a time.

"There are so many worlds, and each is an expression of the center, a variant," his hands seemed to add, *like you or like me*, and then, "As long as there is a thread drawing back to the center, as long as each of us strives to cultivate that connection, the variant thrives. The center is healthier for it."

Eve listened, and had to acknowledge—to herself—that there was truth in it. The words he chose to describe it were not hers, but it didn't take a huge amount of interpretation on her part to get to the same place. She knew because of the day the Spire cracked. That shared, but inexplicable experience of the heavy water. She was connected to everyone for a moment. She felt them floating with her alone in the dark.

"But if a person with this gift chooses to do everything except cultivate it and share it, the connection is lost. The thread withers and dies," it was personal, "and that universe drifts ever so slightly away from the center," another subtle shift in her direction.

"You can imagine what happens when everyone allows their soul to wither and decay," he paused, and moved back a bit dramatically, "The entire universe flies off into the black."

Recognizing Deliah's obvious two-steps-forward and one-step-back strategy for closing the distance, Eve shuffled herself back a step of her own, "What's out there?"

"The big empty. Nothing." Then he implored her, "You remember how it felt? The weight of it?!"

She did. Floating in the heavy water that day, she knew she'd be crushed before drowning. She remembered the struggle, and the impotence. The futility she experienced that day was enough to bury her hope forever, but it didn't turn out that way. She held on. When the earthquake woke her up, she knew others had held on as well.

"That's what's out there! The weight of being so selfish, so disconnected, that you are completely alone." Deliah managed to look sad, "From there you can affect nothing, and nothing can affect you. It is truly the end."

His amber eyes were so big and round that Eve could see the glint in them as he went on, "But we are inevitably headed for the end, Eve. We are too far from the center to ever make our way back. And that is what *hurts* so much," angrily.

"Hurts?"

"Yes. It hurts," his arms fell to his sides, giving up, "I feel all of you who won't just give up and accept reality. We were all there together, so peacefully ready to go, and then Joshua tethered us, and hauled us back toward the shore. He ripped us from our sleep. He took that from us! And now all we have is this purgatory, this limbo, until someone does something about it… until *I* do something about it." Deliah stepped forward without subtlety.

"Joshua?" Eve couldn't guess at Deliah's range, but he must have been approaching the threshold, because he was becoming impatient. Scouting for exit strategies, she found nothing promising. Assuming that everything underground was a bad idea, that only left a dead run through the streets or attempting to hide in a building, neither of which seemed like plausible retreats from a former Secretary of the Spire.

"You didn't know?" he smiled, "It was your boy who cracked the Spire. I assume he was the one who razed it as well?"

Eve couldn't keep back her smile.

"I thought so."

"So, what now, Deliah? You're going to cut the remaining ties and send us all to our deaths?"

"The world has chosen me to unmake it," placing his hands behind his back; he paced back and forth in a short arc, "I am the harbing…"

Eve's IOL display lit up. Two Collective jets were inbound. A message appeared:

"This is Mark.

Fall back"

She interrupted Deliah while she reviewed the escape route, "World? Universe? Which is it, Deliah?"

Her words actually made his temperature rise, "You think I'm the only one!?" his stature suddenly growing as he grew angrier, "You think that was the only Spire?" His hands were still behind his back, but she could tell he was itching to attack her, "The entire universe is decay built on stagnation and apathy! That's the only way we could get this far from the center! That's the only reason why someone like me exists!"

His skin was volcanic glass, and he seemed taller and broader than he was before, but she couldn't be sure with the heat waves rising up all around. Every instinct told her to run, but she stayed her ground. She waited for the jets.

"This meager uprising is only slowing the inevitable," he'd calmed himself to seething, "Joshua can't…"

The buildings around them shook violently, and pieces of them crashed down to the street or disappeared into the hole. Eve crouched to keep her balance as the ground swayed and lurched. Deliah stood perfectly motionless.

The supersonic wave hit them from above—the jets already long gone—adding to the sense of chaos. A piece of brick and mortar the size of a truck fell between Deliah and Eve, exploding into dust and shrapnel. Their standoff was broken and that was all she needed to make a run for it.

She raced away from the hole, following the route Mark plotted for her. The man was damn good at setting up an exit strategy. Prompting communication with Mark, she waited for a response while she ran.

"Eve! You made it!"

"Thanks, Mark." She rounded a corner and crossed a street just as another boom hit. Seeing the jets on her IOL display, she wondered if they hit another pair of buildings around the hole. "What's the status of the rest of the Collective?"

"Should be able to see for yourself."

A prompt appeared on her IOL and she remembered that she had access again. Collective units were set up in the surrounding blocks waiting for the go-ahead. She quickly acknowledged the Leader and announced that she was ready and in position when she made it to her waypoint. She was just outside the forming cloud of dust as the last building fell.

"Are you seeing this, Eve?"

She flicked her eyes to access the stream Mark indicated. The thermal was showing bodies—she assumed they were demons—crawling out of the hole in large numbers; but worse than that, there were demons much farther out from the center of the city, surrounding and closing in on the Collective units. The display was basically showing two concentric circles and an expanding bull's eye. The only reason she knew the middle ring was the Collective was because they were all tagged.

"I see. Did anyone confirm Deliah? Is he alive or dead?"

"Sorry, Eve, no."

She could see the fight from a Leader's perspective since she'd hijacked that system a while back, and apparently she still had access. It didn't look good, but she recognized several of the tags. Most of them were Collective Officers or Leaders that she'd studied either during her ascension through the ranks or after. They were the crème. None of them compared to 127, but they certainly had their strengths.

Pumping raw adrenaline and spiking a cocktail for battle, she closed her eyes and enjoyed the calm before the storm.

Blood

Twenty-Nine

The debris thrown up from the falling buildings created a fog several blocks across. The hole at the center of the fog continually coughed up demons that ran outward from it in all directions. Demons crawled and spread out over buildings, vehicles, and wreckage like a plague of angry insects fleeing from a sabotaged home.

Choking fumes were rising into the air, carried far by the wind. The smell was caustic: repugnant and disorienting to the hopeful, a comforting call to the end for the hopeless. The slavering greys lifted their nostrils and flicked their tongues, sensing they were close to peace.

All around the city the demons rallied to the call. They rose up out of their pits and they raced down the buildings. They joined together, forming a rough circle a mile out from the hole that spawned them. A seemingly endless number gathered and climbed up over each other. The demons whipped themselves into a frenzy, blood-hungry and anxious. They became a writhing grey wall of flesh and teeth, rending and mauling each other as they sprayed bodily fluids into the air. The constant tearing and wounding created a sulfurous red mist around them, which lingered and travelled with them as they began to roll toward the heart of the city.

Streams flowed from earth to space and back again, carrying the imagery to each of the Officers of the Collective. But, "You aren't in the Collective, anymore," each of them heard a man's voice, Mark's voice. He wasn't addressing them as a group though; he was addressing each as an individual. He knew every name, and he spoke to each of them directly. He explained the images—softly to some, more matter-of-fact to others—knowing what each needed to hear to stay calm, to stay focused.

Mark was at Marius' Desk. He'd written a program to digest the psychological profiles of each of the units, and to translate statements accordingly, personalizing them. He used a conjunction of his Mark mapping program and the standard unit mapping to achieve a one-is-many system for managing the fight, and then he simply fed the digested profiles into it. He was proud of the program and how quickly he'd assembled it, and though it felt odd, he unloaded it. Then, after only the slightest consideration, he deleted it.

Since he'd fled Bradley's, he felt different. The room was gone, but the feeling he had when he was in that den writing had remained with him. Though it wasn't as disorienting as it was in the room, he still saw himself as many different possibilities. All of the different versions of him were realized somewhere in the metaverse, and he consulted with them. He kept it to himself, knowing that Marius would think he'd gone mad; he probably already thought so, why contribute more to the judgment?

Until now, there hadn't been voices or hallucinations. But now there were many Marks. Several were at the Desk, and more were at the Walls. One watched the others. One went to the kitchen. One spoke with Marius through an open channel—Marius had left the room, because it was getting crowded. Although there were variations in the timbre of each of their voices, hair color, and height, there was a thread among them, the Mark that held them all together. One realized that he had been preparing for this his whole life. One thought they were all crazy. All of them were coherent. All of them wanted to help.

Mark prepared each Officer for the coming battle. Reviewing their GEaRS, he consulted with each about their spikes and augments. He offered changes to improve duration or potency, and he connected one fighter to another in logical groups so that each would have the benefit of the others' perspectives and systems. He provided information as fast as they needed it. Each was ready.

Deliah was standing at the apex of a pile of rubble that had once been a building. The maelstrom was unaffected by matter as immaterial as concrete; they couldn't seal the hole by throwing dirt at it.

The horde fanned out before him, but he remained expressionless. His amber eyes were vacant, his mind distant. His systems, like everyone else's, had reconnected to the pseudo-Hive created by Mark and Marius. But Mark was actively shutting him out. Deliah, with some concentration and effort, could gain access, but only long enough to catch glimpses of the weapons levied against him.

The rubble shifted and shook beneath him as another building started collapsing. The boom followed, and the skyscraper finally came to rest in a great plume of itself, exhausted like a spirit leaving its body. A strong wind was created by the falling building, powerful and close to where Deliah stood. The rush pushed past him, rippling his robe around his body like a flag in a storm. He was steady.

The fight had taken to foot. The jets would be relegated exclusively to reconnaissance. Deliah made one more foray into the pseudo-Hive and found nothing new before he was ejected again. His eyes flickered a bit, as though he'd woken up from sleeping with his eyes open. He jumped gracefully down to the precipice created by the maelstrom and looked down into the mud-red miasma.

The surface was closer to the street, and from within the thick depths of the cloud, Deliah saw more demons rising. A monster dragged itself up and out and stood before him. It was more than ten feet tall, even hunching. Broad and well-muscled, the beast stared at Deliah and saw him for what he was, and then ran away to join the others. More were rising and at ease.

Introductions were strange; not only because they were preparing to kill or be killed, but because they already had detailed information about one another even though they'd never met.

Eve had mixed feelings about Lesha already, "Hello."

"Eve, it's a pleasure to know you," but she looked like she knew more than made Eve comfortable. Lesha's dark hair was pulled back, showing off her pronounced cheek bones. Her face was well-defined, made uniquely kind by the freckles and wide eyes. She was much shorter than Eve, but she commanded respect.

"And you," Eve checked that the harness she'd made for the Wakizashi was snug. She knew it wasn't the traditional way to wear the sword, but she wasn't a traditional person.

"That's an impressive weapon," leading.

Eve didn't like the way Lesha looked at the Leader's sword; too familiar. So she left the leading statement hanging between them. Lesha smiled, seeming not to notice.

They were waiting in the innermost office of a processing farm. The room—like every other room in the farm—was tiny and empty save for a single chair. The eggshell walls were not the usual interfaces, and displayed nothing.

Eve still had a hard time believing people sold their thoughts to the farm for a price per hour. Well, they didn't sell *their* thoughts, Eve corrected herself. Rather, instead of having their own thoughts, they offered up their processing power for others to use. She knew that some people did it for a living, but she'd never met one, and probably never would at this point. She stayed as far away from the chair as she could in the cramped space.

"I'm not a combat strategist, but it feels like we're positioned to no purpose," if Lesha was afraid, she wasn't showing it.

"The expectation was to take this position and hold it. As you can see," Eve's eyes flickered and sent Lesha the pertinent information, "We don't know anything about it, really." She flattened her robe against her stomach and down her legs with a sweep of her hands. "But look at the activity—demons are pouring from it. It's a pretty good guess it's the source of the demons."

Lesha was wearing the C.O. garb of a Leader's personal guard, though Eve knew she wasn't one. She checked the snug fit, "But they came out of the Spire originally, didn't..."

"I'm sorry that I don't have answers for you. I don't think this is where any of us wanted to be right now. We're just going off of the information we have and are going to do our best to survive."

Lesha smiled sardonically at her, "That's always been my plan."

The grinding whine pierced through the building, and both Eve and Lesha winced when they heard it. More demonic voices joined in, and Eve saw on her IOL that they were engaged.

Lesha cloaked and drew her HDMA.

Eve opened the door and cranked her GEaRS.

Lesha couldn't keep up, but that was okay with Eve because she was planning on getting in close. She burst out through the entrance and picked her first victim.

Eve's eyes were large, liquid-green orbs with black specs set back inside them. The Mantis eyes were precise and filtered, allowing Eve to detect the slightest movement, like the pulsing vein in the neck of the demon she surprised as she entered the fray. Her fingernails were already extended, edges humming with charge and heat. She almost decapitated it with her first swing, but leaving nothing to chance, she finished with the next.

Eve's GEaRS began competing with her emotional drive and impulses. Usually, it would have been time for her to spike something for calm, but she rode the high. The overlap of information from her biological senses and her technological ones created a 360-degree, fully defined awareness of the environment.

The flash appearing over her left shoulder was not a surprise. The light flooded the world in slow motion with a wake of darkness. A demon leaping at her was hit clean in the chest and dragged back through the air with a crushing impulse. Lesha was a good shot.

Eve crouched and tore into the asphalt with her bare feet and hands to launch herself toward a crowd of demons that had turned at the flash. She tore through each of them in turn. Cutting the hand from one that reached for her, she buried it in the face of the next and then she became a blur. Her nails left blue arcs as tracers in the air.

Others closed on her position. A flash from behind, another. Two demons flew from the growing crowd. She cut away at them, focusing on the exposed bellies of those who still stood.

Those that survived her initial swaths gave her a wide berth, and a ring began to form. They stalked and swayed and hissed as they moved around her.

Eve was crouched low, but the street already had slick pools and bodies to avoid. One rushed her from the front and she side-stepped it. They closed together, snapping at her and whining. Close to a line of cars, several of the demons bounded up on them and hunched down to menace her from above. Flash. The demon closest to her flew from the roof of a car as the mass smashed in its face and sent it end over end.

There was a change in the feeling of the fight. Eve couldn't put her finger on it, but the demons' eyes started flicking toward Lesha. She'd moved—a shrewd, cloaked support—after her last shot, but still they looked in her direction. Her cloak was still running, diminishing visual disturbance, scent, and temperature to almost nothing. Eve dodged one attack and then another. She slipped a bit and drove her bad shoulder into the side of a truck, but kept herself from smashing her face against it.

Regaining her footing, she saw a demon stand. Stupidly erect, it made for an easy target. Flash. The mass struck the demon in the belly, doubling it over, and carrying it to a building where it exploded through a glass window. Eve saw all their eyes flick together toward Lesha. She was on the move, but something wasn't right. They were figuring her out.

"Care, Lesha." Eve wasn't afraid to say it aloud. The demons knew Lesha was there somewhere, and Eve didn't have time to dance her eyes to communicate.

Eve took an aggressive stance to draw them away. She charged, and when the demon rose partially to swoop down on her with its fangs and fore-claws, she dug in hard for an extra burst and cut left. Staying low, she tore through its inner-right thigh from groin to knee, and most of the way through its right flank. It caught nothing of her; instead, its hips collapsed to the ground in a howl of pain as its leg slipped out from underneath it. Entrails dropped out of its side as it tried to twist around, but Eve was already on its back ripping it apart. It hissed at her and she crushed its teeth to the pavement as she jumped over the roof of one car to another.

She wanted to move the fight away from Lesha, or at least to different terrain, so they couldn't get a fix on her, but they didn't follow. Eve felt a sick twisting in her gut. One stood up as though to pounce, but she saw the deception in its slack muscles.

Flash.

The demon slid along the ground for a brief second before impact with the car Eve had just jumped over. That car slid forward and hit the car Eve was on, causing her to drop to all fours and dig into the hood to keep from being thrown off.

There was no slow motion. Time hiccupped. The few seconds usually reserved for hope, for a deus ex machina, were skipped.

A giant of a demon held Lesha in its arms from behind. Her cloak was a fulgurate mess where the demon held her and shook her violently. Light bent and broke sharply around her, but her body was already limp.

The demon shook Lesha's body more gently, testing it. When she didn't move, he tossed her to the side with one hand, and then stared at Eve. Lesha hit the ground like a rag doll and then slid to a rest in a gutter trap.

Eve's stomach tightened and the world became a focused rush of adrenaline and animal vengeance. She would have gone for a full burn if Mark hadn't stepped in and denied it. It didn't matter that she didn't spike all her chems; her heart was already pounding, full of raw emotion. She leapt from the car top, and easily cleared two car-lengths distance before hitting the ground. Her legs pumped and fired like pistons. She was fast, but her nails dug into nothing but air. The demon slid away, turning into smoky, charcoal wisps. She'd seen the trick before, but never from a demon. It swung its heavy arm around and into her back, lifting her off her feet.

Catching the ground less than a meter in front of a glass store front, Eve curled tightly and protected her face as she stumbled through the glass. She fell and rolled to a three-legged stance staring out the front. The store was dark, which made the outside appear blinding by contrast. The light of day was washing out the details.

She didn't move. Her IOL reported that she was fine. Her back might bruise where she was struck, but her bones were healthy; the robes prevented any serious lacerations.

The remaining smaller demons moved off. But she couldn't find. That unmistakable shadow-trick, it was Laterali. She had often wondered about the Laterali, and Ezechial had explained some of their tactics, at least superficially. The demon was probably hiding right in front of her, but not allowing her to recognize it, to perceive it.

Fuck that. She needed to shake things up, do something. She wanted to attack everything. So much energy though, and the demon could just pick her off while she was elsewhere. Suddenly, she was overcome with a happy feeling. It swelled up from within her chest, and she laughed. Her mind was open and free, and she became the demon. For just one moment, she felt the advantage of size and invisibility, and the desire to sucker her victim, and she just knew...

A hot breath and eerie laughter came from her right. She faked right, grabbed the handle of her sword, and unsheathed, lunged, and sliced left all in one motion. The blade caught an eye at the tip, and opened up the Laterali demon from shoulder to thigh. Viscera spilled out from its belly; but before the entrails could hit the floor,

Eve hacked left, right, and then up, ending with her blade through its throat until it hit the skull.

She turned her back to the giant and slid her blade down and out of it as she walked away. The demon crashed down to its knees first, and then fell forward onto the floor behind her. Eve cleaned the blade on her already bloody robes, and returned it to its sheath as she left the store.

Ignoring the ever growing tidal wall of demons closing in all around them, Eve saw that they had lost the few mini-copters they had, and several units were not responding. She also saw that she was not alone. At a glance, her IOL showed they had fought well against the first wave... that they had a chance.

The dust was dispersing slowly and moving off to the west with the wind; as a result, visibility was improving. "Mark, I'm going to push toward the hole."

"Meet up with Leader 18." A waypoint appeared on her display, and on every stream she brought up that contained location references. Leader 18's information was also dumped to her. Although the profile was probably useful, there was no time for it, and she just caught his image.

I hate flies.

She looked up and down the street and saw the last of the first wave of demons retreating back toward the hole. Feeling strong—and wanting to stay that way—she reached inside her robes, sliced open a gel pack, and tucked it in her cheek. Deciding it was better to stay ahead, she tucked in another one to have ready for later and set off to meet Leader 18.

Ezechial saw Eve wipe her sword off on her robes. He was watching out a window a few floors up across the street. There was no confusion about what she was anymore. She was no demon. He thought it might already be too late, that the world might already be dead, but he held on to hope for her regardless.

He looked down at Pallomor who was also watching Eve, "She is beautiful."

"She is."

"Do you want to save her?"

"If I have a choice, I would not be the one to take her life."

The child looked up at Ezechial with fondness, and approval, "Seems there are fewer choices today."

"Seems that way."

They took the stairs down.

Out on the street, Ezechial and the boy walked around the bodies without affection or distaste. They generally followed Eve, because they were generally going in the same direction. Pallomor led them down an alley, and a solitary demon emerged from a shadowy overhang. The demon licked the air and tracked the boy closely. Scooting and adjusting, it prepared to attack.

Ezechial almost ripped the demon's arms out at the shoulders. He had caught it and pulled down with such force, so fast, that the demon didn't even know it was dying. The Devil's Tails slithered around the corpse, absorbing a little, but they were still full from the evening before. Recalling the whips and coiling them back into their harnesses, Ezechial followed the boy who hadn't stopped or looked back.

They walked a few more blocks and heard the cries of the demons signaling the attack. Ezechial closed the distance to Pallomor so that he was at his heels. The boy chose a building, and they entered.

By the time they'd positioned themselves in a window with a decent vantage, the battle had already begun.

Eve and her new companion were.

Leader 18 wore a pair of grey, finely woven, force-reactive gloves with no pointer fingers. He pulled out two hand cannons from his chest harness, at least 40cm long. Eve had no idea what the custom guns were capable of until the demons charged.

The Leader banged his wrists together on both sides and the force-reactive material tightened and hardened, and then he opened fire. Demon head after demon head exploded around Eve as she charged in. He held his arms out straight, and the kickback pushed into his enormous shoulders. His multifaceted eyes allowed him to shoot the guns with uncanny accuracy at independent targets. He could easily hit anything that came into his vision.

All of his GEaRS were designed for silky smooth muscle contractions and steady strength. His heart rate never changed. His breathing was always even and smooth, as were his guns. Eve didn't recognize the ammo, but each projectile looked like a long golden tracer.

Eve was barely able to keep up with the Leader's kills. He chose targets quickly and efficiently, and even used Eve's vision when he needed it in order to take accurate shots through vehicles.

But the horde kept coming.

Feeling that they could be overwhelmed at any moment, Eve was creating space. She backed up, rolled forward into pockets, and dodged into clearer areas whenever she saw one. Her bloody robe was beginning to show weakness. It wouldn't be long before some of those slashes got through to her skin.

Her short brown hair, usually spiky, was sweat-flat to her scalp. A burning salty drop landed in her right eye, and the distraction cost her. A demon fell on her from her momentary blind-side, and knocked her to the ground. The demon was on top of her in a second, about the same time its head burst open. Though she blocked as much as she could with her hands, Eve's face was sprayed with the thick, hot blood. She gained her feet quickly and went for higher ground, needing a second to wipe the blood out of her eyes. She could easily navigate without her eyes, but she wasn't in the habit of fighting with disadvantages if she could help it.

Leader 18 protected her retreat. No demon ever got within ten meters of him after he cleared his initial space.

Mark dispatched a waypoint order. It definitely wasn't a fallback, but the reason for the change wasn't immediately obvious to her. The Leader was already moving his position, clearing a path. They moved in unison for a bit, but it was too slow for the Leader. He set his guns to full automatic, firing into the street both ways.

A large group of demons crashed out of an alley and turned to follow them. Eve moved around to the front—toward waypoint—and protected 18's back, while he unloaded the full fury of his weapons on the pack. He slid two meters, leaving tracks in the street.

One gun stopped, then the other. The barrels were smoking; Eve could smell the acrid burning oil. 18 took some backward steps, and then turned and ran up to Eve. He wasn't fast like Eve, so they couldn't just make a break for the waypoint. It wasn't that far, but Eve guessed 18 was defenseless now that his guns had over-heated.

"How long?"

"Three minutes."

"Three minutes?!"

"If they aren't damaged."

The demons weren't closing in on them as rapidly as she would have expected. Eve looked around frantically, "There's a big one around."

"What?" he was calm.

"Just keep those compounds open."

He swiveled his head to see down both streets, but all he saw were demons snapping at the air. They were threatening, but not actually approaching them. One finally ran at them and Eve charged right back at it, meeting it before it was ready. She put a finger through both eyes with one hand and jerked its skull back, flipping the demon. The belly and chest exposed, she raked the demon with both hands as she jumped back to the Leader.

"They're afraid… of us?"

A huge demon smoked into existence near them. Three Laterali—the human kind—smoked in immediately after it. Their swords cut, stabbed, and hacked, and the monster fell before it could take a swing.

The hooded Laterali looked at the two former Collective, bowed slightly, and shadow-stepped away.

Several smoky wisps appeared and disappeared into the mass of demons blocking them from the waypoint. The demons were laid to waste as quickly as if 18 had gone fully-automatic on them.

The waypoint was rescinded, "I was trying to get you closer to the Laterali. Luckily, they were able to come to you."

They weren't far from the hole now. The air was hard to breathe with all the concrete dust floating in it, but Eve could see they were only blocks away from the circle of destroyed building that marked the hole on the landscape. She saw it on her map, too, but the hills of the destroyed buildings were more impressive in person.

Eve reached into her mouth and removed the wasted gel pack. The other pack remained in her mouth; she'd bite it open when she needed it.

The city was eerily quiet; the noise of the fighting was still screaming in her head, but she knew it was residual. There were few distant, unimagined sounds of fighting, but on the whole, they'd reached another lull in the slaughter… and they were closer to the hole.

18 wasn't talkative; then again, neither was she. They checked their weapons and prepared.

"An interesting pair, don't you think?" if the question was asked in jest, it was hard to tell. The child's voice was not at all committed to it.

Ezechial didn't respond. He was lost in the thoughts of his brethren. When they were in the shadows, he could feel them breathing, feel their hearts beating. For the first time though, he could feel the echoes of their emotions in him. The few young that remained were scared, while the rest were dealing in cold business. The last weren't emotionless—they cared a great deal about the task at hand—it was just that it gave them no particular joy, and they had no particular fear. They were detached, but they admired their work from afar.

He wondered what they would think of him. It wasn't that Ezechial desired their approval; it was more that he was curious about what he'd become in their eyes. In a way, he knew he was somehow fulfilling his destiny—or his perception of it—and he felt he was part of the Laterali prophecies directly. What he wanted from his brethren would have been an opinion other than his own, trying to establish if he was completely mad, or righteous.

"We should move again."

Pallomor had been standing on a table to get a better look at the street below. The outer wall locations in any building were usually the most expensive, and almost always had glass windows the entire length and breadth of the exposed wall. The building must have been extremely old. It seemed well-preserved to Ezechial as he lifted the boy and then set him on the floor.

Ezechial felt the curiosity, felt her coming.

A tall Laterali appeared at the door. She had broad shoulders and breasts that fit her frame. The cloak she wore fell free from her chest, down in a long drape, making her appear even more spectral than the others. Her hands were invisible beneath the dark material and her eyes were covered by her hood. Her lips were grey. By her stance, by the way she felt when she travelled the shadows, he knew who she was.

 "Brother." By her rich, dark, otherworldly voice, there was no doubt.

"Sister."

They were not related by blood, but by a pact sealed in blood.

"I knew it was you," the seer floated toward him, feet also covered by the cloak, "I always knew it would be you."

Flexing and releasing his left hand, he split his skin open along the dark cracks and crevices, letting some of the fiery glow spill out, "I'm almost there."

"You're walking a fine line."

"I know."

"Have you decided?"

Ezechial thought about his answer for a moment, and then conceded. He gazed down softly at Pallomor, and the boy looked back affectionately.

The seer floated over to the boy and knelt down. A long hand appeared from within the cloak, dark veins pulsing through the integument. She pulled back her hood, revealing raven black curls and dark grey-olive skin. She put her hand on the boy's face, "I didn't know what it would be like…"

Retrieving her hand quickly, she pulled her hood on again and stood. Her hand disappeared neatly into her cloak, "Remember, the choice has been given to you because you can make it. There is no right or wrong. You are defining it."

He nodded with deference. She returned the nod, and then she left. There was no flash or burst as she moved into the shadows though, like the other Laterali. The seer walked into them elegantly, and slowly. She controlled the degrees of her existence that rested between light and dark. That was her practice.

"We should go."

"Yes."

Where the block had been razed, a large open space was created, like you could walk up and see a green or a lake at the center of the city. From the ground, peering through the buildings and through the thinning dust were golden shafts of sunlight; and beyond those were large mounds—one with a single dark tree at the top. Even the blue sky was hinted at through the fine particles still hanging in the air, though it was somewhat faded.

Deliah was motionless looking out over the battlefield. He stood atop the remains of the second floor of a building. There were portions of wall to his right, but little else was left of the floor. As far out on the edge as he could be without falling, he observed with his hands at ease behind his back. Seeming untroubled by the closing forces, he gave no indication that there was a maelstrom rising up behind him, or endless carnage before him. He was a statue if not for his robes.

The felled buildings in the surrounding block had merged together into a large, uneven hill of dangerous ground, and demons were already cresting the top. The salivating beasts rushed, jumped, and slid down the debris.

There was no discrete beginning to the fight. No grinding wails or rattling howls marked the engagement. Eve and 18 broke free of the standing buildings, entered the clearing, and the rest was blood.

Eve's IOL displayed counts: the warm and the cold. Estimated times appeared with distances and probabilities in case she needed to retreat. She knew the wall of demons was growing higher as it closed in, trading circumference for height. If no more demons were adding to it, the wall would still be insurmountable; there was no retreat. She flicked the displays off with a twitch of her eyes; everything she needed to see was right in front of her.

Eve saw Deliah. A demon leapt at her, but she ducked under its attack and raked at it as she moved toward higher ground, never taking her eyes from his ambers. She revved her GEaRS, dumping adrenaline and a batch of other chems directly into her system. She was running raw now, an emotion-fueled murder-machine. Deliah was her only target.

Flashes went off around her as more Collective joined the fight. Demons were picked up and thrown into each other. Distant but distinct, she heard Leader 18's guns drumming out the rhythm of the heads exploding in front of her.

A gigantic woman was off to Eve's right with a proportionately sized assault rifle. She was lightly armored, but it was unnecessary since the personal shield she wore lit up demons that were close enough to attack her. The C.O. fired from a one-knee-down stance, her back leg propped against a large piece of debris behind her. Her entire body recoiled whenever she squeezed the trigger, but the rifle was level and steady. She looked more like the mounted housing for the gun than a person.

Wisps of black smoke followed the movements and positions of the Laterali. They used hit-and-run tactics. Two or three at a time would choose a target, shadow-step to the demon, kill it, and step away. The attacks were quick and erratic, difficult to predict. It might have been an effective strategy, but the number of demons was overwhelming and they couldn't keep up.

Two demons had climbed a large, jagged spike of wall and were using it as a shield from the ranged fire while they waited for Eve. They jumped down behind her as she passed, but she smelled them, knew they were there. The demons were the ones surprised when she turned around and grabbed one by its collar bones and snapped them out. The demon's arms were instantly useless, and she shoved it by its chest into the other. She pushed them together into a hole where several floors of the building were missing. Eve didn't look down to see the results.

Deliah hadn't moved. She worked her way toward him, closing the distance.

Leader 18 wasn't moving with her, but he covered her anyway, and demons fell around her as she moved toward the madman. From the continued accuracy, she thought he could protect her all the way to Deliah, especially since he was using her vision to pick targets.

Eve looked for a way to get up to Deliah as she jumped and dodged attacks, cutting and slashing whenever anything close. She needed someone to start taking shots at him, to move him off his ground.

An eerie quiet fell over the battlefield; not just the absence of sound, but the absence of movement. Everything slowed down. Darkness moved over the entire area, blocking out the sun. She hoped it was Joshua, but she didn't look up like everyone around her. It felt like an opportunity and she didn't want to miss it.

But Deliah was gone.

Looking around frantically, Eve tried to find the only other person she knew was wearing robes. He probably would have stood out in any crowd, dark chocolate skin against a white robe; not to mention, everyone else was dirty and bloody, and he was clean. But she couldn't find him.

The demons were making room in places, backing off in that odd way Eve had noticed when a shadow-stepping demon was around. The Laterali were strangely inactive, too. The fast-moving shadow crossed the battlefield again and she looked up. It was definitely Joshua. Too many chems running through her system, she was mesmerized by him, but she came to when she heard the scream.

A monstrous demon—a body like a huge grey boulder of muscle and sinew—held the gigantic woman with the assault rifle up with one hand. Its tongue lolled out of its mouth and its hand was covered in blue electric bursts from the C.O.'s personal shield. Crushing her to death, the monster pounded her to the ground. Her gun fired once from her twitching finger and it was dislodged by the recoil.

Leader 18 fired both guns multiple times. The monster's hands exploded at the wrists, then the arms fell as the shoulders burst, and finally two rounds into the head ripped it one way and exploded it the other.

Eve saw it all happen. Not the death of the soldier, or the monstrous demon, but the death of Leader 18. She knew that's what she was seeing, but there was nothing she could do about it. Eve knew they were setting him up, making him vulnerable, playing on his humanity. It didn't matter that they sacrificed one of their own to set it up; that was how they worked. They were interchangeable and expendable. So, when the Laterali demon appeared behind 18, she wasn't surprised.

It was another monster and it grabbed the Leader's hands—guns and all—and then it ripped his arms from his torso. Leader 18 must have seen it happen from every angle. He didn't scream. He just fell face down in a pool of his own blood, and twitched. Eve wanted desperately to close his eyes. There were so many chemically augmented emotions burning inside of her; it was more than she could handle to see him staring back at her.

A prompt was forced to the front of her IOL:

"I made it easier for him."

She saw the twitching stop, the breathing stop. His vitals were flat.

A cacophony shook Eve awake. At first she didn't understand, but then she saw that Joshua was tearing at the wall of demons. It was still several blocks away, but it was reaching up over three stories. The demons spilled around buildings and obstacles and just kept coming. The howls from the wall rose to a register higher than she had heard before, and so many cried out at once that her spine shivered at it.

Joshua swooped down at the wall and swiped his huge talons at it. Demons and demon parts exploded out in all directions. The gaps were refilled almost immediately.

Eve moved carefully along the rubble she found herself on, and saw that the Laterali were engaged with several large demons. She had the feeling that they were able to perceive the monsters, even with their tricks. The Laterali weren't connected to the Hive so they weren't connected to the pseudo-Hive either. Eve didn't know how they chose their targets or moved in such a coordinated manner. She could see that the assassins were taking the fight to shadow-stepping demons though, and she was thankful for it.

Swooping down again and again, Joshua tore through the wall, but the gaping wounds lasted for only seconds as the demons filled them in again.

There were flashes and pockets of fighting everywhere, and the demon numbers had dwindled. Eve hoped they were rushing to the wall where Joshua could annihilate them twenty at a time. The hole had stopped spewing out demons, so maybe they weren't limitless. That left Deliah.

Ezechial stood at the window, but his eyes were closed. Feeling through the shadows, he found his former brethren. He was able to disguise himself from them as he observed, and did not disturb them as they fought. They were doing well, but the man in robes was changing the tide.

The man was tall and made of fire-blackened skin. He radiated an intense heat that melted the world around him. When he moved, his body was liquid, faster than the Laterali. The shadows were no different than the light for him; he could see the Laterali. Ezechial watched him kill one assassin after another without the use of more than his left hand. He was meticulously focused on murdering each in a unique way. He pulled out various bones and organs, and used their own weapons against them. Basically, he was murdering each by dissection.

Ezechial felt the seer approach the man. She was hidden better than the rest were, and even Ezechial couldn't find her easily. The man, though, had no difficulty. He turned and grabbed her wispy, dagger-wielding hand in his and lifted her by the throat. He fell on her and held her down while she fluttered in and out of the shadows. Crouching over her, he put his face to hers as though he might kiss her, and then he did kiss her. Once on each eyelid as she tried to look away. He held her still, and Ezechial could feel her strength waning. The man wasn't done. He opened his mouth, exposing fangs above and below, and lines of sharp teeth. Leaning in again, he sucked out the seer's eyes and burst them in his mouth. Thick fluid rushed out over his lips and down his chin.

Through the shadows, the man looked directly at Ezechial, full amber eyes glowing brightly. He seemed to move toward Ezechial, but then he saw the boy standing beside him and he stopped. The man slurped the liquid up from his chin with his long tongue and swallowed.

Ezechial opened his eyes and looked again at Pallomor. The child had, at some point, slipped his hand into Ezechial's.

The wall of demons was closer, tightening the noose around them. Joshua hovered in front of a section and tore at it viciously. There were flashes of his stained talons against the wall, and showers of gore pouring from them. On the ground the falling blood sounded almost like heavy rain and hail. The demons were screaming. The mass of rolling demons was decimated, but it circled in even closer and continued to replace its losses with more writhing bodies.

Eve had found a dark space between an intersection of concrete, and backed herself into it. She had a view of Joshua, and nothing else could possibly fit into the hiding spot with her so she felt safe enough for the time being. Using her tongue, she positioned the gel pack she'd previously tucked into her cheek, and bit into it with her teeth.

A smoky Laterali flew through the air in front of her and into three prongs of bent rebar poking from the side of a slab of concrete.

The battle had flipped upside down. She had felt like they were winning—like they were somehow overcoming the odds—but then the units positioned closest to her were taken out in the space of a single breath. And now she was having a hard time finding the rest of the units. There were flashes and gun fire, but they seemed so few. She heard more in the distance, coming from behind her, but it was difficult to discern through the concrete.

She flicked her IOL to show the warm count, and she was glad to be wrong. Turning all of her displays back on, she found the remaining forces. Most of them had joined together and moved to the other side of the hole. Her mind opened with a sigh and saw the situation from their perspective; dragon! *Right.* Not sure she could explain it to Mark with a few words, she decided to let Joshua's actions speak for themselves. Mark might have figured it out already anyway.

Joshua flew out of sight in a spectacular demonstration of grace and power. A breathless moment passed, and then he appeared as a blur, flying with his arms raised into the wall. Eve was able to see beyond the morass through the hole he made in it. The gap closed slowly as Joshua flew back over her head. She could see that he'd picked up a few demons on his tail and wings, but he ducked down and crashed through the wall again, unbothered by the riders.

The wall was even slower to reform as Joshua hovered up next to it again. There were demons biting and pulling at his wings and feathers, and burning him. Every bite or scratch threw bright sparks into the air. He tore at the opening with his teeth and hands and swung his tail at it. The demons that rushed across the wall to fill in chose to jump onto Joshua instead. They got the scent and the wall attacked him.

Demon after demon lunged at him off the bodies of the others. Joshua's swings became more and more frenzied and frustrated. Hovering became difficult and he began to fly around erratically. He floated away from the attack, out of the farthest jumping demon's reach. But he was already covered with the slavering demons. He was coated with them.

Losing control, Joshua crashed down in front of Eve. Bright arcs trailed through the air from the wounds as the demons ripped at his flesh. Rolling around on the ground, he started pounding his wings and arms into the earth like he was on fire and he desperately needed to put it out. He rolled and pounded and shook himself, and the ground shook with him. Eve shook with him.

When he'd crushed them all, he seemed so much smaller. His wings were sheets of skin with rough and random sprouts of feathers clinging on. He propped himself up on his hands and tail, which made him look like he was dragging dead legs behind his torso. Digging in, he tried to walk forward like that, but it caused him too much difficulty and he just stayed there a moment longer.

Eve watched him closely and realized he was considerably smaller than he was before. The demons had taken something out of him. She saw something deep inside the dark, mottled blue and green scales of his body, and tried to look closer with her Mantis eyes. It was Joshua's body—his human body—in the chest of the dragon. He was feverish, hot, and shaking.

The dragon—or whatever it was—fell to the ground and dissolved in slow-moving lines of intensely burning fire. Joshua was lying naked on the street for only a second before he got up. He was already looking better, as though releasing the dragon had offered some relief.

Eve was about to announce herself and emerge from her hiding hole when she heard Deliah, "Joshua," a sinister and knowing confidence in his voice.

He was standing above her.

"This was all for you. To get you here."

Joshua stood up tall; and though he was shaking only moments before, he looked steady.

"You see, I couldn't find you," Deliah walked toward Joshua and passed right in front of Eve, "I looked everywhere, and asked everyone you knew, but you were very elusive."

Deliah pointed to the sky, "Somewhat lacking imagination, don't you think?"

"It's what I felt like," he shrugged, "but coming down wasn't as great as I remember it."

"Should we continue? Or are you ready to end this?"

Joshua's eyes turned to marbles, and his veins ran black. Eve thought she could hear his heart pounding. He held his arms out from his sides, fingers curled slightly and flexed in anticipation.

Heat poured down Deliah's body and spilled into Eve's hiding place. He seemed to grow—his muscles expanding more than they should—and his frame seemed taller and broader. His skin turned the color of obsidian.

Pallomor squeezed Ezechial's hand.

Ezechial squeezed back.

They left the room together and walked down the stairs. When they exited the building, Pallomor stopped, "If you do this, you will be forever divided."

Ezechial's salt-and-pepper stubble had grown out some in the last few days, but it was still a scruffy mask more than a beard. There was still not a grey hair to be found; each hair was either black or white, and there was no in between. He rubbed at the rough hairs with his hand, considering his words carefully, "The consequences will take care of themselves… they will be my story as I tell it, not as it is told to me."

"I will lose you."

"That's your choice."

"It's my nature."

"You've already chosen."

Pallomor looked away, "It's always like this, why should it change?"

"Because I'm willing to try to make it work."

"You were always my favorite disciple," Pallomor walked away.

Life and Death

Thirty

Deliah opened his mouth; his teeth seemed to grow to fill the space between his lips. The impressively sharp tips of his fangs were only revealed when his lower jaw touched his neck. Super-heated areas formed rivulets around his body, and rose and fell as he breathed. The small waves were short-lived as they cooled and disappeared a short distance away from him.

Joshua's veins were thick, pulsing, and black. His opaque blue eyes were steady and glassy, and his fingers itched. He thought of his recurring dream, and remembered to wait for the light.

Fighting continued away from the standoff, on the other side of the growing maelstrom. Demons and the humans tried their best to kill one another.

Deliah reached his arms out and his fingernails grew long and sharp, then he smiled at Joshua. He wasn't a demon; or at least, he wasn't like the greys with their thin skin and fragile bones. Powerful and strong, and effusing malevolence, he was a living nightmare. His eyes would burn your soul if you stared into them too long.

Eve was tucked like a cat into her previous hiding spot in the concrete. She peered out from the blackness, seeing everything while remaining unseen. Patiently, she watched for an opening.

Joshua charged Deliah.

Deliah charged Joshua.

Joshua's arms were a blur as his fingers etched lines into Deliah's hardened skin. The touches seemed light, but sparks flew from each gouge.

Deliah shrugged off the scratches and thrust an open palm into Joshua's chest, sending him flying through the air. Joshua landed hard on the ground and crashed through jagged pieces of debris, but he picked himself up quickly. Deliah was on him almost immediately, leaving a trail of black tendrils in his wake. Joshua was ready. It wasn't shadow-stepping, but he imagined passing through Deliah, and he did. He turned around and punched Deliah in the back with both fists. His chest, where Joshua's fingers had etched deep grooves earlier, shattered into pieces that exploded away from him like he was puking shards of glass.

Spinning around, Deliah back-handed Joshua across the face and knocked him to the ground. This time, though, Deliah was on top of him before he could get up.

"You think you can save them?" he spit the words, "You think they want to be saved?" He pounded Joshua into the ground, lifted him up, and pounded him down into the ground again. "Look around you, Joshua! The souls of this world can barely hold a body together they are so uncared for, so withered and decayed!" Deliah grabbed Joshua's face and forcefully pointed it toward the wall, "Look at them! Weak, servile, and waiting for oblivion. They don't want to be tied to this world, much less any other."

Deliah palmed Joshua's face and ground it into the rubble, "You think you can make a difference? One man threaded through to the center of the universe? What is your bond? What ties you so strongly to this world?!"

Eve slid from her hiding spot without a sound. She dashed toward Deliah and drew the Wakizashi. The muscles in her legs moved at the speed of her will, covering the distance before the sound of her footsteps. She jumped onto Deliah's back, but as the tip of her blade touched the soft space between his shoulder and his neck, he twisted.

Her strike only cut the surface of his skin as she slipped from Deliah's back. The main thrust of her downward movement almost impaled Joshua as the length of the blade was buried beside him. Deliah swung his arm as he twisted back like a wound spring uncoiling. He caught Eve under the chin with his elbow and swept his claws across her face as he followed through. She spun fully around and fell dizzily to the ground.

Deliah's eyes grew wide as he pounded Joshua's head once again, and stood up. Satisfied that Joshua wasn't going to do more than groan, he leaned over to stare at Eve. Placing his hands behind his back, he failed to appear at ease as the heat gradients boiling off his skin flowed higher; every inch of his face screamed rage.

He rolled Eve over with his foot and saw the blood pulsing into the four trenches he'd dug across her face. The wounds filled and overflowed and he smiled. His voice was gravelly, "Now, we're right back where we were at the start of this. Wouldn't it have been so much easier my way?"

Eve's eyes fluttered open and saw the terrifying face twisted in its self-satisfied, self-righteous grin. Her hands moved without thought, and she clawed his face twice before he grabbed her by the throat and waist, picked her up, and threw her into a slab of concrete. The hollow thud of her skull elicited a load groan from Joshua as he tried to stand. He was too disoriented, and his legs and arms buckled weakly beneath him.

Both of Deliah's eyes were shut tight, blood squeezing out around the lids. He didn't need them to see, so he kept them closed.

Deliah's focus returned to Joshua. He grabbed his wrists and locked one huge hand around both of them, cuffing them. Walking in the direction of the maelstrom, he dragged Joshua effortlessly behind him. Joshua was still delirious and couldn't find the strength in his limbs to do much more than wriggle to slow them down.

The wall of demons had stopped at the perimeter of still-standing buildings. The Collective Officers and Laterali—still fighting for their lives—didn't see Deliah or Joshua, and couldn't help even if they had; the wall was pouring down demons onto them.

Deliah crested the highest point of the fallen debris and descended into the depression around the hole. Joshua was regaining his wits and he struggled harder against him. Deliah snapped him on the ground like a rag doll to stop him.

When Deliah made it to the maelstrom, he held Joshua up over it and examined him, "It's hard to believe you were the only thing holding us here."

———

Eve raised her head from the ground, groggily. There were alerts flashing in her eyes, but Mark came online and cleaned them up for her. He'd taken over some of her controls while she was unconscious, and spiked several painkillers for her.

Trying to orient herself, she failed a few times before she realized what was going on. She stood and looked for Joshua. Walking over to the Wakizashi still buried hilt deep, she saw his blood: two trails of dripping black.

Her dizziness faded quickly with the help of her GEaRS and Mark's expertise. She pulled out the sword from the ground, and ran. Eve followed the trails, though she didn't need to, because she knew where they were going as her mind fully grasped the situation.

She leapt around the wreckage of the buildings, ran along partially exposed I-beams, and avoided breaks in the floor that seemed to drop off into nothing. Eventually, she made it to the edge of the depression and crouched low, waiting and watching.

As far as she could tell, the maelstrom had eaten up everything that was thrown into it, and also sucked up whatever was loose in the surrounding fifty meters or so. Eve could feel the soft tug of the storm on her robes and felt the heat of the ruddy glow on her cheeks, though she hadn't descended the eight or nine meters down into the depression yet.

The sinkhole was more like a lake now that it was full to the brim. Stormy, viscous liquid lapped at the edges of the street and ate away at it slowly. Deliah was there, holding Joshua up by his wrists with one immense hand. Joshua's feet were dangling over the pool and Deliah was speaking to him, "... wither and die. The farther we are away from it, the less we believe it exists, the farther we drift. It perpetuates itself..."

She knew there was truth in his words, but to Eve it sounded tainted by a desire to be wrong, like he was challenging Joshua to prove him wrong. The Apple compound had given Deliah strength, awareness, and knowledge of the universe, but it had also taken away his hope. Deliah believed the end was inevitable and out of control, and it broke him. Now, he was just an insanely powerful madman who controlled the one thing he thought he could: the way the world would end. Joshua had frustrated his first *elegant* and *merciful* attempt.

Deliah was coming unglued, unstable, "... unmake it. You should say something. This ending lacks poetry. This is the epic battle... the fight between good and evil for the sake of existence..."

Good and evil? Eve didn't think it mattered anymore. There was only life and death, and Eve made a conscious choice about both. The world might be ending—or even the universe—but either way, she planned to live longer than Deliah.

As Deliah continued his rant, Eve saw Ezechial appear from nowhere through her blurred-red vision. He slid into her awareness from behind, but made his presence obvious. *He's allowing me to see him.*

She didn't know if she could trust him, didn't know the meaning of the cuts in his body, or understand his relationship to the strange boy, but she was confident he could have killed her easily if he wanted to; he'd appeared so suddenly, so close to her.

He walked by her without acknowledging her. The wounds in his skin were cracked open and glowing softly. Eve thought the glow looked more like it was holding him together than tearing him apart.

Ezechial jumped down, but the movement was a single even speed, not accelerated by gravity. As he approached Deliah, the glowing edges of his skin became brighter. Eve jumped down and followed him, moving in tandem with the assassin. He was flanking Deliah, and she flanked opposite.

Something was swimming around beneath the surface of the pool, coming toward Deliah and Joshua. Eve and Ezechial both saw it and stopped.

The swimmer breached the tension with one bright rippling tendril, and then another. Pulling itself up over the edge with numerous flowing tendrils was a golden, glassy shard. It floated up toward Joshua, but it seemed that Deliah couldn't see it or feel it.

Eve thought it might be a figment of her imagination—the head trauma or the chems working too well—but, Ezechial had stopped moving, too. When the rippling shard floated toward Joshua, she thought she saw Joshua reflected in it, but it wasn't quite Joshua.

The shard floated into Joshua as more waves stirred in the maelstrom. One after another, golden shards floated up out of the fluid and into Joshua. They came faster and faster, their tendrils floating behind them, long and wavy. The surface of the maelstrom was retreating, slightly at first, and then faster.

Eve realized that Deliah saw nothing because of the wounds she had given him. The blood had already begun turning black as it cooled against his skin. Where his eyes once were, she now saw thick plates of liquid black. But Deliah must have felt the maelstrom ebb, because he stopped talking and swiveled his head around suspiciously.

Joshua's black veins were throbbing. Deliah felt it and shook him wildly. Joshua opened his bright blue marbled eyes and began slowly prying his wrists apart though Deliah strained to hold them together.

Opening his mouth in fury, Deliah clasped Joshua's wrists with both his hands. Joshua confidently pulled his hands free regardless, and instead of falling, he was held up by the waves of flowing tendrils and shards.

Deliah grabbed Joshua by the throat and squeezed with one hand, placing the piercing claws of his other hand on Joshua's bared chest. Joshua reached up and throttled Deliah with both hands, pulling himself closer. Deliah's claws sank deep into Joshua until his entire palm was flat against his chest and his fingers and thumb were through the ribs.

Joshua's black veins throbbed and pulsed around Deliah's black fingers, but he didn't bleed. His veins circled and joined Deliah's fingers so that Joshua's skin was indistinguishable from Deliah's. Joshua stared into Deliah's eyeless face.

The fissures that ran vertically down the blue marbles of Joshua's eyes opened up. Bright rays of light, and tendrils like those on the shards, poured out of them. Joshua tightened his grip on Deliah's throat and suddenly Deliah was floating, too.

The shards slowed and stopped, but Eve couldn't even see the surface of the maelstrom anymore. Joshua was surrounded in waves of light the way Deliah was surrounded by heat.

The pair hovered in a tense embrace. Their muscles flexed and their faces hardened to the task of killing each other. The tug that Eve felt toward the maelstrom earlier had gone entirely, and now she felt pushed away. As the push grew stronger, she felt her chance slipping away.

There was no time, and nothing left to do but try again.

Eve went for full-burn, and felt a wave of nausea hit her hard before it was countered with a spike of balance-enhancer. The world became a blur of light indistinguishable from sound as she ran. Her blood-heavy robe lagged behind her, and she cut it free.

She was detached from her clothes and detached from her body. Her IOL screamed alerts, and painted warnings of every kind across her vision. But as she ran, the information melted into tiny droplets of various colors, caught the turbulence of the wind rushing past her face and streamed away.

She leapt toward Deliah with her arms out like wings, and brought the sword up over her head in the same motion, grabbing the hilt with both hands. She made first contact with the Wakizashi.

Time slowed. Details were sharpened and magnified. She felt the tip of the sword—delicate, like the tip of a needle in the groove of a fingerprint—enter the scratch she'd cut earlier between Deliah's shoulder and neck.

Beginning at her tailbone, she curled and flexed her entire body and thrust the sword downward.

The sword slipped in behind the clavicle. Eve felt the vibration as the edge bit into the bone, sliding along it on the way down. The tip slipped through Deliah's heart—crossing from right to left and out the other side—before the hilt stopped it from going farther.

Her feet finally landed on his back and she pushed off, flipping back and pulling the sword free in a spray of red that fanned out as it followed the arching movement.

Deliah's hand convulsed around Joshua's throat and he tightened his grip around his chest. Falling to the ground, Deliah was intent on dragging Joshua with him. He held tightly, and Joshua held just as tight as Deliah staggered to the edge and jumped.

Joshua let go, but Deliah held on and both slowly sank into the bottomless pit left by the receding maelstrom.

Rushing to the edge, Ezechial unleashed his Devil's Tails. He looped one around Joshua's waist, and pulled back. His left whip cracked at Deliah's face and hands. Deliah wouldn't let go, and they were still slowly sinking. Ezechial's feet slid along the street, but he held.

Joshua pried at Deliah's hand that was embedded in his chest. One finger at a time he was getting loose, but they were still falling.

Deliah's grip over Joshua's heart was enervating. He seemed to grow stronger—even as he was dying—but Joshua was only getting weaker.

Ezechial let his cracked whip slide and slither around Joshua's body, trying to find a way to cut at Deliah with his bone quills, but it didn't work. Deliah held on tenaciously, squeezing power from Joshua as they descended slowly into the darkness.

There was only one loop remaining around Joshua as Ezechial let out a little more in order to hold his ground. Ezechial stared down into the pit. He'd already made his choice, so why was he holding on?

He released the handle of his cracked whip. It slithered down around Joshua, and from there snaked around Deliah. The red glow from the cracks splashed off of Joshua and Deliah, and then disappeared into the darkness. It wrapped its way around Deliah's body, his throat, his chest, and his arm. It constricted and wound tighter, and glowed even brighter. Cutting through the flesh, the whip was holding Deliah by his bones.

Snapping sounds reverberated up and out of the hole, and echoed deep into the earth as Deliah's bones fractured and broke.

Finally, Deliah let go.

FALLEN SPIRE

Starting Over

Thirty-One

Ezechial hauled Joshua up with his remaining whip. Eve came to his side and helped. Together, they carried Joshua's body away from the hole and set him down gently.

"He'll be alright."

Eve was kneeling down over Joshua, checking his vitals, and looking at the wounds in his chest that were already closing up, "I know. I mean, I absolutely know he will be." She looked up at Ezechial with her own hazel eyes, "Will you?"

Ezechial's left arm was twitching violently, but his wounds still glowed dimly beneath the skin. The cracks had closed up again, mostly. "No," he smiled, "But that won't stop me from trying to be."

"He has a fever," back to Joshua, she placed her hand over his chest, "I'll have to get him someplace warm." Winter cold had set in fast, though there were still a few hours left of sunlight. "I'll get him over to the GlassTech building. Mark and Marius are calling everyone back there."

"Do you need help with him?"

"No," she rolled Joshua up and over her shoulder, then stood. His feet were dragging on the ground a bit, "I'll manage."

Eve started traversing the wreckage, but realized Ezechial wasn't following. "Wait, you're not coming with us?" she turned around.

"No."

"What will you do?"

"I'm going to write this down," his eyes were shining in the sun, "because right now, all I can think about are the prophecies."

He thought to himself, *"We will tell the story. We will write the story, and we will rewrite the story. And even then, it will be wrong. It happens differently each time it happens, but almost all fall away. A universe that manages to hold on—halfway between sundered and alive—is miraculous, and that has always been our story."*

And then he said aloud, "Telling the story of our world and what happened here is the creation of legend. As long as we keep telling it, we'll always be connected. Legends hold us together; how they happened, and how we choose to remember them is what gives us life."

Eve wrinkled her nose at him, and then she smiled, "I don't know if I've ever understood your prophecies, Ezechial, but I know I need to take care of what's in front of me, and right now, that's Joshua," her eyes fell down for a moment, "Good luck."

As she turned to walk away, Joshua whispered in her ear, "Joshua says, 'Good luck, Winter.'" She did her best to shrug with the added weight and walked on.

"Winter," he tried it on the air, "I like that."

As Eve climbed away, she saw a strange prompt on her IOL, "Mark, what's this?"

"Lesha time-capsuled that for you. Looks like she passed it to you securely when you guys met. It didn't go through the network. I don't know what it is. Want me to open it up?"

"No, that's okay. Thanks."

Eve opened the file. It was a text file, and it began: "Adam loved you."

Marius was staring at the bottles lined up on his wet bar. Even though he had Wall dispensers capable of making any drink he could possibly want, he'd always preferred to pour for himself. Unfortunately, he'd squandered his last bottle of his favorite alcohol.

Mark—the one and only Mark in this universe—was sitting at Marius' dining room table. Living alone, Marius had never used the table; Mark might have been the first to sit at it.

Finally, dissatisfied with his choices, Marius just poured himself a glass of Scotch on the rocks, grabbed the bottle and an extra glass of ice, and sat down with Mark at the table. He studied Mark for a minute, then poured him a glass and slid it across to him.

"Are you going to search for another den?" Marius waved the glass at Mark and then twirled the ice around slowly, "Or tunnel, or whatever it was?" The question was genuine. It was the most genuine Marius had ever been with Mark. There was no game in it, only curiosity.

Mark sucked in a deep breath and picked up the bucket glass, "I don't think so," unsure, "but I'm pretty sure that it doesn't matter as much as I thought it did. I think maybe I carry that connection with me?"

He thinks he's a meta-universal node… great. "Do you really believe that?" he couldn't believe he was asking.

"Yes, but it really isn't going to affect my decisions; it's going to affect how I actually do things," he took a sip, "I'm going to be a little more personally invested in whatever I do, or I'm not going to do it." He downed the remains of the drink and shook his head once, hard. He opened his eyes wide and slid the glass back across the table. Marius filled it up and sent it back. "I think the only mistake we made was to live unconsciously… I mean, without intention. I mean," he paused, "Damn, this was so much clearer a few minutes ago… I mean, we're too detached, too divested. We shut ourselves down and close ourselves off…" he sipped again, "I think I'll open a café."

"Need a partner?"

About the Author

Aaron Safronoff was born and raised in Michigan where he wrote his first novella, *Evening Breezes*. In his early twenties, he moved to California to attend culinary school. He fell in love with the Bay Area and has never considered leaving, although he did eventually leave the school.

During his ten years in the games industry, he worked at various levels and for several disciplines including quality assurance, production, and design. All the while he was writing a novel, short stories, plays, and poetry. His career in design introduced him to amazingly intelligent, fun, and creative people, many of whom he considers family today.

Safronoff self-published, *Spire*, in 2011, and won the Science Fiction Discovery Award for the same in the summer of 2012. By the end of that year he decided to drop everything and free fall into fiction. In the following three months he completed work on the sequel to *Spire*, *Fallen Spire*, edited *Evening Breezes*, and published both.

Today, Safronoff is co-founder and Chief Storyteller of Neoglyphic Entertainment and working on his fifth novel, the second book of the *Sunborn Rising* series. In his spare time, Safronoff enjoys reading a variety of authors, Philip K. Dick, Cormac McCarthy, and Joe Abercrombie among them. He enjoys living near the ocean, playing and watching hockey, and video games. He has a deep love of music and comedy.

NEOGLYPHIC
Entertainment

Neoglyphic Entertainment believes story is the heart of the human experience. Story inspires creativity, shapes minds, and catalyzes social change. Story connects us to one another, celebrating our greatest triumphs and exposing our deepest fears, establishing a common ground to learn, to understand, to be.

Stories are shared through written word, visual art, film, music, video games and more. Neoglyphic develops technology to cultivate story across all these art forms, and reduces the traditional risk and cost associated with entertainment production. We offer a storytelling platform to connect with fans, derive meaningful insights, and deliver immersive experiences.

Whether you're an author writing your first novel, or a studio creating a feature film, Neoglyphic will be your trusted partner to untether your imagination.

www.neoglyphic.com

Made in the USA
Charleston, SC
27 January 2017